WHERE HEAVEN BEGINS

Further Titles by Rosanne Bittner from Severn House

FOLLOW YOUR HEART
WHERE HEAVEN BEGINS

WHERE HEAVEN BEGINS

Rosanne Bittner

This first world edition published 2011
in Great Britain and the USA by
SEVERN HOUSE PUBLISHERS LTD of
9–15 High Street, Sutton, Surrey, England, SM1 1DF,
by arrangement with Steeple Hill Books.
First published 2004 in the USA in mass market format only.

British Library Cataloguing in Publication Data

Bittner, Rosanne, 1945-
  Where heaven begins.
  1. Alaska--Social conditions--19th century--Fiction.
  2. Love stories.
  I. Title
  813.5'4-dc22

ISBN-13: 978-0-7278-8000-0 (cased)

To my special and beautiful grandsons, Brennan, Connor and Blake Bittner;
and to their parents, son Brock and wife Lori, and son Brian, and wife, Edna.
When I'm down, all I need is to hear the words "Gwamma, I wuv you" and
I'm on top of the world again. I'm sure that in the future one of my inspirational
stories will involve the love between a grandmother and her grandson. My own
grandsons are the light of my life and truly a gift from God.

All Severn House titles are printed on acid-free paper.

Severn House Publishers support The Forest Stewardship Council [FSC],
the leading international forest certification organisation. All our titles that
are printed on Greenpeace-approved FSC-certified paper carry the FSC logo.

MIX
Paper from
responsible sources
FSC® C018575
www.fsc.org

Printed and bound in Great Britain by the
MPG Books Group, Bodmin, Cornwall.

AUTHOR'S NOTE

Within most of my fifty-plus novels about America's history there has always been an element of faith that was important to each story. When the opportunity arose for me to write for Steeple Hill, I was delighted, as deep inside I have always wanted my writing to inspire hope and faith within the reader. I am deeply gratified to have often accomplished that, or so many of my readers have told me.

Now, by writing for a line designed especially for books with faith in God as the primary theme, I am free to release that little voice inside that has been telling me that this is the kind of book I must write.

In these times when it is important to remember that through all the upheaval in the world today, we can still realize peace and joy deep inside through abiding faith, it is my privilege to write a story that is centered on faith in God.

All Scripture verses used in this novel are taken from the King James version of the Holy Bible.

A good share of the travel details in this novel were gleaned from the authentic diaries of E. Hazard Wells, a reporter who traveled to the Klondike in 1897 and whose notes were published in *Magnificence and Misery*, edited by Randall M. Dodd, Doubleday & Co., Inc., 1984.

As a reader for whom faith in God is a key element in daily life, you will, I hope, find *Where Heaven Begins* worthwhile reading and an uplifting experience.

Rosanne Bittner

ACKNOWLEDGMENTS

To all those who have touched my life in a positive way without even knowing it. I can only hope to do the same in return through my writing.

A special thank-you also to Ann Leslie Tuttle, the editor who originally brought Rosanne Bittner to Steeple Hill; and to my agent, Denise Marcil, for suggesting I try writing an inspirational book. Writing this novel has opened up a whole new avenue in writing for me. I have loved every minute of it.

And who can write an inspirational novel without thanking God for a talent that comes only from Him. I thank Him too for planting the seed of faith that helped me write this book.

Chapter One

Be not a witness against thy neighbor without cause;
And deceive not with thy lips.

—Proverbs 24:28

San Francisco, August 4, 1898

"We've taken a vote, Elizabeth. We understand you will need to find a job and a place to live, and we are ready to help you there, but you will have to leave Reverend Selby's residence."

Elizabeth Breckenridge felt as though the blood was leaving her body, beginning with her head and draining down toward her feet. She had no doubt what had caused this meeting of church deacons who sat circled around her with looks of condemnation on their faces.

"May I have an explanation?" she asked, fighting not to cry. Elizabeth always cried when she was extremely angry, but she refused to shed tears in front of these pious judges, especially the two-faced Reverend Selby. *Lord, help me not to hate these men.*

"Surely you know the reason for this." The words came from Anderson Williams, who'd once been a good friend to her father.

Liz faced him squarely. "And surely you know me better," she answered. "How can you do this, Mr. Williams? You were one of my father's staunchest supporters. You know my family well, and you know how I was brought up."

Williams shifted uncomfortably, and Liz could see that he was bound to abide by the decision of the rest of these church leaders, six deacons in all. And, of course, the Reverend Thomas Selby himself sat in judgment.

"I'm sorry, Elizabeth, but I do understand it's possible after all that's happened to you that...well, my dear...it would only be natural for you to turn to someone for comfort, and perhaps for you to...well...yearn for the safety and steadfastness of a man's love," Williams said.

"Love? Is that what Reverend Selby told you? That I turned to him for comfort? That I said I *loved* him?" Still fighting tears, Elizabeth continued. "Gentlemen, my father always taught that we should not condemn. According to St. John, Chapter 7, Verse 24, *Judge not the appearance, but judge righteous judgment. You* have made a grave *misjudgment*, I can assure you. I am not the one who should be cast out of this church, but I can already see that none of you is ready to listen to the truth, so I will not sit here and beg you to believe me! Only our Holy Father knows the truth, and true judgment will prevail when all of you stand before Him!" She turned her gaze to Reverend Selby.

"Including *you*, Reverend, but I forgive you, *for if ye forgive not men their trespasses, neither will your Father forgive your trespasses.* St. Matthew, Chapter 6, Verse 15."

Reverend Selby's dark eyes narrowed with what Liz interpreted as a literal threat. "We all understand your sad situation, child."

"My sad situation?" Oh, how hard it was to hold her tongue! That had always been difficult, and right now the Lord was not helping her at all when it came to not harboring hatred and a desire for revenge against the reverend. Deep in her heart she really could *not* forgive this man! "For one thing, I am not a child. I am twenty years old."

She turned her attention to the others, men who had known her since she was a little girl; men who had worked with her father to build this church in San Francisco; men who now fell into the common belief that all women were basically weak and needy and were somehow responsible for any man's basic weaknesses. "My sad situation is not the awfulness of losing both my parents to death and my brother to a higher calling," she continued. "My saddest situation is that I accepted the reverend's offer to remain living with him and his wife until I could get back on my feet and decide what to do next after Mother's death. My saddest situation results from trusting a supposedly godly man and thinking he truly wanted to help me. I misjudged his kindness. Reverend Selby had in mind when he offered his home to me other intentions than just helping the daughter of your former preacher!"

"Daughter, watch your tongue!" The words came from Cletus Olson, another former friend of her father's. "Don't add false accusations to what has already happened. We are ready to forgive and help you."

Liz rose from the straight-backed oak chair in which she sat. She felt like an accused harlot. She took a deep breath, astounded and disappointed at the attitude of these men who'd known her family so well.

"Speaking of false accusations, I can only imagine what the pious reverend has been telling you," she said, turning to meet the eyes of each man directly. "I need no forgiveness, and it sickens me that you would believe him. I assure you that I will gladly leave his home, and in fact I was about to tell all of you the same…that it might be best if I lived elsewhere."

She swallowed, realizing now that this was God's way of letting her know it was time to act on what she'd been wanting to do for a long time. "I had already decided to join my brother in Dawson. I know that many of you believe he only went there to search for gold like all the thousands of others who've gone, but I know in my heart he intended to build a church and minister to the many lost souls who will surely need his services. I've heard some of you joking about his real intentions, but you know what a sincere man of God he is, how hard he worked to save this church after Father was killed. He would never drop all of that for something as shallow as a gold rush. He felt God's calling and he followed it. I intend to go and find him."

"How on earth will you get there, Elizabeth?" Anderson Williams frowned with what seemed true concern. "It's a terribly dangerous trip for a young woman alone. Besides, it's too late in the year to go at all."

Liz held her chin proudly. "That shouldn't concern any of you, considering that you are so eager to ban me from the reverend's house and brand me as something I am not. Traveling to the Yukon won't be any worse than struggling to find work and fend for myself with absolutely no family left here…and a congregation that is apparently whispering behind my back."

Elizabeth folded her arms, angry with herself for not speaking up sooner about Reverend Selby instead of keeping quiet and allowing him the chance to speak first and turn everyone against her. It had always been obvious to her that the man was jealous of the fact that her father had founded Christ Church, and that her presence reminded the congregation of that. Selby didn't just want to preach here. He wanted to "own" Christ Church and its members. He didn't want to be known as the man who tried to fill Reverend William Breckenridge's shoes. He wanted all the glory for himself. He'd done what he could to malign the Breckenridge name and get rid of the last bit of Breckenridge influence in this church so that he and no other would be the number-one leader of his flock. Winning over these men, former friends of her father's, was his final victory.

"We've taken a collection for you, Elizabeth," Jeffrey Clay spoke up. He was always the most quiet, reasonable man among the deacons. "It was intended to help you find a boarding house and keep you on your feet until you could find a way to support yourself, perhaps by teaching. If you choose to use the money to get you to Alaska, that's your choice." He rose and cleared his throat, walking up to her and handing over an envelope. "There is four hundred dollars here. That should be of considerable help. We are aware that your mother also saved some money, which she put in your name before she died."

Elizabeth took the money with a gloved hand. "I am told that traveling to Alaska could take much more than this, what with the embellished prices of goods there. But somehow I'll make it with this and what little else I have. I apparently have no choice."

She turned to leave, wanting nothing more now than to get away from the accusing glares of these pompous men who knew nothing of what she'd suffered since her mother had died three months ago. She should be angry with her brother. This was partly his fault. If he hadn't up and left last summer... Oh, Peter, if only you were here, none of this would have happened!

"Elizabeth, wait!"

Liz stopped short at the sound of Reverend Selby's booming voice. Even before he'd started making advances toward her, he'd always had a way of looking at her as though she were some kind of evil temptress. She turned to glare back at him.

"Our love and prayers go with you, daughter," the reverend told her. "Know that I forgive you, as does my wife. You are welcome to stay another few days until you can make your arrangements, or until you find work. Surely you could teach, or perhaps work as a nanny. And there are any number of young men in our fold who would like to court you. Marriage could bring you all the security you desire."

Oh, Lord, why are You making it so impossible not to hate this liar!

"I'll not marry just for security," she answered aloud. "And yes, I will look for work, but not in San Francisco. I'll not stay here any longer than it will take me to go home and pack my things. I'll find a hotel room for tonight and however many days it takes to procure passage to Seattle. I'll leave as soon as I can!" She moved her gaze about the circle of men again. "And how dare any of you talk about forgiving me! *I* am not the one who needs forgiving! I am the one who will be praying that God forgives all of *you* for what you've done today!"

With that, Elizabeth quickly left the brick building that had been built next to Christ Church as a gathering hall for potlucks and the like. She rushed around behind it, clinging to the envelope of money. She let the tears come then, deep sobs of humiliation, disappointment, mourning for her dead father and mother, and fear of the unknown. What choice did she have now but to go and find Peter? All she wanted was to be with her brother, the only family she had left.

"Lord Jesus, help me do this," she wept. How afraid Jesus Himself must have been so many times, but He trusted God to give Him the strength and wisdom necessary to bear the accusations thrown at Him, and to travel where others dared not go. Now Elizabeth knew that she must do the same.

Chapter Two

Thou hast rebuked the proud that are cursed,
which do err from Thy commandments. Remove
from me reproach and contempt; for I have kept
Thy testimonies.
—Psalms 119:21 & 22

Feeling guilty over her anger, too guilty even to pray about it, Elizabeth stuffed clothing into two worn carpet bags that had belonged to her mother. Tears stung her eyes at the longing in her heart to be able to turn to the woman now. The day three years ago that the police informed the family that Liz's father had been murdered was the day Edna Breckenridge's health began slipping downhill. She never really recovered from the loss of her husband, but she insisted that no one in the family lose faith in God because of it.

Still, this last hurt did indeed bring a challenge to Elizabeth's own faith. What more terrible things lay in wait for her? What had she done to deserve this? First, her father, a faithful servant of the Lord, cruelly murdered while bravely ministering to miserable drunks and thieves and prostitutes who plied their dastardly trades on the Barbary Coast. Then her brother, another faithful servant of the Lord, as well as her best friend, felt a calling to follow the hordes of men headed for the Yukon to find gold. God meant for Peter to go there, too, and to build a church and bring His word to men who would too easily forget God even existed in their quest to get rich, or so her brother believed.

After Peter left, one of the more respected deacons, Thomas Selby, had offered to take over as preacher for the church. Deep inside, Liz had always suspected Selby of wanting the job even when her father was alive. Even her mother had doubted that Selby had anything like the abiding faith and love for mankind in his heart that Liz's father had possessed.

"They'll never replace Reverend William Breckenridge," Elizabeth seethed. She closed one carpet bag and threw her only other pair of shoes into the second bag. Her whole family had given up so much so that the church could grow, to the point that they had few possessions. She and her mother had been allowed to continue living upstairs in the parsonage after Thomas Selby became the new minister, but her mother's health failed rapidly and the woman eventually died from what the doctor claimed was cancer. It was a long, painful, cruel death, another blow to Elizabeth's faith.

Now this. So unfair! Thinking she was some kind of helpless, needy waif, the pious Reverend Selby had "consoled" Elizabeth with a little too much hugging and touching, as far as she was concerned. It was not until the night one week ago when the man had come into her bedroom and sat on the edge of her bed, waking her when he leaned close and tried talking her into letting him "help" her by coming to bed and "filling her with his strength" that Liz had realized the man's true intentions.

She'd screamed for him to get out, pushed at him, her reaction waking the man's wife. The false accusations that came out of the reverend's mouth then had shocked her. Of course, his wife believed him when he'd told her that Elizabeth had asked him to come to her room to pray with her and then had tried to tempt him into her bed.

She shuddered at the mere thought of the much older, supposedly righteous man being such a hypocrite. He had two grown sons older than she was, and he'd even preached sermons about the sin of adultery! After the incident, Mrs. Selby and other women in the congregation, women who'd been friends of her mother's and who'd often offered their help in her grief, became cold towards her.

Oh, how it hurt to lose not only her beloved father and mother, but to be lied about and thus to lose others who had been her only source of comfort. Before the disgusting meeting with the deacons today Elizabeth had already decided to leave San Francisco and go to live with Peter. She'd received letters from him, knew he had indeed founded a church in Dawson. He most surely would not want her to make the trip, but he had no choice in the matter. Once she made up her mind to do something, she did it! Her mother used to tease her about such stubbornness.

She drew in her breath and closed her eyes. *"God,*

forgive me," she prayed. *"I have never been so full of anger and...hatred. Yes, that's what it is, Lord. It's hatred. I'm so sorry that I feel this way."* She went to her knees. *"Please guide me in my journey, Lord. Help me make it safely to Alaska. Help me find my brother. Show me what it is You want of me. Take away this anger so that I can better serve You with a heart that is not full of malice."*

She moved to sit down on the bed, reaching to take her Bible from the nightstand. She pressed it to her heart and let the tears come. Oh, how she missed the days when her family was all together, working hard to build their own church. Since she was eight years old, when her family had arrived in San Francisco after an arduous journey by wagon from Illinois, a life of serving the Lord was all she'd known. She'd been so involved with helping first her father and then her brother that she'd never even taken time for her own life, for allowing young men to court her or attending any social functions except those involving the church. She'd taught Sunday school, helped her mother minister to sick members and then had spent months nursing her own mother until she died.

"Why, God? Haven't I served You well? Why have You taken so much from me?"

She opened her Bible to the New Testament, always believing that wherever she opened the Gospels she would find answers to her problems. She believed it was God's way of talking to her, leading her.

"Beware, lest any man spoil you through philosophy and vain deceit," she read, "after the tradition of men, after the rudiments of the world, and not after Christ."

There, as always, was her answer. She could not allow the hypocrites who'd kicked her out of this parsonage to spoil her faith.

She closed her eyes. *"Lord, I believe You have a reason for the turns life hands us. Surely You mean for me to go to Dawson. I'm afraid, Lord, but I know You will be with me. And I believe there is a purpose for what has happened that You have not yet shown me. Whatever You have planned, Lord, I will accept whatever You entrust to me."*

She rose and packed the Bible into the second carpet bag, along with what was left of her clothing, such as it was. Her family had never owned many material things, and she dressed simply. She breathed deeply as she buckled the second bag, feeling more confident now. God had a purpose for her. She did not doubt it.

She walked to the dresser where she used to sit while her mother brushed her hair for her, always praising its thickness and luster—*a lovely red glint to your dark tresses when the sun hits your hair just right*, her mother would say. Liz sometimes felt guilty for admiring her own hair during those times, but she was proud of it, and it felt good to remember how she and her mother used to talk about so many things, and to remember how kind and loving Edna Breckenridge had been.

A lump rose in her throat at the memory. She tied on her bonnet, remembering her mother's warning to always wear a hat with a brim to *protect the beautiful, flawless skin God gave you. When the Lord blesses you with good health, you should respect your body and take care of it.* That included, of course, giving her body to a man someday only out of love and through God's divine blessing. So far she'd not met one young man who came close to giving her even the slightest feelings of desire in that respect. And the night Reverend Selby had come into her room with his hideous suggestions only made the thought of being with any man repulsive. It would be a long time before she forgot that awful night!

She forced back another urge to cry as she smoothed her plain green dress with a tiny white ruffle at the high neck. It matched her small green pill bonnet. She wore black ankle-high button shoes and looked properly prim and respectable, certainly not the harlot the Reverend Selby had tried to convince others she was.

It was midafternoon. Neither the Reverend nor Mrs. Selby were home. Good. She'd not bother telling them or anyone else goodbye. She'd go to the church graveyard and visit her father's and mother's graves one more time. Oh, how it would make her heart ache to leave them and Christ Church behind, but she had no choice now. They would want her to be with Peter. Steamships left every day for Alaska; and she'd pay passage on one of them and leave.

She took a last look at the room she'd occupied since she was a little girl and shared with her mother for those last months of suffering. Then she straightened, hooking the strings of her handbag on her arm, a handbag that carried all the money she possessed in the world. She picked up her carpet bags and turned, walking out the door. This was it. There was no turning back.

Chapter Three

*I am a stranger in the earth; hide not Thy
commandments from me.*
—Psalms 119:19

August or not, it was foggy and chilly today. Elizabeth
was not unaware of the stares of the hundreds of men who
milled about. She could not forget the letter she'd received
just this past spring from Peter, in which he'd casually
stated that any women who came unescorted to Alaska
were generally considered to be there for prostitution,
although a very few managed to open legitimate businesses
such as eateries, or to find work as seamstresses.

Elizabeth had practically memorized Peter's letters, of
which she had only two. It was not easy getting mail out
of Dawson and all the way down to San Francisco. She'd
received one letter over the winter after his arrival last fall,
and the more recent one this spring. She'd written Peter
right away about their mother's death, and it was possible

he'd not even received that letter yet, let alone the letter she'd written two nights ago.

Now she stood on the wharf waiting for passengers to disembark the *Alaskan Damsel,* a steamer that had made numerous trips to Seattle and on to Skagway via the Inside Passage throughout the past two summers.

As she'd suspected would be the case, not many people left the boat, yet hundreds waited, ready to board. For most who made this journey, it was a one-way trip, and like most of them, she'd purchased a one-way ticket herself. Once she found Peter, she had no intention of ever returning to San Francisco.

She shivered from the damp fog, then jumped when the high smokestacks of the *Damsel* billowed black smoke, accompanied by three shrill whistles, beckoning all who intended to board her. She wondered if that included the three painted, gaudily dressed women who stood not far away batting their eyes at some of the men. It made her ill to think what such women did to make their money. Not far from them stood a group of Chinese, conversing in their strange sing-song tongue. The men's hair was worn long and braided into tails at the backs of their necks. Other Chinese as well as black men worked at the docks loading and unloading supplies.

Different. All so different. Did God actually expect his followers to love people like that? She liked to think that she could, but if she actually had to associate with them... *Oh, Lord, I fall so short of Your will. I am surrounded by heathens and harlots and men whose hearts are filled with a lust for gold and painted women. How can I truly love such people? I know that I am no better than they, and yet it is so hard to think of them as equals. Teach me how to love all people.*

Perhaps if her father had not been murdered by people very much like these.... The memory still brought a stabbing pain to her heart. Her father used to come home and ask the family to pray for thieves and murderers, alcoholics and drug users, harlots and men who visited them. He'd truly been a man of God, for she believed he honestly loved these people in the way God intended. He'd died serving the Lord. The same people to whom he'd ministered had turned around and murdered him for a mere three dollars. They had even stolen his clothing, leaving him naked and disgraced.

To realize God meant her to love that kind of people brought a great struggle to her soul. The congregation mourned, but they also had repeatedly warned her father not to go to such dangerous places as the Barbary Coast, a section of this dock area not so far away from here. No one else in her father's church, most certainly not Reverend Selby and the deacons, had anywhere near the courage of her father when it came to bringing God's Word to the lost souls of the world. The remaining members of Christ Church had decided it was best simply to serve the current congregation and the surrounding, more civilized neighborhood. If anyone on the Barbary Coast wanted to find God, they were welcome to come to the church and be saved.

Only her brother understood what their father's calling was all about. He was following William Breckenridge's footsteps, heading into dangerous, wild country just to minister to those who would have no other source of hearing God's Word.

She took a deep breath, praying she could drum up the same courage it would take to make this journey. Baggage and supplies were being unloaded from the boat, as well as several large, well-guarded crates that took several men to load onto wagons.

Gold ore? She'd heard that thousands, maybe even millions of dollars worth of the treasured ore arrived almost daily in Seattle and San Francisco, to be shipped to stamp mills. Her brother's last letter revealed that stamp mills were already being built in the Yukon so that the ore could be processed there. Rumors of the value of the gold coming out of the mines in the Yukon abounded. It was difficult to know what to believe.

The crowd around her grew more excited as they watched the armed bank guards that surrounded the ore wagons. Men began shouting about gold and getting rich, whooping and laughing.

"I ain't never gonna have to work again!" one man yelled.

"I'll build my Sarah the biggest house in San Francisco!" yelled another.

Elizabeth began to see what the term *gold fever* meant. Why was being rich so important? She thought about how Christ had never owned a thing to His name but the clothes He wore and the sandals on His feet. If her brother were to, by chance, find gold, he would use it to build his church and help the poor.

The wharf gradually became even more crowded. The wagons surrounded by men with rifles rumbled past, and

Elizabeth picked up both her carpet bags and made her way
to a less-congested area, getting bumped and shoved as she
struggled through the crowd, keeping the *Alaskan Damsel*
in sight so she could get on board as soon as the boat took
on its passengers. She'd paid the cheapest rate possible,
deciding she would have to bear the discomfort of sleeping
below deck using one of her bags as a pillow. She would
need the greater share of her money once she arrived in
Skagway for the clothing and supplies it would take to
make the journey to the Klondike, or so she'd been told by
the man who'd sold her the steamer ticket. He'd advised
her not to make the trip at all, most certainly not alone, but
she'd made up her mind and there was no going back. She
might end up stranded in Skagway without enough money
to go any farther, but at least there she'd be closer to Peter.

"God will guide me," she'd told the man. Deep inside
she struggled against fear and doubt, secretly praying
almost constantly for the Lord to help her do this.

She removed one glove and ran her fingers over the
buttons of the bodice of her dress, making sure none had
come undone. Today she wore a simple gray frock with a
black velvet shawl and black velvet hat, wanting to appear
as plain as possible to make sure strange men realized she
was a proper lady. Her hair was wound into a bun at the
base of her neck, and she checked to be sure the pins were
still holding it tight. It was so thick she always had diffi-
culty holding it in place, whether with pins or combs.

Her handbag dangling from her arm, she reached behind
her neck to tighten the hairpins when suddenly her arm was
jerked painfully backward and her handbag ripped away.

She screamed with the pain, then took no time to stop and think. Her money! It was all in that handbag! Following her first basic instinct, she ran after the culprit who'd stolen all the money she had in the world, screaming for him to stop, screaming to others please to stop him for her.

Dear Lord, please stop him! Please don't let this happen! Help me!

She began screaming the words aloud. "Help! Help! Please stop him!"

It was then that someone rushed past her and tackled the thief, throwing him to the wooden planks of the pier, then jerking him up and landing several vicious blows, bloodying the man's nose and mouth. Her apparent aide was tall and obviously strong and knew what he was about, for his blows were well aimed and the thief had no chance against him. Then, to Elizabeth's wide-eyed shock, the stranger picked up the thief and threw him over the edge of the dock into the water.

He whirled then, as two more ragged-looking men approached him with knives. The stranger whipped out the six-gun he wore at his hip so quickly that Elizabeth barely saw the movement.

"Back off!" he ordered.

The two men looked at each other and backed away. Still holding the gun on them, the stranger walked over to pick up Elizabeth's handbag and a wide-brimmed hat that had been knocked from his own head in the fight. His two would-be attackers melted into the crowd that had gathered to watch, and finally the stranger holstered his sidearm. He put his hat on and stepped up to Elizabeth, still breathing hard, a slight bruise forming on his square jaw. He held out the handbag. "I believe this belongs to you, ma'am."

Speechless, Elizabeth took the bag, staring into deep-blue eyes that looked back at her from beneath the hat that now covered wild, wavy strands of dark hair. He was the best-looking man Elizabeth had ever seen, and she felt a sudden, inexplicable jolt to her heart.

Chapter Four

*If thine enemy be hungry, give him bread to eat;
and if he be thirsty, give him water to drink...*
—Proverbs 25:21

The savior of Elizabeth's handbag began to walk away before she found her voice. "Mister, wait!"

From several feet ahead the man turned, pushing back his hat slightly and looking her over. Elizabeth wondered if perhaps he thought her one of the loose women heading for the gold fields. Surely not! Who could think such a thing, the way she was dressed? No matter what he thought, she had to at least thank him, but... "What about that man you threw into the water? He could drown!" she called to him.

The stranger frowned. "Who cares? Any man who steals from a woman is worthless anyway. You of all people shouldn't be concerned with what happens to him."

"But...he's a human being. If he drowns, I'll be responsible!"

"What?" He grunted a laugh. "He stole your purse, and *I'm* the one who threw him into the water."

Elizabeth glanced toward the spot where the man had been thrown off. She noticed a couple of men helping him climb back onto the wharf.

"There, you see? He's wet and mad, but he's all right. The water probably helped sober him up," the stranger told her.

The voice was closer, and Elizabeth turned to see him standing right before her. It was then she realized he was a good six feet tall and well built. She backed away slightly. "Well, I...I'm glad, in spite of what he did. And I thank you, sir, for recovering my handbag. All the money I have in the world is in it."

He grinned and shook his head. "Then I suggest you take that money and put it inside your girdle or your camisole, someplace where a man can't get to it so easily." He frowned teasingly then. "Unless, of course, you're not the prim-and-proper lady you appear to be."

Elizabeth reddened. "I beg your pardon!"

He tipped his hat. "Just some friendly advice, ma'am." He started away again.

"What's your name?" Elizabeth called after him.

Again he turned, removing his hat and running a hand through his thick hair. "Clint Brady."

Still feeling heat in her cheeks, Elizabeth nodded to him. "Well, thank you again, Mr. Brady. I'll...take your advice."

Brady looked around and stepped closer again. "You headed for Alaska?"

Elizabeth nodded. "Yes. My brother is building a church in the Yukon. I am going to join him."

The man frowned, his blue eyes revealing true concern. *"Alone?"*

Elizabeth glanced down at his gun and suddenly wondered if she was revealing too much information. Still, he'd risked his life to get her purse back for her. "Yes."

"And your brother approves?"

"He doesn't know. I sent him a letter, but I'll be well on my way by the time he gets it. He'll have no choice in the matter. He's all the family I have left and I'm going. God will get me there safely."

Brady's eyebrows arched quizzically, and Elizabeth could see he thought she was silly to make such a remark. "He will, will He?" He chuckled. "Well, ma'am...what's your name, anyway?"

"Elizabeth Breckenridge."

"Well, Miss Breckenridge, it's nice to have so much faith, but if I were you, I'd still be more careful of my money. And I'd find a guide of some kind. The trip to the Yukon is daunting for the strongest of men, let alone a woman on her own. You able to carry a thousand pounds of supplies on your back up a mountainside?"

Elizabeth swallowed. "Well, I...I'll find a way. Perhaps I'll find a guide once I reach Skagway...and a mule or a horse."

"Mmm-hmm. And how are you going to know who to trust?"

She held her chin higher with pretended confidence. "I'll know, that's all. However, I doubt I have enough money to pay a man for such work anyway. Perhaps someone will take me for the cost of his own supplies... grubstaking, I think they call it."

Brady nodded. "That's what they call it." He looked around the crowd as though watching for someone in particular. "Come on. I'll walk you back to your bags, if they're still there."

"Oh, my goodness! I forgot all about them! What if someone has stolen them!" Elizabeth began a rushed walk back to where she'd left her things, and Clint Brady walked beside her.

"They're probably all right," he tried to assure her. "Believe it or not, most of the men headed for the Yukon are just common good men, a lot of them family men who respect proper ladies." Elizabeth's bags came into sight. "There, you see?"

"Thank you, Jesus," Elizabeth said as she hurried up to the bags and picked them up. People were now boarding the *Damsel*. "I'd better get on board." She looked up at Clint Brady. "Thank you again, Mr. Brady. I didn't even ask if you're all right."

"Oh, I've been through worse, believe me."

"Oh, my." She glanced at his gun again. She wanted to ask more, but it might seem too intrusive; besides, there was no time. She had to get on board. She smiled nervously and nodded a goodbye, turning and climbing the wooden plank that led to the steamer's wooden deck. The *Damsel* was one of the larger steamers available, painted bright yellow with white trim, three stories of expensive cabins looking inviting. Again, Elizabeth wished she could afford a cabin, rather than staying below deck.

Only God knew how she was going to reach her destination safely—or if she would reach it at all. She had to keep the faith. Whatever was God's will for her, so be it. Fate, or more likely God, had led her this far.

She stood at the rail of the ship for several more long minutes, staring out at the hilly streets of San Francisco. So many memories there, mostly good ones until her father had been murdered. And Mama. Her eyes stung with tears. Mama! She might never again be able to visit her mother's grave. Oh, how she missed her! She could not imagine finding happiness here ever again. Her only hope for that was to be with Peter.

Her heart rushed faster when the steamer again blasted three short whistles from its tall smokestacks. Several black men working along the wharf unwrapped heavy rope from around thick wooden dock posts and tossed them to the deck of the *Damsel*. Elizabeth noticed again what a montage of races mingled at the wharf, and that many of them had boarded the *Damsel*. Negroes, Chinese, painted women, a couple of men who looked Indian, perhaps even Eskimos. She realized that in all the years she'd lived here, she really couldn't tell one Indian tribe from another. She only knew that most of the California tribes had become nearly extinct from war and disease. And, of course, there were many Spaniards among the crowd and several on board.

She realized that the members of Christ Church were nearly all white, and that many of them did not openly welcome other races. Her father would have welcomed anyone, and he'd died going out to find those who truly needed to hear God's Word. Since his death the church had strayed far from what her father meant it to be. He would expect his children to love and welcome other races, for he'd often preached that Christ taught that all should love one another, no matter how different that other person might be.

She turned to glance around at those who'd boarded the *Damsel*, and there were those very three women! And standing there talking to them was none other than Clint Brady! She'd not even noticed him come aboard.

So, he, too, was going to Alaska. To look for gold? She suspected it was for some other reason. Why did he wear a gun at his side? She couldn't remember seeing a badge on the man, but maybe he was a lawman. That would explain why he knew how to handle her attacker. He obviously had a good side to him, or he wouldn't have helped her…but he also had a violent side…and apparently a sinful side, or he wouldn't be standing there talking to harlots!

Why did that bother her? It was ridiculous to care. He glanced her way, and again she felt that little jolt to her heart, that little, uneasy feeling that Clint Brady had some kind of connection to her…some strange reason for coming into her life in such an odd way.

She turned away. How silly! Besides, the man might only be going as far as Seattle. Still, why did she actually feel relieved that he was on board?

Slowly the docks of San Francisco Bay began to disappear into the cold mist. The sound of other steamers' shrill whistles pierced the thick fog that began to shroud the *Damsel*.

She was on her way. *Stay with me, Jesus. I'm so afraid. My strength and courage come only from You.*

Chapter Five

*And the scribes and Pharisees brought unto him a
woman taken in adultery; and when they had set
her in the midst, they said unto him, Master, this
woman was taken in adultery, in the very act...such
should be stoned; but what sayest thou?
...Jesus...said unto them, He that is without sin
among you, let him first cast a stone at her.... And
they...went out one by one.... And Jesus said to the
woman, where are thine accusers? Hath no man
condemned thee? She said, No man, Lord. And
Jesus said unto her, Neither do I condemn thee:
go, and sin no more.*
—St. John 8:3-11

Elizabeth studied her Bible by lantern light, the only
kind of light available on the lower deck, although the
cabins and upper decks had electric lights, for what that
was worth. For the first two days of the trip men grum-

bled that the lights constantly dimmed or went out completely.

Elizabeth could barely sleep because of the deck's vibration, due to the steamer's engines rumbling directly beneath her. Added to that noise was the noise of others talking, particularly the painted women who were situated only a few feet from her. The first night they'd laughed and visited half the night, talking about things that made Elizabeth feel like a sinner just by hearing them.

Then last night the women had put up a makeshift tent made of blankets, and one of them lay inside the tent groaning in pain most of the night. The other two sat just outside the blankets whispering about something. Elizabeth assumed the woman groaning must be sick to her stomach from something she ate.

She fished through one of her carpet bags and took out a bottle of ink and a pen, as well as a notebook she'd purchased before leaving San Francisco. She had decided to keep a diary of her journey, partly to keep herself occupied so she wouldn't think about all the frightening things that could happen to her, and also because if she died on this journey, someone might send the diary on to Peter as a keepsake. She began by writing a note as to what to do with the journal should she not make it to Dawson.

August 10, 1898...This is only my third day, and we should make Seattle very soon. This part of my journey is, of course, the easy part, but I will try to make note of what happens every day. So far, other than when a thief tried to steal my handbag before I could board the steamer, things have been quite uneventful.

I am camping here below deck with Chinese and Indians and even three painted women whose occupation I suspect is unmentionable. One of them is sick. I have no idea...

She set her pen aside when she noticed that one of the painted women was coming toward her with what looked like a wadded-up towel.

"Miss?"

Elizabeth swallowed. Should she be seen associating with such women? Don't forget the adulteress, and how Jesus forgave her. She capped her pen and set it and her diary aside. "Yes?"

The woman crouched closer, and in the lantern light Elizabeth realized the woman was not much older than she was!

"My name is Collette. My friend in the tent over there that we set up, her name is Francine." Collette kept her voice lowered. She looked around, as though keeping a big secret. "My other friend there is Tricia, and we were all wondering...I mean...we've noticed you reading a Bible and all...and maybe you know enough about it to... well...pray over a dead body."

Elizabeth's eyes widened in surprise. "Did Francine *die?*"

"Oh, no, miss," Collette answered in a near whisper. "I think she'll be all right. We have experience in these things. That's not what we'd want you to pray about...except, of course, if you'd be so kind as to do that. Francine just lost a baby. I've got it right here in this towel. There's not much to it, but, well, you know, it just doesn't seem right not to pray over it, 'cause it's still what's left of a little human life. But me, I'm not much good at such things, so I thought maybe you'd consider coming up top with me and saying a prayer before I drop it into the water—kind of a burial at sea I guess you'd say."

Elizabeth felt her heart pounding in her chest. *Dear Lord, help me know what to do!* This woman of the streets was asking her to pray over an illegitimate child delivered by yet another prostitute! "I...well, I..."

"I know it seems awful to somebody like you, but like the Good Book says, we're all God's children, even this tiny little bit of life that's hardly recognizable. I sure don't intend just to throw it in the garbage."

Elizabeth wondered at the fact that the woman seemed to understand a little bit about God and the Bible, and she actually respected the bit of life she held in the towel. She felt ashamed about worrying what others would think of talking to such women. God surely was placing this duty in her hands, and so she would pray over the poor little soul in the towel. She reminded herself as she stood up that her father would have done the same. "I...of course I'll pray over the baby, and I'll pray for its mother. Are you sure she's all right...physically, I mean?"

"I think she'll be all right, but there's an awful lot of bleeding. We're getting off in Seattle to get her some help. It's kind of you to ask." Collette leaned a little closer. "And we understand somebody like you wouldn't want to be seen consorting with us, so I won't bother you after you do this one thing."

"It's all right. My father was a preacher, and he used to minister to people along the Barbary Coast."

Collette brightened, raising painted eyebrows. "Well, he must have been a real good man."

"Yes, he was." Elizabeth realized she needed to think about what God's love truly means. "Let's go to the main deck," she told Collette.

Nervous and unsure, Elizabeth led Collette to the main deck. It was early morning and the sea was quite calm today. They managed to find a place away from others, as many men were still asleep and not milling about. Elizabeth touched the towel and prayed for God to bless the bit of life inside and take him or her into His arms for blessed eternity.

"'Suffer the little children and forbid them not to come unto me,'" she said after praying, "'for of such is the Kingdom of Heaven.'" She noticed tears in Collette's eyes.

"Thank you, ma'am." Collette hesitated, then turned and threw the towel overboard. Gradually the towel soaked . into the water. Collette turned and gave Elizabeth a quick hug. "I'll be leaving you now. You're a kind woman. What's your name, honey?"

"Elizabeth...Elizabeth Breckenridge."

Collette nodded, then turned and left. Elizabeth felt confused by why Collette would live the way she did if she believed in God. She realized she had so much to learn about real people and real life.

She breathed deeply of the morning air and looked up at the sky. It was then she saw him...Clint Brady... watching her. Surely he'd seen her with Collette. What was he thinking? And why did she have this feeling that he was *always* watching her? He gave her a smile and a nod and turned away.

Elizabeth looked back out over the ocean. She could no longer see the towel, and it struck her that just as that tiny bit of life was now in God's hands, so was hers. *"Lord, just don't send me more than I can handle,"* she murmured. *"But I do have so much to learn. Just show me the way."*

Chapter Six

Beloved, let us love one another: for love is of God; and
every one that loveth is born of God, and knoweth God.
—1 John 4:7

Seattle, August 11, 1898

Elizabeth stood beside the railing of the *Damsel*'s main
deck watching supplies being unloaded and a very few passengers disembark at Seattle. Even more men and supplies
waited at the dock to board. Among those leaving the
steamer were Tricia, Francine and Collette, who stopped at
Elizabeth's side for a moment before leaving the ship.

Collette wore a rather plain dress, but it was cut low
enough to show sinful cleavage. "We're going to find a
doctor for Francine," she told Elizabeth.

Elizabeth glanced at Francine, astonished at how young
she, too, looked—as well as how pale, with dark circles under
her eyes. "I hope you feel better soon," she told the girl.

Francine nodded a thank-you and looked away, covering her head with a shawl. She left with Tricia, the only one of the three who appeared to be perhaps as old as thirty.

Collette patted Elizabeth's arm. "Francine truly appreciates you praying over that poor little piece of life, and praying for her, too. I hope you don't think too dreadfully of her. She's had a hard life—never knew her father, and her alcoholic mother abandoned her when she was only ten. Her stepfather treated her...well...not like a daughter, that's for sure, if you know what I mean."

Elizabeth thought a moment, feeling ill when she deduced what the woman was trying to tell her. "Oh, how awful!"

"Well, honey, I don't mean to upset you. I just thought maybe it would help for you to understand how some people end up the way they do. Say, how far into Alaska are you headed, anyway?"

Elizabeth's emotions reeled with pity and shock, and she swallowed before replying. "Uh...Dawson—really it's not Alaska at all—it's up in the Yukon."

"Oh, we know where it is. That's where we were headed. Hey, maybe we'll see you up there!"

Elizabeth wasn't so sure she should be glad about that. "Yes, maybe you will. My brother is building a church there, and I'm going to Dawson to join Peter and help him with his ministry."

"Really?" Collette looked her over. "Well, why am I not surprised? You're such a nice, gracious young woman. By gosh, maybe we'll find that church and go there—that is, if your brother would allow it."

Elizabeth smiled, unable not to like the woman in spite

of her occupation. "He would never turn anyone away for any reason. He's a lot like our father, who accepted all people. He was…killed while ministering along the Barbary Coast. His name was William Breckenridge. Perhaps you've heard of him?"

Collette frowned. "Could have. I mean, I remember hearing about some preacher being killed." She shook her head. "I'm real sorry to hear that, Miss Breckenridge. And I hope you have a safe trip to Dawson, but you should know how dangerous it is for you to be doing this alone. The girls and I would have gladly watched out for you, but we'll be taking a different steamer the rest of the way now." She glanced toward the upper deck. "Then again, I have a feeling somebody is already watching out for you."

Elizabeth glanced in the direction where Collette looked, and there stood Clint Brady. She reddened and looked back at Collette. "I don't even know that man. I mean…he helped chase down a man who'd stolen my handbag, but that's the extent of it."

"Well, the girls and I saw the whole thing. We talked to him briefly the day we all boarded the *Damsel*, and he told us about how you were traveling alone and that it worried him."

"Why? He doesn't even know me."

Collette shrugged. "I expect he's just the kind of man who hates thieves and the like—kind of a lawman at heart. He's a bounty hunter, you know."

Elizabeth's eyes widened. "What?"

"That's right. He showed us a drawing of the man he's after, wanted to know if we'd seen him around San Fran-

cisco before we left. He's pretty darn sure the man is
headed for Dawson, since that's where he's from. So, your
Mr. Brady is going there to find him. There's five thousand
dollars on his head. Heck, it's probably a quicker way of
making five thousand bucks than panning for gold in that
miserable back country." She chuckled. "Anyway, he's obviously a man who knows how to handle himself, so if he's
got an eye on you, that's good." Collette leaned closer.
"And your Mr. Clint Brady is just about the most handsome
specimen of man I've ever set eyes on." She winked. "And
I've set eyes on plenty!" She laughed then. "I wouldn't be
too quick to turn down his attention, sweetie!" She gave
Elizabeth a quick hug. "You have a safe trip now."

The woman turned and walked away, and a rather
stunned Elizabeth watched after her. Again her thoughts
whirled with indecision about people and God's love and
what the Lord expected of her. Was he throwing these
people at her to teach her something? Thieves. Prostitutes.
A bounty hunter! Didn't bounty hunters search out men
and kill them for money? What if the men they looked for
were innocent? And even if they were guilty of whatever
crimes they were accused of, what gave another man the
right to pass judgment to the extent of shooting them down
without a trial? How could one man treat another man no
better than an animal, killing them as they would kill a
beaver for its pelt?

No wonder Clint Brady had been unconcerned about
whether the man who'd attacked her got out of the water!
What would compel a man to have such little concern for
human life? She watched the swarm of people on the

docks. From what she could tell, she just might be the only woman on the *Damsel* for the rest of the journey.

She drew a deep breath for courage. So be it. In spite of what she now knew about Clint Brady, she couldn't help hoping, deep inside, that he really would look out for her.

Lord, what would compel such a nice-looking man who apparently cares about other people to be able to kill another human being for money? Have You brought Clint Brady into my life for a reason? How on earth can I be of any help to such a man?

She watched Tricia, Francine and Collette hail a horse-drawn cab and climb inside. Had she been of any help to them? Any influence? "God be with them," she muttered. She looked around, catching a glimpse of Clint Brady talking to some other men. He was showing them something, most likely the drawing of the man he was hunting. "And be with Mr. Brady," she added.

Chapter Seven

*Jesus saith unto him, I am the way, the truth and
the life: no man cometh unto the Father, but by me.*
—St. John 14:6

Where heaven begins. That was how Peter had described
this land, and Elizabeth was beginning to see what he meant
as the *Damsel* chugged past some of the most magnificent
scenery Elizabeth had ever seen. Because of the stale stench
below deck, she'd spent most of the past three days above
watching the landscape, often pulling her cape close around
her against the cool, misty air. The weather had become
totally unpredictable as the steamer moved through fjords
bordered by mountainous islands that appeared to have no
beaches. It looked as though the deeply forested slopes
simply rose from the sea straight upward.

The mornings were chilly, often followed by a very
warm midday as the sun appeared through the mist, and
yet it could rain within minutes of sunshine, followed by

bright sun again. Every day it rained in spurts, and she had to keep an umbrella with her at all times.

Most of the almost crushing crowd of men on board seemed to have no interest in the gorgeous landscape beyond talk of how much gold lay beneath the distant mountains. She saw a different kind of treasure there, visions of God's beautiful heaven. She realized how right Peter had been in saying that he would be needed at the gold seekers' final destination, for surely there would be hordes of people there who might be hungry for God's Word: people like Collette, who needed to hear about God's forgiveness, men who needed to know that gold was not their God, and men like Clint Brady, who needed their hearts healed by God's love.

Why couldn't she get him off her mind? Why couldn't—

"Miss Breckenridge?"

Elizabeth turned at the words, spoken in a deep voice, Clint Brady's voice. A quick rush of cool air sent a shiver through her, and she drew her cape closer again as she looked up into steel-blue eyes. "Yes?"

He stepped up beside her and leaned on the deck rail. "I have to tell you that I was hoping you'd change your mind and get off at Portland."

Elizabeth frowned in surprise. "Why? You don't even know me. Besides, it's really none of your business where I'm going." She stood next to him, leaning against the railing. Both watched the deep-green mountains as the *Damsel* made its way through currently calm waters.

Clint paused long enough to fiddle with something. Elizabeth waited, not even looking at him, but soon she smelled smoke as he let out a long, deep breath. She glanced at his hands hanging out over the railing, and noticed a cigarette between his fingers.

"Ma'am," he finally spoke up, "I don't think you have an inkling of what you're in for. Even *I* can only guess, from what the rumors are. Either way, it's not an experience for a proper young lady like yourself. A good deal of *men* who make this trip won't manage to even get over the first pass to Dawson. The Canadian North-West Mounted Police are demanding that men tote a good thousand pounds of supplies, because last winter hundreds of men died either trying to get over the passes or from starvation on the way or once they reached Dawson. It's a trip a lot of men can't withstand, let alone a woman alone who doesn't have near the necessary strength to tote a backload of supplies for hundreds of miles. And if that alone isn't enough to make you turn back, you're headed into country where you'll often be caught alone with a pack of men who haven't seen a woman for months. Even the most proper among them would be tempted to forget gentlemanly behavior."

Elizabeth felt a warmth coming into her cheeks at what he was suggesting. "I told you before that God will provide. I trust Him completely, Mr. Brady. Somehow He will help me reach my destination safely."

She heard him give an almost moaning gasp signaling his disbelief. He clearly felt that she was probably stupid and naive to believe what she was saying. He took another long drag on his cigarette.

"Perhaps you don't know much about God and putting your trust in Him, Mr. Brady, but I—"

"Oh, I know all about those things," he interrupted. "I know all too well about trusting God, and how He can completely fail you. Don't preach to me, ma'am. I'm just trying to prevent you from suffering or maybe even losing your life, that's all."

Oh, the bitterness in his comment about God! What was the story behind this man? She remained confused about why he would care about her, and she again asked him that very question.

Clint shifted as though uncomfortable with the entire conversation. "Ma'am, I don't even know why myself. I guess it's because I had a wife once, about your age, and she met with a terrible misfortune. I saw you standing all alone on the dock back in San Francisco and have watched you ever since. I'm worried your simple trust in God is going to make you do something very foolish. It's obvious you aren't very well schooled in life in the real world, and since I don't have much of anything else to do on this journey till I reach Dawson, I figured I'd occupy my time with looking out for you...kind of a leftover from not being there for my wife when she needed me."

So, this had something to do with his wife. Was the life he led also related to what happened to her? She swallowed, not sure just what to say. "Well, Mr. Brady, if you want to go out of your way for me, I suppose I should tell you I appreciate it, but I certainly don't expect it of you or anyone else. It's very kind of you to think of me that way, and I'm deeply sorry for whatever misfortune hurt your wife. Is she well now?"

Another pause, another long drag on the cigarette. "She's dead." The words came flatly, angrily.

"Oh, I'm so very sorry. Truly I am." It was all beginning to make more sense now. Was his wife murdered? Was he searching for her killer?

"I should have made that point in the first place." He sighed and cleared his throat. "I, uh, just want you to know that if you need anything, you can ask. And if I were you, I'd pack some kind of handgun."

Elizabeth had to smile at the very thought of it. "Mr. Brady, that would do me no good. For one thing, I can't afford one, and for another, I wouldn't use it anyway. I could never in my life shoot at someone."

"Not even if they threatened to steal everything you own, or steal what's most precious to you?"

"Most precious?"

She looked up at him curiously. He faced her and rolled his eyes, now appearing rather better-humored. "You don't know what I'm talking about?"

Elizabeth thought a moment, then turned away. "Oh!" She felt ridiculous, embarrassed, angry with him for mentioning such a thing. "God would never allow such a misfortune. Thank you again for your offer, Mr. Brady, but I'll be fine."

He leaned closer. "I meant what I said. Other men might offer the same thing, but I wouldn't trust any of them, understand?"

She drew in her breath, drinking in a bit of courage along with it, and faced him again, hoping her cheeks weren't too flushed. "And why should I trust you and not all the others?"

He looked her over in a way that made her feel safe and warm. It disturbed her to be unable to ignore the fact that he was incredibly handsome. Wasn't it sinful to notice such things about a man?

"Maybe because I'm the one who risked his life to help you out at the docks," he told her. "I didn't see anyone else doing that. Maybe because I've handled some pretty bad characters and know more about that than most of the men on this ship. Maybe because I know how to handle my fists and a gun, which I guarantee you are going to need before this journey ends. And maybe because your God intended for me to notice you. You said yourself that He would be sure you get to Dawson safely. Maybe I'm the reason."

She raised her eyebrows in surprise and grinned. So, he *did* still believe, at least a little. "Are you saying *God* brought us together?"

He gave her a rather sneering smile. "If He did, it was because of you, certainly not because He cares anything about me."

The door was open! "Oh, but He *does*, Mr. Brady. He most certainly does."

Clint took one last drag from his cigarette and tossed the butt into the water. "No, ma'am, I don't think so." He looked around. "Look, there are only three more days left until we reach Skagway. Believe me, when we get there, you'll be thrown into a wide-open, lawless, crowded, wild town where there won't be one man you can trust, and the only women there will be like Collette and those other two who got off at Portland. And, by the way, you need to be careful who you're seen with."

"God loves everyone, Mr. Brady. I can do no less as

His servant. One of them needed my help. I could not turn her away."

He folded his arms, giving her a stern look. "Do you really think that I or the other men on this ship didn't know what was going on?"

Elizabeth's patience was rankled. "It's none of their business, nor yours! They asked me to pray for them, and so I did. I am *not* as naive as you think! My own father was murdered on the Barbary Coast, ministering to harlots and thieves and murderers! I know a little bit about the real world, sir, and I know that *you* are a bounty hunter! You hunt men down for money, so as I said, why should I trust you?"

Why had she said that? She hadn't meant to. She wasn't even going to bring up the subject, which she now knew surely had something to do with his wife! She saw hurt and anger in his eyes. She looked away. "I'm sorry."

"No matter," he said coldly. "I didn't say I was any better than the harlots and murderers you just mentioned. I'm only telling you that I do care what happens to a young woman alone against the odds you'll be facing. In fact, what I was going to say was that for what's left of this journey, you're welcome to use my cabin if you want. I hate to think of you down there with a bunch of men who haven't bathed since God knows when and who I don't doubt are using language you'd rather not listen to. But then since you're more worldly than I thought, I guess it's not so bad for you. And you wouldn't want to stay in a cabin that's been inhabited by a bounty hunter, now, would you? Enjoy the rest of your trip, Miss Breckenridge."

He left her then, and Elizabeth wanted to kick herself.

He'd given her an opening to help him learn about God's love, and she'd missed it! She'd let her own pride and orneriness get in the way. She leaned over the railing again, putting her head in her hands.

Oh, Lord, forgive me! I failed You miserably! Clint Brady had offered to help her, protect her, give up expensive quarters for her, and she'd behaved abominably. What a fool she was! And what a poor servant of the Lord!

Chapter Eight

He that is of God heareth God's words:
ye therefore hear them not, because
ye are not of God.

—St. John 8:47

Clint felt frustrated, angry, anxious, guilty, worried and bored. He tried to think of one positive thing about his life, and he couldn't come up with anything...except Elizabeth Breckenridge, which seemed pretty ridiculous, considering he'd known her all of ten days. Most of that was by sight alone, and the one and only real conversation he'd had with her ended disastrously.

Why in heck did she get to him the way she did? He was making this trip for one reason alone—to find Roland Fisher and either take him back to San Francisco alive, or return with a notarized certificate of his death...by a bullet from Clint Brady's gun. It made no difference to him which way it was. The man was a murderer of innocent people, which meant his life had no value.

The intrusion of Elizabeth Breckenridge into his thoughts and emotions was an unexpected infringement on his life and purpose. Why did he allow it to perplex him? There was absolutely no reason for it, and he wished he'd never run after the thief who took her handbag. Maybe then she would have missed the *Damsel* altogether and he wouldn't be in this mess of emotions.

How could a woman be so ridiculously stupid about her decisions? She was apparently just as misguided as her father had been, actually believing that God would watch out for her and see that she reached Dawson safely. The thought was enough to make a man laugh. Sometimes he wanted to, but the thought of what could really happen to the poor girl sobered him.

He lit another cigarette, glad he'd brought plenty along. Pacing around on the *Damsel* was driving him nuts. He couldn't wait to get off and get away from Miss Naive. At least those below ate at a different time from those with cabins, so he didn't have to see her in the dining room, such as it was. He wondered how her stomach was handling the doughy, half-baked biscuits and tough meat the ship's cook served.

At least once they landed at Skagway he could get away from her. If she was so sure she could make it to Dawson all on her own, then let her find out the hard way that God was *not* going to provide! It would serve her right to discover that maybe there was no God at all. She'd find out how crushing it could be to realize that simple faith wasn't enough when it came to the real evils of the world.

And faith in God was also no use when trying to forget the pain of the past, to get over the loss of loved ones. And forgiveness—that was totally impossible. How can a man forgive those who've robbed him of what was most precious in his life? No, forgiveness is for fools, as is faith in a cruel God. What a mean lesson Miss Breckenridge had yet to learn!

Fools! Half the world was made up of fools. Fools like the men on this ship who'd deserted loved ones to look for a treasure most of them would never find. Fools like Elizabeth Breckenridge. Fools like he'd once been, thinking life could be perfectly wonderful and peaceful and full of joy. He'd almost forgotten what true joy was, forgotten how to smile because of love rather than because of bounty money. He wasn't even sure what to do with all the money he'd gradually built up in a bank in San Francisco. The only things he spent money on were a few clothes, tobacco, the horses that would arrive in Skagway ahead of him on a cattle boat and the best Winchester rifle and Colt handgun money could buy.

A group of men toward the *Damsel*'s bow began singing a risqué song about the women of Skagway and the places they liked to stuff gold nuggets. He wondered if poor Elizabeth could hear the filthy words, then chastised himself for caring. He finished his cigarette and walked over to join the singers, laughing at the dirty lyrics. Laughing. Crying inside.

Elizabeth shivered into her cape, surprised at how cold it was today compared to the lovely day yesterday, with sunshine and no wind. She closed her eyes and concentrated on the beauty of the mountains, softly humming a hymn in her attempt to shut out the dirty, suggestive words of the men singing nearby. Finally the singing stopped when a pod of orca whales began following the ship, sometimes jumping high out of the dark, foggy waters in a magnificent display of black and white majesty.

After nearly a half hour of staying close enough to be seen in spite of the fog, they swam off to the distance, disappearing into the mist. Only minutes later their show was replaced by the antics of a huge herd of chattering dolphins that jumped and rolled and played alongside the ship. The comical sight made Elizabeth and others laugh, and it seemed the blue creatures were laughing with them. They reminded Elizabeth of little children.

It felt good to laugh. Elizabeth glanced around to see if Clint Brady might also be watching the dolphins. She saw him standing farther down along the ship's rail, and yes, he, too, was laughing. She whispered a little prayer of thanks to God for creating something so sweet and beautiful that it could make a man like that forget whatever was burdening him and genuinely laugh, if for just a few moments.

She quickly looked away so he wouldn't catch her watching him, for she suspected he'd fast lose his smile if he knew she'd seen him actually enjoying himself. As little as she knew about him so far, she was pretty sure he'd be stubborn about admitting any kind of brief happiness. Mr. Clint Brady was determined to be mad at the world and at God.

The dolphins disappeared as suddenly as they had appeared, and again the ship was shrouded in thick, cold fog. It was unnerving to know there were islands and rocks and other ships all around, as they'd been watching other steamers ahead of and behind them throughout their voyage. In just one more day, so she'd been told, they would make Skagway, and she would be more than happy to get off the *Damsel* and out of the worsening conditions in the lower deck.

"One more day, fellas," a man nearby shouted.

All the talk was of Skagway and White Pass and Chilkoot Pass and the cost of horses and gear and hope that those who'd gone before had "left some of that there gold for us."

In the distance she could hear another ship's steam whistle. The *Damsel* sounded her own wail in reply, the steam pouring from her stacks only adding to the denseness of the fog. Something about the thick mist made the whistles seem louder than normal, and the other ships' haunting horns seemed all too close.

Suddenly Elizabeth could barely see past her hand, couldn't even see those standing next to her.

How close were other boats? They were in fairly narrow fjords now, no room for error. *"God, protect us,"* she whispered. She'd no more said the words than she felt a jolt, and in what seemed no more than a second she felt the rail on which she leaned give way. She was falling…falling…

She hit the icy water, and the weight of her leather shoes and many layers of under slips, her dress and her fur cape…all caused her to sink…sink…ever deeper.

Chapter Nine

And Jesus said unto him, Receive thy sight:
thy faith hath saved thee.

—St. Luke 18:42

"*Lizzy.*"

Mama?

Elizabeth was sure she'd heard her mother calling her. No one else ever referred to her as Lizzy. She searched the dark waters. Nothing. Was her mother calling her home to heaven? Should she allow her lungs to give up and just breathe in the icy water, allowing herself to drown?

"The Father is with you," her mother told her.

Something strong bumped her, then grabbed her, lifted her. She was near the point of passing out from holding her breath, and from futile efforts to bring herself back to the water's surface. She felt herself rising, rising now instead of sinking. Someone had found her! Who? How many others had fallen overboard when the railing broke?

Thank you, Jesus!

In the next moment her head broke above water and she gasped, desperately gulping air, blessed air. She was alive!

"Hang on to me!" a man's voice commanded.

She obeyed, still not even aware of who it was. He clung to her with one arm and used his other arm to swim.

"Kick your feet a little," he told her.

"I can't swim!"

"Just kick your feet the best you can."

This time the words were shouted. She obeyed, surprised that kicking her feet actually helped. She dug into a muscled back with her right hand as she clung to whoever held her. "Don't let go!" she found herself begging, her words coming through chattering teeth.

The arm holding her tightened. "I didn't jump into this ice bath just to let go of you after finding you," he shouted in reply.

Clint? It sounded like Clint Brady! Had he also fallen in from the broken railing, or had he deliberately dived in after her? Those thoughts flickered through her brain as she struggled against the cruel cold of the water and kept kicking in spite of the weight of her dress and shoes. Between the heavy fog and the water splashing into her eyes, she could barely see a thing, including the man rescuing her. A small boat appeared out of nowhere, and the man led her to it, lifting her slightly.

"Grab on!"

Now Elizabeth could hear other voices, men yelling for help. Two men in the boat reached for her, and the man who'd helped her put his hand on her rump and gave her a boost. She managed to climb over the side of the smaller boat and literally fall into it.

"Hello!" one of the men in the boat shouted. "We're here! We've got a boat. Swim toward our voices."

Coughing and shivering, Elizabeth managed to sit up and stare over the side of the boat. What had happened to Clint?

"You'll be okay now, ma'am," one of those in the boat told her. "We got rammed by another steamer, but the *Damsel* will make it to the closest island. We'll get help right quick, and we'll still make it to Skagway."

Breathless, Elizabeth couldn't even answer. She recognized the man as one of the *Damsel*'s crew. Another man removed his pea coat and put it around her shoulders. Elizabeth very gladly pulled it closer, wondering if she would ever feel warm again. She continued gasping as she waited, watching for Clint to emerge.

After a few minutes two more men came to the side of the boat. To her relief she could see Clint was one of them. The fog seemed to be lifting slightly, enough that she realized Clint had gone out to save someone else. He helped the man to the boat and left yet again, seemingly immune to the cold water.

Minutes later he again returned with yet another man. This time he climbed inside after the man he'd helped. He fell to the bottom of the boat, breathing hard, and Elizabeth noticed he wore only a shirt and pants—no jacket, no gun and no boots or even socks! Surely he hadn't fallen in accidentally at all. He'd taken a moment to half undress so he could swim better, having every intention of rescuing as many as he could.

He sat up and put his head in his hands, still breathing deeply, and there came another cry for help, somewhere in the fog. Clint stood up and dove off the small boat again.

"Clint!" Elizabeth screamed.

Moments later he returned with a third man. Both of them climbed into the boat.

"I hope...that's all of them," Clint panted.

"It's a mighty fine thing you did, mister," one of the crewmen told him.

"Where did you learn to swim so good?" one of those he'd rescued asked.

"Lake Michigan," Clint answered, "a long time ago. I wasn't so sure I'd have the strength I needed, it's been so long." He took several more deep breaths. "Good thing I got the last of you. I was about out of breath." He coughed and glanced at Elizabeth. "You all right?"

"I think so. Oh, Clint, how can I thank you enough? First my handbag, now this—"

"Don't worry about it," he waved her off. He coughed again, then sneezed. "Let's get back to the *Damsel*," he told one of the crewmen, who began rowing.

The crewmen and others from the ship began shouting back and forth to each other, and in moments the *Damsel*, its back end sitting low in the water, came into sight. Another ship sat close by.

"She's takin' on water, but she'll make it to the closest island," one of the crewmen repeated. Men on board threw down ropes, and the crewmen rigged them to trollies on each end of the smaller boat, tossing the ends back up to the deck, where men began hauling the lifeboat upward in even jerks until it was high enough for the passengers to climb onto the deck.

Clint helped lift Elizabeth, and she couldn't help being aware of his strength. Men on deck helped her the rest of the way up, then helped Clint climb on deck. Those he'd rescued were already telling others what Clint had done and what a good swimmer he was. There came a round of thank-yous, and Clint took Elizabeth's arm.

"You're coming to my cabin whether you want to or not. No arguments! You're getting out of those wet clothes and under some covers, and then you're going to pray you don't get sick."

The words were spoken with such command that Elizabeth didn't even consider arguing. She had to half run to keep up with him as he directed her to the wooden steps that led to cabins on the second level. She lifted her soaked dress and managed to climb the stairs, feeling more and more weary with every step, worn out from her struggle, shivering fiercely from the cold. She followed Clint through a door.

"What about the steamer? Isn't it sinking?" she asked Clint.

"They said we'd get to the closest island, and I believe them. Other ships will come along to help us. They'll figure it out." Clint closed the door. "Meantime, we're on the second level. We can probably stay right here until help arrives."

We? "I...what will I change into? What about my things below?"

"I'll go get them for you. You get yourself undressed and under those covers."

"But...I don't have anything to wear!"

Looking rather disgusted, Clint dug through a duffel bag and threw a shirt at her. "Put this on and just get under the covers. I'll be back."

Still soaked and shivering himself, he left before Elizabeth could say a thing. She looked around the tiny room, lit by a lantern and warmed by a small, potbelly stove. She could see glowing embers through the partially open vent. She felt totally bewildered, full of questions, as she began undressing.

Realizing Clint could come back any time, Elizabeth hastily removed her dress, her many slips, her now-squishy high-button shoes, her stockings, and her camisole. Her money fell out. She gasped and quickly gathered it up, looking around for a place to put it, then turned and shoved it under the feather mattress of Clint's narrow bed.

She then removed her wet drawers. "Oh, dear Lord!" she lamented. She was completely naked, but how else was she to dry off and get warm? Still, she was in a man's cabin, about to crawl into a man's bed! How humiliating!

She hurriedly put on the shirt he'd given her, which was far too big. It fell past her knees, but as far as she was concerned, it still didn't cover her legs enough. Elizabeth looked around again, noticing Clint's six-gun hanging over the back of a wooden chair, looking so intimidating and dangerous. She noticed a towel lying beside a bowl and pitcher, and she grabbed it up to dry her hair as best she could, taking out the few pins left in it.

Suddenly she felt nauseated and dizzy. She crawled under the covers, pulling them over herself and settled into the pillow, relishing the warmth of the room, the comfort of the first bed she'd slept in for over a week. She could smell Clint's scent in the pillow, a very pleasant, manly scent, much nicer than the smells below deck. The room itself smelled of cigarettes, leather and wood smoke.

She watched the red coals of the stove, and thought what a blessing fire could be.

"Thank You, Jesus," she whispered, *"for fire, for saving me...for Clint Brady."* Oh, how wonderful felt the warmth of that potbelly stove! She thought about hearing her mother's voice. "Thank you, Mama," she whispered.

Chapter Ten

*Fear ye not therefore, ye are of more value than
many sparrows.*
—St. Matthew 10:31

Elizabeth stirred, for a brief moment remembering lying
in bed at home in San Francisco, the smell of bacon
cooking downstairs, knowing her mother was in the
kitchen preparing breakfast. She loved those moments, the
peace, the feeling of love and safety.

In seconds she came fully awake, realizing she was not
in her own bed at home at all and gradually remembering
where she really was. She lay still a moment, blinking open
her eyes to see through the porthole in the steel door of the
cabin. It was light out. How long had she slept? She turned
over, at first watching a small fire in the potbelly stove, then
realizing through the bit of light that came through the
porthole that a man was sitting on the floor near the stove,
quietly smoking. He had long legs and wore denim pants.

It was only then that she became fully aware of where she was and what had happened. She jerked the blankets to her neck. She put a hand to her hair, realizing it was entirely undone.

"Good morning," came Clint's low voice.

Elizabeth thought a moment. Morning? The accident had happened midmorning. Had she slept such a short while? "I...good morning," she answered, feeling embarrassed and awkward. "What time is it?"

He took a long drag on his cigarette, then reached over and flicked it through the slats of the wood burner. "About nine-thirty."

Elizabeth frowned. Nine-thirty? "But...it was later than that when I fell overboard."

"Yup." Clint sneezed before continuing. "About twenty-two hours ago."

"What! You mean it's the next *day?*"

"Yes, ma'am. You've had a right good sleep."

Astounded, Elizabeth put her hand to her mouth. "I don't believe it!"

Clint stretched, sneezed again, excused himself. "Well, it's true. We've been stranded here since the accident. They're hoping to load some of the passengers onto the next ship that comes by, then more on the next and so forth, till we're all off and on our way to Skagway. We ought to be able to get off later today and make Skagway by tomorrow morning."

Elizabeth rolled to her back and stared at the ceiling. "Oh, I'm so embarrassed, and so sorry! Where on earth did *you* sleep last night?"

"Outside under the stars. Doesn't bother me much. I've spent plenty of nights sleeping on the hard ground with a saddle for a pillow. I just now came in to get warm."

Elizabeth struggled to untangle her thoughts. She pulled the blankets clear up to her nose. "This is terrible. I'm so sorry, and so embarrassed."

"You already said that, and I have no idea why you think that way."

"But I've put you out…and what must the other men think, me sleeping here in your cabin."

He sneezed yet again, then cleared his throat. "They can think what they want. Besides, most of them are only concerned with how soon they can get on another ship and get themselves to Skagway. They're all pretty upset that they've had a setback, all anxious to get to their gold. I can tell you right now that most of them won't find any. I can think of a lot of ways to make good money a lot faster and with less discomfort."

By killing wanted men? She wanted to ask.

Clint leaned forward and rubbed at the back of his neck, squinting slightly as though in pain. Then he sneezed again.

"Are you catching a cold, Mr. Brady?"

He reached toward a saddle bag and pulled out a handkerchief. "I'll be all right."

She watched him quietly a moment. "You could get very sick, after what you did yesterday. Those men and I owe you a lot, me especially. That's the second time you've helped me." Her throat swelled with a sudden urge to cry. "I was so sure I was going to die. How can I ever, ever thank you enough?"

He shrugged. "I just reacted. I used to be a pretty good swimmer." He leaned his head back against the wall.

"I think I remember you saying something about Lake Michigan to someone. Is that where you learned to swim?"

He waited a moment to answer. "I was a kid," he finally told her. "I grew up near Chicago. Then my folks got tired of city life and moved to Nebraska to farm. My mother died when I was seventeen, my father the next year, which left me on my own. I didn't much like the humidity and the mosquitoes in that part of the country, so I headed for California. I'd heard others talk about how nice it was there."

Elizabeth listened to the sound of heated wood snapping and popping in the stove. It relaxed her. "My parents came west from Illinois, too, only farther south from Chicago. I never got to see the Great Lakes. Are they as big and beautiful as I've heard?"

He drew a deep breath. "From what I can remember. It's been years. I do remember that Lake Michigan was so big that you couldn't see the other side of it. Big ships, much bigger than this steamer, would dock in Chicago, bringing goods from practically all over the world, mostly from Europe and, of course, from places like Boston and New York City." He rubbed at his eyes. "But that was a long time ago. Chicago is probably all changed and a heck of a lot bigger by now."

"I'm sorry about your parents. It must have been hard for you. It sounds like you had no brothers or sisters."

"Neither one." The air hung quiet for a moment. "I still miss them sometimes. They were good Christian people." He sneezed again and kept rubbing at his eyes.

Elizabeth was surprised at his reference to "good Christian people." This man apparently had had a Christian upbringing. What on earth had turned him to the life he led now? Youthful curiosity left her dying to ask, but good manners meant not prying into other people's business, especially not a man she suspected gave such information only when good and ready.

"I'm sorry you're not feeling well," she told him. "If you will leave for a while I'll get dressed, you can have your bed back." Privately she thought how wonderful it would feel to stay in the bed all day. "And again I'm sorry to take it from you for so long. I must have been far more exhausted than I thought. All the time I've been on this boat I've barely slept for all the noise and stench below, and worrying about someone trying to rob me. And then nearly drowning yesterday..." Again she remembered her mother calling to her. "My mother's sweet spirit must be very strong."

Clint frowned. "What do you mean?"

Elizabeth turned on her side and curled up. "She called to me. She's the reason you jumped into the water, you know...my mother...and God."

He grunted a laugh. "They were, were they?"

"I'm serious, Mr. Brady. They used you to help me."

He simply chuckled wryly and shook his head.

"You don't believe in the spirits of dead loved ones being able to reach out to you?"

He took several long seconds to answer. "Maybe... sometimes." Again he sneezed. He took a moment to blow his nose. "I'm surprised you believe in such things. Isn't it anti-Christian to believe in spirits?"

"Oh, on the contrary. For one thing, we don't really die anyway, not those who truly have loved and served God. We just travel heaven's pathway to a beautiful home filled with peace and flowers and the glory of God. I like to believe that since our spirits simply take on a new form and live on with God, He allows us to hover close to our loved ones still living on earth and to help them however we can. God surely has enough to do. I believe He uses our spirits to help Him with His constant vigil to protect and love His children on earth."

He shook his head again, grunting a little as he stood up and stretched. "Well, I don't see where He does a very good job of protecting those still on earth. And me managing to find you like I did was just a quirk—nothing special."

She smiled softly. "You don't really believe that. The other men you helped were thrashing and yelling, easier to find. But me, I was sinking far below the surface, yet you found me. No one could ever convince me that God and my mother didn't have something to do with that."

Clint rummaged in one of his own carpet bags and pulled out yet another clean shirt. He began unbuttoning the one he wore, and Elizabeth's eyes widened when she realized he was going to take it off in front of her! Other than black men working on the wharf in San Francisco, she'd never seen a man with his shirt off! She pulled the blankets over her head. "Mr. Brady!"

"What?"

"Couldn't you wait until I'm gone to change your shirt?"

This time his light laughter sounded genuine. "You've never seen a man with his shirt off?"

"Of course not!"

"Not even your father or your brother?"

"Heavens no!"

Elizabeth heard the soft rustle of clothes. "Lady, your situation is even worse than I thought."

Elizabeth waited, refusing to uncover her eyes.

"You can look now," he finally told her.

Slowly she pulled the covers away to see him wearing a shirt and a leather vest. He was leaning over pulling on socks and boots.

"I think these boots have dried out," he told her as he finished dressing. "By the way, in case you didn't notice, I brought your things up from below, and I laid your wet clothes around the room to dry out." He sneezed again. "I'll leave for a while and you can dress and go to the kitchen and get something to eat, such as it is. At least you can get some hot coffee. You might as well pack up as best you can and be prepared to leave the ship later today. Next stop is Skagway. It's a good thing you got some rest. You'll need it when you reach that town. Rough and lawless, they say." He straightened. "Did your money survive?"

"Yes, it's under your mattress."

He grinned and shook his head again. "Don't tell me you thought I'd *steal* it."

"Well, I...I just wasn't sure where to put it."

He chuckled. "Just make sure you stuff it back into your camisole." He winked. "Where it's dang sure safe."

He walked out the door, and Elizabeth wanted to crawl through the cracks in the floors and disappear. She looked around the room to see that Clint had indeed hung her clothes all about the cabin to dry—including her camisole, under slips and drawers!

She closed her eyes in humiliation.

Chapter Eleven

For now we see through a glass, darkly; but then face to face: Now I know in part; but then shall I know even as also I am known.
—1 Corinthians 13:12

Skagway, August 20, 1898

Clint could see the outline of Skagway in the distance, visible only because of smoke and steam from the stacks of other steamers docked there. The crew of the *Damsel* had managed to keep the steamer's leak in check enough to bring the ship into the "jumping-off" town with the help of a tugboat sent from there. That meant that everyone on board the *Damsel* could stay there and be towed in, much to the chagrin of some who were bent on getting to the town a day sooner.

Clint wouldn't have minded if not for the fact that waiting the extra day had meant letting Elizabeth Breckenridge sleep in his cabin one more night. Try as he might, he couldn't get the picture of her in his bed out of his mind.

If ever his resolve to resist temptation had been tested to the limit, the last two nights had been it. He'd managed until now not to think about how long it had been since he'd been with a woman. After Jenny was killed, all desire for any other woman in his life had left him. After a matter of time, he'd not even cared about being with easy women, let alone giving one thought to truly having feelings for any woman ever again.

So why had Elizabeth Breckenridge changed all that? It made him so angry he could spit. This was never supposed to happen to him again. For one thing, it was dangerous to care. That meant risking having his heart shattered yet again, and it wasn't even mended from the first disaster. Besides that, he was full of too much hatred and anger to find room for caring about anyone. He hadn't even cared about himself for the past four years. How many times had he wished that in pursuit of a criminal he'd get shot and killed so the pain in his heart would go away forever? Then he could be with Jenny… and little Ethan.

There came the sharp pain again, so real that it made him grasp the rail and bend over. For months now he'd managed to stop thinking about his son altogether. Maybe, just maybe, he could have gotten over Jenny, if only he still had his little boy…his sweet, innocent, joyful little blue-eyed, blond-haired son named after his daddy. From the day he'd had to look at that beautiful child lying dead he'd never again used his real first name, because every time someone would call him Ethan he'd think about that baby. He used only his middle name now. That helped some.

A hard sneeze brought him out of the pain of the past long enough to remember how lousy he felt today. This was the worst cold he'd ever experienced, and it hadn't helped sleeping on the deck last night. It had rained, as it seemed to do several times a day in this place, but at night it was a cold rain that went to the bone. He'd covered himself with a tarp, but the dampness had enveloped him anyway. Every bone and muscle in his body ached. It hurt to breathe, hurt even more to cough, hurt to look at bright light, hurt to move at all.

As soon as he reached Skagway he hoped to find one available hotel room where he could stay in bed for a day or two before heading into God-knew-what in his effort to reach Dawson. He could only hope that the holdup wouldn't mean missing his chance to corral Roland Fisher. If he somehow heard Clint was after him, he might slip away.

Life sure had taken a strange turn since he'd first tackled the man who stole Elizabeth's handbag. Something about this whole trip just didn't seem right, kind of like he suddenly was not in full control of his life. Elizabeth weighed on his mind like an anvil, and try as he might, he couldn't keep from feeling like he should watch out for her. He thought he'd be glad to reach Skagway, where he could let her go her own way. If that meant she'd really be dumb enough to try to reach Dawson this late in the year, then so be it. And yet the thought of it drove him nuts. How could he let her try to do that alone? Stupid as the idea was, he had to admire her gumption...and her unending faith that God would help her.

At the same time, he couldn't help feeling sorry for her having that faith. God would find a way to shatter it, just as his own faith had been shattered. Fact was, he hadn't even given much thought to God for the past four years, until Miss High-and-Mighty-Holy-Roller had come along, constantly throwing God in his face. There again, he had no control over having to listen to her rhetoric about God and Jesus and prayer and all that bunk. That's what made it so senseless to think about helping her get to Dawson, which was exactly what he'd been thinking about doing...probably the worst decision he could possibly make.

Another sneeze. Could a man feel any worse than this without being dead?

"Clint?"

Someone touched his arm. Naturally it was Elizabeth.

"You're even sicker, aren't you? I'm so sorry you had to sleep on the deck last night. I told you I'd gladly go back below."

He sneezed again, which only increased his irritation with her and then enhanced his anger with himself for *being* irritated with her, because the way he was feeling inside wasn't her fault. It was his own. Still, that didn't stop his sharp retort. "I wish you'd stop bringing it up. I told you that you could have the bed and that's that." He sneezed, and she leaned closer to study him as he blew his sore nose.

"Oh, you poor man. You look awful!"

"Gee, thanks." He coughed, his chest so sore that he hadn't even craved a cigarette.

"I hope you will see a doctor when we reach Skagway."

"I don't need one. I just need a day or two of rest. I'll be fine."

"I wish there was something I could do. You've done so much for me."

"I'll get over it."

"Well, I think you should definitely see a doctor."

"Will you just leave it alone? I'll be all right." He knew she was right about one thing. He must look terrible. He kept his handkerchief over his nose so she couldn't see how red it was. He leaned over the railing again, looking away from her as the outline of Skagway came ever closer. Other men on deck were getting excited, some whooping and hollering at the sight of their jumping-off point. He heard Elizabeth take a deep breath, for courage, he suspected.

"I guess this is it," she told him. "I hope you stay in Skagway and rest up a bit before you go on, and I will pray for your health and for a safe trip."

"Pray for yourself. You're the one who will need help, not me."

Another sigh. "If you are so adamant that it was all right that I use your cabin again last night, Mr. Brady, then please stop being so angry and making me feel so guilty about it."

How he wished that she would just magically drop out of his life. "Sorry. I just feel rotten, that's all." He sneezed again. "I am not in the mood for small talk." He blew his nose and finally looked at her again. She looked as pretty as ever, and it irked him that he'd taken a cold and she seemed to be just fine. Wasn't the man supposed to be the stronger one? How humiliating! He hated showing any kind of weakness.

"Well, then, I'm sorry I bothered you," she answered, looking almost ready to cry. "I just wanted to let you know that I have everything out of your cabin. Once we reach Skagway we might not see each other again, so I just...I truly, truly am grateful, Mr. Brady, for everything you've done for me, and for being so kind as to let me have your cabin the last two nights. You're a good man at heart. Anyone can see that. I will pray that whatever is eating you up on the inside, God will bless you with a way to overcome the pain and be happy again. And I pray that you will be able to stop doing what you do for money. God will forgive you, you know, because only He understands why you do it. I just wanted to tell you that He loves you and—"

Clint rolled his eyes. "Thank you, but save the sermon. I hope the best for you, too. And I still advise you to get yourself a handgun, and be very, very careful who you trust. Find someone to travel with, preferably a man who is taking his wife along so you'll be with another woman." He sneezed. "Good luck, Elizabeth. You'll need it," he said as he moved away.

The *Damsel* let off three loud whistles then, as the tugboat hauled her even closer. Skagway was very visible now, and her docks were crowded with men who'd just disembarked from another steamer that had arrived ahead of them. The men on the *Damsel* began getting even more excited, shouting about gold and land and women and whiskey and dogs and horses and sleds and the best route to take for Dawson. They pushed and shoved to get a better look, some of them forcing Elizabeth away from the railing.

Clint looked back to see her watching him with tears in her eyes. She had to be scared to death. He turned away. She'd made her decision. He had his own agenda.

Chapter Twelve

*The Lord is my shepherd; I shall not want. He
maketh me to lie down in green pastures:
He leadeth me beside the still waters. He restoreth
my soul...I will fear no evil, for Thou art with me.*
— Psalms 23:1-4

It was all Elizabeth could do to hang on to her bags, there
was so much pushing and shoving to get off the *Damsel*.
Most of those who pushed their way past her seemed
hardly aware she existed. The day had turned sunny and
warm, but because of the constant spurts of rain, she
stepped into mud as soon as her feet hit land.

She had no choice but to follow the crowd and walk past
a literal town of tents on the beach, her shoes sinking into
the damp sand. Men and dogs and supplies were absolutely
everywhere. Stove chimneys stuck up through the tops of
the tents. Stacks of barrels of flour and crates of canned
goods were piled so high it appeared they would surely

topple. Some of the men literally ran toward Skagway's main street, and she had no choice but to go with the flow or be knocked over.

The throng shoved her into the main, muddy street, through slop and horse manure. After a desperate search to get out of the way, she finally spotted an opening to her left that brought her to a boardwalk and directly in front of swinging doors. From the other side she could hear a piano playing, men shouting and women laughing. The smell of whiskey and smoke permeated her nostrils, and she quickly moved away from the doorway. She couldn't help peeking through a window, and her eyes widened at the sight of women dancing on a platform, lifting colorful ruffled skirts to show their legs.

She turned away, feeling guilty for looking in the first place. Still, the sight made her wonder about Collette and her friends. She hoped Francine was all right.

She shook away the thought and hurried on, facing the fact that for the time being she had to look out for herself and not worry about others, including Clint Brady. He'd said something to her yesterday about having to locate three horses he'd sent ahead. He'd been worried about someone making off with his horses, as he'd heard the animals were worth plenty in Skagway. Most men arrived here without them and had to pack their own gear over the passes, which meant constantly backtracking all the way over the passes as the gear often weighed hundreds, even thousands of pounds. Word was, many never even made it over the passes to begin with.

Elizabeth had decided that would not be a problem for

her, as all she intended to take were her bags. She would visit the sawmill and see if perhaps someone there could build her a sled that she could attach to her waist and use to pull her bags and however much food she would have to bring along. That would probably take whatever money she had left, but she certainly wouldn't need any more money before reaching Dawson. Once she was with Peter, she'd be safe and never alone again. Whatever Peter did, wherever he went, she would stay with her brother. She couldn't wait to see him.

Yes, that's what she would concentrate on. She would forget about those poor, lost women, forget about Clint Brady, forget about her own fear of the journey ahead. Collette and her friends were likely not at all concerned with what had happened to her, and Clint Brady had brushed her off like a pesky fly. Why should she care that the man was sick and lonely and wayward? Her attempted words of comfort had only angered him, and he obviously did not want her bothering him any more. So be it.

She put her head down and charged forward, ignoring other people, watching her step as she walked down wooden steps, crossed in front of an alley, walked up more steps to the next block of boardwalk. She looked at every window she passed, and every other establishment seemed to be a saloon. In between were supply stores, attorneys' offices, banks, a newspaper office and finally she came across a hotel. She had to climb even more steps to reach the entrance, and from that standpoint she could see another hotel, a blacksmith's barn, more supply stores, a sign that read Boats, another that read Book Store, and a

few restaurants. The words Saloon and Bank far outnum-
bered all others.

Above some of the saloons were balconies upon which
stood brightly dressed women, many of whom wore
dresses cut so low that they barely covered the merchan-
dise being advertised. She noticed one woman who wore
only underclothes. She was laughing and waving at the
throng of men in the street.

The sight was difficult to believe. Now and again a supply
wagon would splatter past, churning up the mud. She
smelled the sweet scent of fresh-cut pine, and in the distance
she could hear the grinding sounds of the sawmill that
created the smell. She recalled someone on the *Damsel*
saying something about Skagway being nothing but a
couple of buildings just a year ago, then becoming a huge
tent city almost overnight. Now most of the tents had
become real buildings, and more building was continuing.
The air rang with the pounding of hammers and the scraping
of saws and was redolent with the smell of fresh lumber.

Smoke rose into the air from a hundred sources, mostly
from the stacks of the steamers at the shoreline and from
wood-burning stoves inside most of the buildings. Elizabeth could not help thinking what rich men the suppliers
must be, and those who made wood stoves and guns and
shovels and boots and the like. She thought how, if she were
not alone and unsure of what to do next, this could be
terribly exciting. As big as San Francisco was now, she had
never seen so many people crowded together in one small
place, or heard so much noise or seen so much bustle and
commotion. She imagined San Francisco must have been

like this during the gold rush in California, but that had taken place long before she was born.

Without even realizing it, she found herself scanning the throngs of men for one face. Tall as he was, Clint Brady would surely be easy to find. He usually wore a leather vest and a wide-brimmed, Western hat, different from the wool felt derbys most men wore, whether dressed in suits or in more rugged clothing.

She searched patiently, but caught no glimpse of Clint. Then she rolled her eyes in disgust with herself for wanting to find him. She'd just convinced herself it was stupid to look, and even though God surely intended for her to help him in some way, there was nothing she could do if he was determined to keep her out of his life.

She turned and picked up her bags, going into the hotel. It had been a long day, and she felt literally banged up from struggling through the crowd to get this far. She walked across a plank floor to greet the desk clerk. "Might I be lucky enough to find a room for the night?" she asked.

The very short, bespectacled man frowned. "I'm very sorry, lady, but I'm full up."

Elizabeth's heart fell. "Is there *any* hotel in town that might have room?"

The man pursed thin lips and thought. "Well, you seem like a nice young lady, and I know for a fact you won't find a room anyplace else, either. I hate to put you out." He looked past her. "Did your husband bring a tent along or something like that?"

She hated telling a stranger that she was alone. "I'm…I don't have a husband, but my brother is meeting me in town from a different boat in a few days. I really need a place to stay in the meantime. I'll take anything. It doesn't have to be fancy."

He rubbed his forehead, then ran a hand through thinning hair. "Well, my own wife would be real upset if I sent you back into the streets without shelter." He leaned closer. "Don't tell anybody, but I can let you stay in a storeroom in the back. I can set up a cot in there, and there's a wash bowl and pitcher, and a privy just outside the back door. It's the best I can do. I'd have to charge you fifty cents."

Elizabeth breathed a sigh of relief. "That will do fine!" It was a relief to actually find a kind man who was truly concerned about her well-being. His smile was warm and genuine. Yes, God was looking out for her after all!

She dug into her handbag for some of the loose change and smaller bills she kept in it and dug out the required fee. "As far as I know it will only be one night, but is it all right if I let you know tomorrow if I find I need a second night's stay?"

"Sure thing. Fact is, by then one of my roomers might leave and you can have his room."

"Oh, thank you!"

The clerk turned the registration book around so she could sign it. "Awfully wild and raw place for a nice lady like yourself," he told her as she dipped the pen into an inkwell and signed her name.

"A person just does what she has to do sometimes, Mr.— Oh, what is your name?"

"Michael Wheeler, ma'am. Wife and I came here last summer from Seattle—figured we'd make more money putting people up than looking for gold, so we sold everything and came here to build this hotel. Don't serve any food, I'm afraid. You'll have to go out for that. I can bring you an extra pitcher of water for drinking, though."

"That would be wonderful."

Wheeler closed the book and signaled for her to follow him. He led her to a room behind his office, where stacks of blankets and pillows and towels were stored, as well as a few brooms, crates of soap bars, several oil lamps, a box of ink jars, several books and ledgers and a few extra bowls and pitchers.

"The wife and I live in an apartment in back of the second-floor rooms," the man told her. "Right now we only have ten rooms, but we plan to add on a third floor and expand the first two."

"Well, I'm glad you're doing so well," Elizabeth told him.

"There's a bolt lock right here on your side of the doorway, and the back door there, it has one, too, so once you're down for the night, just slip both locks closed and you'll be plenty safe. Me or the wife might end up knocking on the door to get something, but that almost never happens once everybody is bedded down for the night. Trouble is, this is a town that never sleeps, if you know what I mean, so you're better off back here anyway. You won't hear the noise from the streets near as bad back here."

"Thank you so much. You're very kind. Perhaps in the morning you can advise me on what things I'll need to journey to Dawson."

The man's smile faded. "*Dawson?* You're headed for *Dawson?*" He spoke the words as though she was insane.

"Yes." She remembered the story she'd told him about

her brother. "As soon as my brother arrives, we'll go together. I just thought I'd get a head start on supplies."

Wheeler shook his head. "Ma'am, brother or not, I wouldn't advise you to head for Dawson till next spring. I mean, I know a lot of the new arrivals here are headed that way, but they're men and they're determined to find gold. Most of them are going to regret leaving this late in the year. But…I mean…men can take care of themselves, you know? And maybe your brother can, too, but he ought not to take you along. You should wait and leave next spring. It's a rough trip, miss, a real rough trip. A lot of the men headed there will never make it."

His words dashed the excitement and affirmation she'd allowed to build within her spirit. Her chest tightened with trepidation. "Nevertheless," she replied, "it's important that I…I mean we…go this year. But thank you for the warning. I'm sure we'll be all right. God is with us, Mr. Wheeler."

He shook his head. "Well, I sure hope so, ma'am. I sure hope so." He shook his head again. "I'll go rummage up a cot for you. There's an extra one in one of the rooms."

Wheeler nodded to her and left, closing the door behind him. Elizabeth drew a deep breath against the sudden urge to cry. She sat down in a wooden chair and put her head in her hands. *"Dear Lord, help me to be strong,"* she prayed. *"Show me the way."*

Chapter Thirteen

*For I was an hungered, and ye gave me meat: I
was thirsty, and ye gave me drink: I was a
stranger, and ye took me in: ...I was sick, and ye
visited me.*
—St. Matthew 25:35 & 36

Mr. Wheeler was right. Skagway never slept. Even
though Elizabeth was at the back of the hotel, she could
still hear talking and laughing, sometimes a scream, even
gunfire a time or two. More conversation with the hotel's
owner enlightened her to the fact that the crowds of men
in town were a grand mixture of those planning to head for
Dawson and many more who had started the journey and
turned back because of the hardships. There were also
those who had already been to Dawson and been disappointed to find most good claims had already been laid.
And many, like Mr. Wheeler himself, had come to
Skagway with the intention of staying put and making

their money off the other groups of people. These included the men who owned the saloons and other business establishments, and those who owned the steamers that brought men here and would take many of those same men, and the gold, back to the States.

Tired as she was, Elizabeth lay awake wondering if indeed she should wait until spring to make for Dawson. But what in the world would she do over the winter to survive? Perhaps she could find some kind of work here in Skagway, but this was such a wild town, and she was already tired of being so alone and unsure.

She finally fell into a fitful sleep filled with crazy dreams, the purgatory between asleep and awake. She dreamed that the whole town of Skagway was under water, and she was trying to swim to the top of the hotel. Her mother stood near the chimney, smiling at her. Then Peter floated by in a rowboat that had smokestacks on it, but he didn't stop to pick her up. Collette and her friends sat on the roof of a nearby building laughing at her. One man swam past her and stole her hat. She tried to swim after him, but he was too fast for her. Reverend Selby threw a Bible at her, and she clung to it to stay afloat.

Finally she floated past some steps where a man stood. It was Clint Brady. He smiled and reached for her, and she grabbed his strong arms. He pulled her up, but then he started sneezing and dropped her. Then both of them began coughing, and she began drowning. She cried out for help. Help. Help.

"Help," she murmured in her sleep. In the dream she was screaming the word. She jumped awake, only half aware at first that she'd been trying to cry out in her sleep. She sat up and shook her head, deciding that if she went right back to sleep her brain would return to the silly but stressful dream. Even awake she could swear she still heard Clint coughing.

She stood up, running a hand through her hair and shaking it out, realizing only then that she *was* hearing a man cough. It was a terrible, deep cough, and it came from not far outside her door. Then came the sneezing. It all sounded familiar.

"Clint?" she said softly. It couldn't be. She went to the door that divided the store room from the lobby, then slid the bolt, cracking the door open slightly to peek out. If someone was out there, she didn't want them to see her in her flannel nightgown.

There came the coughing again. A man lay in a bedroll behind the clerk's desk, apparently having been allowed to sleep there for the night. The hotel did not yet have electricity, and by the soft light of a lantern Elizabeth could see he was a big man. Was it Clint? Whoever it was, he sounded very sick. Surely the Lord would want her to see if there was anything she could do for him. He shouldn't be sleeping on a hard, drafty floor.

She quickly turned and pulled on a flannel robe, tying it tightly. She walked into the lobby, looking around to see that no one was there but the sick man. She walked noiselessly over to him and leaned closer.

"Clint!" she said in a half whisper. His breathing was horribly rattled.

"Liz...beth?" he murmured. Immediately he started

coughing again, a cough that made him sit up and lean over. He held his chest and gasped for breath.

Elizabeth dared to reach out and touch his face. "Dear Lord, you're burning up! Clint, you're a terribly sick man! Come into the back room and lie down on my cot. You shouldn't be out here on the floor."

"No...rooms..." he choked out.

"I know. That's why I'm in the storeroom. Please, Clint, let me help you back there. I'll try to find a doctor for you."

"Be...okay..." He coughed again, and his whole body trembled. "Don't want to...put you out."

"After what you did for me? And I wasn't even sick! You will *not* lie out here like this! Please, Clint, come to the back room. It's warmer in there. There is a little wood-burning stove in there that Mr. Wheeler let me use. I'll see if I can find a teakettle back there and heat some water on it. And I'll wake up Mr. Wheeler and see if his wife can lend me some tea. Maybe Mr. Wheeler can send for a doctor."

"No. I can't...let you..." He coughed again. "Never... felt like this...in my life."

"And you *are* going to let me help you, whether you like it or not! If you don't come lie down on my cot I'll find some men to come and *drag* you in there! I swear it!"

Clint groaned again, clinging to his chest as he managed to reach up with his other hand and grab hold of the desk top to pull himself up. Elizabeth put her arm about his waist and let him lean on her. She led him into the back room and ordered him onto her cot, which he seemed to take gladly. She helped him remove his boots and jacket, and he then curled onto the cot, the raspy, deep cough consuming him again as she threw her blankets over him, even though he was still fully dressed.

"Don't you get up from here," she ordered, tucking blankets around his neck. "I'm going for that tea and a doctor!" His condition frightened her. She'd never seen anyone so sick, other than when her mother had died of the ugly cancer. This was different. She knew that sometimes people died from pneumonia, and surely that's what poor Clint suffered from.

That's when it struck her that she'd be absolutely devastated if he did die. She still hardly knew the man, and yet the thought of him being dead tore at her heart. She blinked back tears of distress, not really sure what to do to help him, not sure whether there was a decent doctor in Skagway... realizing that if Clint died, she would have failed to help him find God again before his death. He would die so terribly lonely, and an unsaved man!

Chapter Fourteen

Then they cry unto the Lord in their trouble, and
He saveth them out *of their distresses.*
—Psalms 107:19

Elizabeth managed to dress quickly behind a shelf of supplies so Clint could not see her, although he seemed in no shape even to be aware of what was happening around him. She'd managed to wake the Wheelers in their upstairs apartment. Mrs. Wheeler loaned her some tea and a strainer, and Mr. Wheeler promised to find a doctor. However, it was now dawn, and still no doctor had arrived.

She finished buttoning her dress, leaving off most of her slips. Quickly she pulled her hair back and twisted it into a bun, shoving hairpins into it. On stockinged feet she searched for her shoes. Before she could find them, someone knocked at the back door. She walked closer. "Who is it?"

"It's Michael Wheeler. I found a doctor," came the reply.

Elizabeth unbolted the door and Wheeler walked in with another man who appeared to be in his fifties, with thinning hair that needed cutting, a scraggly gray beard and a mustache badly in need of a trim. He'd pulled on a woolen jacket and pants, but he wore no shirt. Rather, the top half of his long johns showed under his jacket. Elizabeth was relieved to see that he'd apparently realized the seriousness of Clint's situation and had hurriedly dressed, however, he certainly did not fit her idea of an educated physician.

"Doc Williams," the man mumbled as he hurried over to kneel beside the cot, where Clint still lay curled up.

"He coughed so hard that he threw up blood," Elizabeth told the man. She suspected Clint was not even aware of it. "I'm afraid I soiled one of your towels cleaning things up," she explained to Wheeler. "I'm so sorry."

"Don't worry about it," the man replied.

Again Elizabeth silently thanked God that she'd found at least one person with a bit of compassion in this wild town.

"I tried to get him to drink some tea," she told the doctor, "but he's so far gone I couldn't even get him awake enough to take any. He's burning up, Doctor Williams, and when he threw up blood like that—"

The doctor waved her off, pulling back the covers and forcing Clint onto his back. Clint flopped over as though half dead. Doctor Williams ripped open his shirt and the top half of his long johns without even stopping to unbutton anything first, then placed a stethoscope to Clint's chest. He moved it to his ribs, then managed to roll him forward so he could move the stethoscope to Clint's back. After a moment he pulled the stethoscope from his ears and took

Clint's pulse. Then he sighed and rose, facing Elizabeth and Wheeler.

"It's pneumonia, all right."

Elizabeth gasped with dread. "What can we do?"

Williams shook his head. "Not much, really. I've got some horse liniment you can heat up and rub on his chest, and if you keep a cool towel on his head—"

"*Horse* liniment?" Elizabeth interrupted.

"Yes, ma'am. Generally what works for a horse with pneumonia will work for a man with pneumonia, if it's God's will that he lives."

Elizabeth looked at Wheeler with a frown. Wheeler rubbed at the back of his neck. "He, uh, he's a horse doctor. Best thing I could find under the circumstances. Most doctors who come through here are on their way to Dawson. A real doctor is supposed to be on his way here to stay, but he hasn't made it yet."

Elizabeth looked back at the doctor, confused as to whether she should be grateful or angry. "A *horse* doctor?" she repeated.

"Ma'am, I've took care of humans lots of times. I've pulled teeth and delivered babies and even took out bullets a time or two. A horse has a heart and lungs and organs and blood and guts same as a man. Like I said, what works for pneumonia on a critter can sometimes work for a man, too." He reached inside his black bag and took out a fair-sized brown bottle. "This here stuff smells mostly like lemon, but it has a stink to it, too. Fact is, it's just possible the smell alone will rouse him and make him want to get better just so he can wash the stuff off. I guarantee it'll sink through and break up all that congestion inside of him so he can get rid of it, but he'll do a lot more coughin' first. This stuff will help bring down the fever, too. That's the most important thing."

Elizabeth was still trying to deal with the fact that a horse doctor was treating a man who was close to death.

"You take this here liniment and warm the bottle in hot water, then rub it all over his chest and a little on his back if you can manage to do that. Then keep him covered good and keep cold wet towels on his forehead to help bring down the fever. If God's of a mind to let him live, then he should be feelin' a lot better within about twenty-four hours."

Elizabeth blinked. Rub the liniment on his bare chest? "I...I wouldn't feel right touching his chest. Can't you do it?"

Williams frowned. "Well, he's your husband, ain't he?"

Elizabeth hesitated. She didn't want to lie, but she also realized how bad it might look if she didn't. She glanced at Wheeler. "Mr. Wheeler, I met this man on the ship coming here. He's just a friend because he helped me out a couple of times. I only brought him in here because I could see how sick he was and I felt responsible. I fell off the ship and he dived in after me. I fear his condition is worse because of going into that cold water to help me. I found him out in the lobby and gave him my cot to get him off the drafty floor. I can't...I mean, I shouldn't stay in here alone nursing him. How would it look? Isn't there someone who could help?"

Wheeler looked at Williams, who shook his head. "You're lucky I came over here at all," the doctor told her. "I'm leavin' in an hour or so for Dawson myself, so don't count on me." He walked up to Elizabeth and handed her the liniment. "Lady, if the man saved you from drownin', then the least you can do is rub some liniment on his chest and do whatever else you need to do to help him live." He headed for the back door. "Oh, and keep him a bit elevated," he added, "else his lungs could fill up and drown him."

"But—"

Williams turned to face her with a look that told her he'd done all he could do.

"How much do I owe you?" she asked.

"Nothin'."

The man turned and left, and Elizabeth faced Mr. Wheeler with questioning eyes.

Wheeler sighed and glanced at Clint, then back to Elizabeth. "Ma'am, most folks in this town are either coming back from somewhere or going somewhere or running businesses. I wouldn't know who to tell you to go to for help, and I kind of hate to have my wife help on account of she tends to take chest colds easy anyway and at her age—"

"I understand," Elizabeth told him. "I guess I'll just…do what I have to do."

Clint fell into another round of pitiful coughing and groaning, and Wheeler looked anxious to leave. "I'd help you myself, but if I get too close I could maybe somehow take something home to the wife, you know?"

Elizabeth closed her eyes, hiding her exasperation. "I understand. Thank you so much for going out in the dark and trying to find a doctor. That was very kind of you. I hope you don't mind letting me…us…use the room for however long it takes for Mr. Brady to feel better."

"That's fine. I won't even charge you."

"I deeply appreciate that, Mr. Wheeler."

The man patted her arm and left. Elizabeth bolted both doors and stood there a moment, clinging to the bottle of horse liniment, and in resignation leaning her forehead against the door, eyes closed in prayer.

"Lord, for some reason You have placed this burden on me. And so I accept it. And if I am the one who has to... touch Mr. Brady's bare chest, please understand that it's necessary to save his life and not a sinful act. Please work through my hands to heal this man who has done so much for me."

Steeling her resolve, she turned to face Clint, who lay hanging over the side of the cot coughing up more blood. It seemed incredible to think a man could drown lying in bed!

"Heaven help me," she whispered. She walked over to take the lid from the kettle of water on top of the potbelly stove, then loosened the cork on the horse liniment and set it into the water to warm it up.

While waiting for the horse liniment to warm, Elizabeth took a towel from a stack of several on a shelf and hung it over the elbow of the stove pipe to warm. She knelt beside Clint. His face was flushed with fever, and his rattled breathing was interspersed with groans. He appeared barely cognizant of her presence. God had given her a job to do, and do it she must.

She took a deep breath and grasped hold of one of Clint's hands, closing her eyes.

"Heavenly Father," she prayed, *"help me to look upon this man as Your child and not a stranger. Use my hands*

to help heal, and help me say the right words to him when he recovers. Guide me in every way, Lord Jesus, and please let Clint Brady live. More than that, I pray that somehow he finds his way back to You and can stop living the life he lives now. Thank You, Jesus. Amen."

With that, she rose and leaned closer, touching Clint's shoulder. "Clint, try to roll onto your back so I can put some liniment on you."

He did not respond.

"Clint? I need your help here." She pushed at his shoulder, and he groaned. "Clint, roll onto your back."

"Jenny?" he moaned.

Who was Jenny? His dead wife? Did he think she was Jenny? "Yes," she answered. "Roll over, Clint."

Finally he moved to lie flat on his back. Taking a deep breath for courage, Elizabeth pulled open his shirt, which had only two buttons left on it because of the way Dr. Williams had jerked it open. She turned and took the liniment from the kettle and poured some into the palm of her right hand, her eyebrows arching in reaction to the strong scent. If not for the mild scent of lemon, the concoction would literally stink, and she wondered that the strong aroma did not stir Clint fully awake.

She smeared the oily substance onto Clint's chest. She worked it along his ribs and around under him as far as she could get with him still on his back. By then she'd used up the first dose and poured more into her palm to smear over his upper chest, all the way to his neck. Hard as she tried to ignore it, she could not help thinking what a big, strong, brave man he was, or noticing how hard-muscled he was.

Nor could she avoid the odd curiosity touching his bare skin aroused in her thoughts.

She suddenly drew away, ashamed for wondering. *"God, forgive me,"* she whispered, turning to take the warmed towel from the stove pipe. She laid it over Clint's chest and pulled his shirt closed as best she could, then covered him. She washed her hands of the liniment and then poured fresh water into a bowl and wet a washrag with it. As she washed Clint's face with the cool rag, she realized he was already growing quite a stubble of a beard. Should she try to shave him? Surely he had a razor in his gear, but she'd never shaved anything in her life, and she feared cutting him. With any luck he would be well enough to shave himself in a day or two.

She rinsed the rag and wrung it out again, folding it and laying it across his forehead. Then she took hold of his hand again. "You're going to be all right, Clint," she said softly. "I'll not leave you until you're completely well."

To her surprise, he squeezed her hand. "Jenny?" he said again. "I'm so...sorry."

Elizabeth frowned, a thousand questions running through her mind. "For what?" she asked daringly, hoping to learn something more about this man's past.

"Couldn't...help," he muttered.

To Elizabeth's amazement, a tear slipped out of Clint's right eye and trickled down toward his ear. Pain tore through her heart at the sight. "It's all right," she answered, not sure if it might help. "I'm happy now. I'm safe and well."

"Take care of little Ethan," he whispered.

Ethan? There was someone else? A child? Did Clint

Brady have a son? If only she knew all the facts, she would know better the right things to say to this man. "I will," she answered. What else could she say to such a statement?

The moment was interrupted by another round of pitiful coughing and spitting. Clint groaned, and Elizabeth adjusted the pillows under him to make sure he remained slightly elevated. She gasped when Clint suddenly clamped his arms around her and pulled her tight against him, breathing the word *Jenny* into her ear.

"Don't go," he mumbled. "Stay...home."

Elizabeth was both stunned and touched. His grip was surprisingly strong, forcing her to move the rest of her body onto the side of the bed and lie bent over him, her head on his shoulder. The poor man actually thought she was his wife. If that thought might help him get better, she supposed she should stay in this position until he fell into a deeper sleep and let go of her again. He could, after all, be dying. Why not let him die thinking he was holding his wife?

Chapter Fifteen

A soft answer turneth away wrath:
but grievous words stir up anger.

—Proverbs 15:1

Clint awoke to an odd smell, what seemed a mixture of lemon and alcohol and God knew what else. It created a vapor that actually made it easier to breathe, although he remembered feeling so rotten that any kind of breathing would seem a relief.

He stirred, surprised to realize that he was not lying on a hard floor at all, but rather on something soft. He stretched and took a deep breath, realizing immediately that doing so was a bad idea. He coughed until it felt as though his very innards would come up through his throat, then noticed a bowl sitting on the floor by the bed. Having no other way to get rid of the phlegm that nearly choked him, he spat it into the bowl, then felt so weary he collapsed back onto the pillow with a groan.

"Clint?"

A woman spoke his name. He heard a rustling sound, and someone knelt beside him then, touching his face.

"Well, at least it seems your fever is gone," she said. "How do you feel? You haven't sneezed for quite some time, and it sounded like you were breathing just fine through your nose. Everything must have settled in your chest."

Clint squinted at her and saw by the dim light of an oil lamp that it was none other than Elizabeth Breckenridge. "Elizabeth?"

She smiled. "Yes. And it's so good to see that you seem to be getting a little better."

He raised up on an elbow again and looked around. "Where am I?"

She stood up. "You are in the storeroom of the hotel. Actually it's my room—the only room the manager had when I checked in two days ago."

He ran a hand through his hair, then felt the stubble on his face. "How long have I been in here?"

"For two days." Elizabeth pulled a wooden chair close to the bed and then told Clint about how she'd found him and the horse doctor who'd treated him.

Clint lay back down, staring at the low, sloped ceiling of the back room, trying to straighten his thoughts. "Two days?"

"Two days. For a while there I truly feared you would die. I've been praying constantly for you."

He coughed again, but not as deeply this time. *Two days.* His chest ached fiercely. He felt under the blanket and discovered he was still dressed. "What about...you mean

I haven't..." Lord, his bladder was full! "Is the manager out there?"

"I'm not sure. What's wrong?"

"What's *wrong?*" He rolled his eyes. Of all people to be left in charge of taking care of him, it had to be Elizabeth Breckenridge. Why not some whore from down the street? He felt humiliated at being sick and weak in front of her, embarrassed to tell her he needed the chamber pot or a privy, ashamed at how he must look, let alone how he must smell by now. "I haven't emptied my bladder for two days, *that's* what's wrong!" he answered, angry that he should even have to explain.

"Oh!" Elizabeth jumped up from her chair and practically ran out the door, returning a few long minutes later with a nearly bald man sporting a red beard and wearing the typical denim pants and calico shirt of most men in the area.

"There he is," Elizabeth told the man, before quickly shutting the door.

"Name's Victor Macklevoy," the man told him. "The lady grabbed my arm out in the lobby and told me you need to get to the privy out back. She told me to come help you out so's you don't fall down on the way." He chuckled and held out his arm. "Let's go."

Furious with humiliation, Clint refused the man's arm. "I can do this alone, thank you. All she had to do was tell me where the blasted outhouse is!" He wrapped a blanket around his shoulders and reached for his boots, grumbling profanities as he yanked them on. "Appreciate the help, mister, but you can go on about your business."

Fighting dizziness and determined not to lean on

someone else, he managed to get himself outside to take care of things. Going back inside, he vowed to wash and change and get out of Elizabeth's room.

"Of all people to be taking care of me," he muttered. Pain seared through his chest again, and by the time he reached the bed he realized with great frustration that indeed he was too weak even to wash himself, let alone change his clothes and leave. It felt as if a volcano was erupting inside him, and his muscles felt like mush. He'd never been sick a day in his life! How did this happen, and why now?

He knew why. Because he was so involved in feelings for Miss High-and-Mighty-Perfect Breckenridge that he'd dived into that cold water to save her. If he'd had any sense at all he would have let her drown! He'd thought he was rid of her, and now here he was lying in her bed and totally dependent on her to take care of him until he could find enough strength to get out of here.

Someone knocked on the door. "Clint?"

"Heaven help me," he groaned quietly. "It's okay," he said louder.

Elizabeth came inside, great concern in her pretty green eyes. "You must still be so weak."

"I'm all right," he grumped. He curled back into the blankets. "Tell the manager that as soon as a room is free, he's to give it to you. I can get by okay on my own now."

"You most certainly cannot! I will go out and see about bringing back something for you to eat. You'll need food to get your strength back, and lots more rest."

"Aren't you supposed to be headed for Dawson?"

She sat down in the nearby chair again. "Yes. But after

everything you've done for me, do you really think I could have left you, as sick as you were?"

He closed his eyes in exasperation. "Why not? You could have got me that doctor and then left two days ago."

"With you coughing so badly that I thought you'd choke to death? Let alone the fact that you were so hot I half expected you to burst into flames! You were, and still are, I might remind you, a very sick man. I kept that liniment warm and kept putting it on you. It truly does seem to have helped."

He thought a moment. *Elizabeth* had put the liniment on his bare chest? Just a few days ago she was mortified that he'd dared even to take off his shirt in front of her. Their gazes met, and she seemed to have read his thoughts. She quickly looked away, getting up from the chair and pretending to fuss with some towels.

"What do you feel like eating?" she asked. "There is a little diner just across the street and a short way down. I tried to get you to eat, but it's been impossible to do anything more than get some water down your throat. You must be famished." She went to a coat stand and took down a cape, putting it around her shoulders, then finally faced him again.

He turned on his back and stared at the ceiling again. "I wish you would just get a room for yourself and leave me alone."

"You know that I can't do that. I have a responsibility—"

"Will you quit with all that? We're even-up now. Thanks for getting me some help. And, yes, if you want, you can get me something that will stick to my ribs, something like biscuits and gravy, I guess. And I could stand a couple of shots of whiskey."

The room hung silent for a moment. "Very well. I'll get you the biscuits and gravy...and some hot tea," she answered. She went out the back door.

"Hot tea," Clint mimicked. He thought about it a moment. The prim and proper Miss Breckenridge had probably never tasted whiskey or even touched a bottle of it. He rolled his eyes at the thought of drinking *tea* after coming out of the worst sickness a man could suffer!

He sat up again, then wrapped himself in one of the blankets and stood up. This was a storeroom. It was a good bet there was some whiskey around here somewhere. He searched through several of the shelves, struggling not to fall down he was so weak and dizzy. Being careful not to disturb the manager's neat stacking of supplies, he finally caught sight of a couple of brown bottles. He pulled one out from the shelf and uncorked it, taking a sniff.

He grinned. "Now *here's* what I need!" he said. With that he took a long swallow. "Best medicine in the world for what ails a man."

Chapter Sixteen

They mount up to the heavens, they go down again
to the depths: their soul is melted because of
trouble. They reel to and fro, and stagger like a
drunken man, and are at their wit's end.
—Psalms 107:26 & 27

Elizabeth lifted her skirts slightly as she hurriedly made her way across the street on wooden planks that had been put down to create pathways at frequent intervals all along the muddy thoroughfare of Skagway. Getting across safely was yet another feat. There was a constant flow of traffic, people, horses, wagons, dogs and sleds.

"Looks like it's blowin' up a good one in the passes," she heard a man comment. She glanced at him, then looked in the direction he was looking. Snow was visible in the higher mountains, which reminded her that it was becoming dangerously late for making it to Dawson.

Once she got some food for Clint, she really needed to

get out today and find someone with whom she could travel safely...and leave soon. Clint was too sick for it, and he'd already made it clear that he did not intend to take her any farther himself. Besides, now he was too sick to leave any time soon.

She made her way past men of such diverse looks and clothing that she wondered if there might be a sampling of every human male on earth right here in Skagway. Some wore neat suits and top hats and were clean-shaven; others sported the bristle of a few days without a shave while yet more sported full-grown beards and mustaches. Many wore soiled, tattered clothing; while most wore the common clothing of the everyday prospector: dark woolen pants, plaid shirts, vests and jackets, woolen caps with ear flaps, most wearing leather boots, some wearing shoes with steel cleats, and some wearing simple canvas shoes. Most were courteous, a few made unmentionable remarks that she ignored, and nearly all eyed her curiously.

She entered the restaurant, where tables full of men stared as she walked through to the back to ask a very tired-looking waitress for some food to take to "a sick friend."

The waitress, whom Elizabeth had never seen before in the establishment, looked her over disdainfully. "Lady, can't you see how busy I am serving the customers out there? You want special service? Go talk to the owner." She nodded toward a gray-haired man who was giving orders to a cook.

Determined not to be intimidated by the rude waitress, Elizabeth walked up to the owner with the same request.

"It'll cost you a dollar," the man grumped.

"A dollar! That's outrageous!"

The man grinned through yellow teeth. "Honey, it ain't outrageous in Skagway! You think I was dumb enough to come here for *gold?*" He leaned closer, his breath atrocious. "I'm makin' *my* money off all the *rest* that's come here for gold! A man's got to eat, don't he?" He chuckled and straightened. "Besides, yer askin' for somethin' extra. Now, do you want what you asked for, or not?"

Elizabeth reminded herself that even this repulsive man who was literally stealing from everyone in his restaurant was a child of God. "Fine," she answered, digging into her skirt pocket. She handed him two fifty-cent pieces. "Please hurry. My friend has been very sick and hasn't eaten in two or three days."

The man shrugged and shouted an order to another cook. Both cooks were women who looked quite harried and overworked. The owner looked at Elizabeth again. "You make sure I get back my dishes and the tray," he told her. "I'll come lookin' for ya' if ya' don't." He grinned. "You wouldn't be holed up at some whorehouse, would you?"

Elizabeth stiffened. "I'm at Wheeler's Hotel," she answered curtly. "And you needn't worry. You'll get your tray back, although for a whole dollar, I should get to keep it!"

Regretting her sharp tongue, she stood back and waited, noticing filth on the floor and hoping that after being so sick, Clint would not end up dying from eating the food she brought back to him. Minutes later one of the cooks arranged the food on a plate and set it on a tray, covering it with a towel. She then poured coffee into a pewter pot and set the pot and a tin cup on the tray. "Here you go, ma'am," the woman told her.

"Thank you, and God bless you," Elizabeth answered, feeling sorry for the overworked woman. The cook just stared at her a moment, obviously surprised at her last remark. She smiled. "Why, thank you," she told Elizabeth. "That's a nice thing to say."

Elizabeth took the tray, smiling in return, and feeling better that she'd said something kind rather than let the owner make her rude to everyone else. She left, thinking how people and places like this were such a test of one's faith and one's desire to be kind to others.

She made her way to the hotel and after briefly relating Clint's condition to Mr. Wheeler she entered the storeroom.

"Here you are!" she told Clint as she set the tray on the only table in the room. "I have eggs and ham and biscuits and coffee! It cost me a whole dollar, but you need to start eating." She turned to face him. "I think you'll—" She did not finish her sentence. There sat Clint Brady, with a look on his face she couldn't even read, a brown bottle in his hand. He held it up.

"How about a toast, Miss Christian-Holier-than-Thou Breckenridge? What does your Bible say about a woman drinking whiskey? Jesus drank wine, I think, didn't He?" He chuckled. "Maybe He wasn't so perfect after all." He waved her over. "Come on. Take a swig. This stuff will cure anything that ails you. I drink enough of this and I'll be back to my old self within twenty-four hours."

Elizabeth's heart fell. "I just spent a whole dollar on you, Clint Brady, and I come back to find you *drunk!*"

He winked at her. "Don't worry. I'll eat the food, soon as I finish this bottle."

Elizabeth felt like crying. "You can finish it alone, Mr. Brady, and if you do, I highly doubt you will be one-hundred-percent cured by tomorrow. It is more likely you'll hardly be able to get out of bed!"

He laughed again. "You have an answer for everything, don't you? What the heck does it take to get you to loosen up, Miss God's-Gift-to-the-World?"

"Certainly not whiskey! And no, I *don't* have the answer for everything. I don't have an answer for why you behave the way you do." She folded her arms, struggling to control her fury and deciding to say something that would wipe the drunken smile off his face. "One thing I don't know is—who is Jenny? You called me Jenny a couple of times while you were your sickest. Was she your wife, Clint? What happened to her?"

The remark certainly *did* wipe the smile off his face—to a greater extent than she'd thought it would. The smile turned to a grim look, his blue eyes suddenly looking much darker. "Get out!" he told her. "Get out of here before I knock you clear out the back door!"

He rose, making ready to come for her, and Elizabeth backed away. The anger in his eyes was unnerving. She grasped the door handle, but before Clint could reach her he wavered, then fell flat on his face.

Chapter Seventeen

An ungodly man diggeth up evil: and in his lips
there is as a burning fire.

—Proverbs 16:27

Clint awoke to a raging headache. Unaware at first of where he was, he rolled onto his back and rubbed his forehead, finding there a swollen knot. He squinted with pain, taking a moment to think. The room was dark except for an oil lamp burning low.

Skagway. He was in Skagway…and he'd been so sick he'd wanted to die. The darkness could mean practically any time of day, since daylight hours were getting shorter and shorter this time of year. Was it morning or evening? With a groan he sat up, running his hands through his hair, which he realized was getting long. He scratched at his face and frowned at the long stubble there.

He took a deep breath, thinking more, looking around the room. He spotted a brown bottle nearby. That was when it hit him. Whiskey! He'd drunk practically that whole bottle of whiskey! It wasn't a big bottle, but big enough. No wonder he felt so lousy. And he remembered something about food…Elizabeth…she'd brought him food…said something about paying a whole dollar for it.

He managed to get to his knees, then realized he'd been lying on the floor. He stood up and stumbled back to the bed. He sat down on it and looked at the floor, groaning. Had he passed out in front of Elizabeth Breckenridge?

He shook his head and ran his hands through his hair yet again. It all came back to him, and he moaned. What had he done? After all Elizabeth had done for him, and he'd threatened to clobber her! What kind of man had he become?

He walked over to the little table where the oil lamp sat, and he turned it up so he could see the room better. On the stove sat a tin plate with food on it, and a pewter coffee-pot. He walked closer to see that the tray held eggs and ham, although quite dried out now. Elizabeth must have put the food there to keep it warm for him…and after he'd as much as cussed her out and chased her out of here. He checked the coffeepot and found it full, and still hot from sitting on the little potbelly stove, which she must have stoked with wood before leaving.

He glanced at the bed and saw that the sheets had been changed. Everything was clean and neat…kind of like Jenny used to take care of things. Clean clothes were laid out for him. For God's sake, had she gone and had his clothes washed?

A further glance around the room showed that all of Elizabeth's things were gone. Hadn't he told her to get a room of her own? She must have done so, which would probably cost her more than this back room had. Or maybe she'd found someone to take her on to Dawson.

No! He couldn't let her do that! There wasn't a man in this town who could be trusted to take her alone on a long trip like that. But then, maybe he couldn't even trust himself under the same circumstances. Apparently not, judging by his most recent behavior.

Never had he felt like such a complete ass. His aching head made him want to lie back down for several more hours, but he had to do something about this mess. He needed to apologize to Elizabeth. He needed to find out if she'd already left for Dawson. If so, he had to go after her and order her to go with no one but him.

He felt as if someone had beat him near to death and dragged him behind a horse for a few miles, but he was better and could do the rest of his healing on the journey. There was no time to be wasted! What was the date? How late was too late to head for Dawson? Were the horses he'd boarded still all right? For all he knew they'd been sold out from under him, or stolen.

The last few days were like a nightmare of sickness and dizziness and being hardly aware of where he was or what was going on around him. Then he'd had to go and drink that whiskey, thinking it would cure what was left of his pneumonia. Thing was, he'd drank it for another reason, like he always did—to forget. Forget. Forget. Whiskey eased the pain in his heart, but then sometimes it only made things worse, so he'd drink till he passed out. When a man was that far gone, he couldn't think about anything at all.

Now he did have to think! He was a mess, needed a shave, needed to change, needed to go find Elizabeth, needed to apologize, needed to get a map showing the best route to Dawson, needed to get the proper supplies, needed to go claim his horses...and he'd practically forgotten about Roland Fisher! The man was worth five thousand dollars!

This sickness had put him behind on everything and had shown him up to be a weak man in front of Elizabeth. He'd sure never let that happen again! What must she think of him!

Quickly he turned and scarfed down the dried, rubbery eggs and ham and toast, washing all of that down with the coffee that had become strong from sitting so long. There, that felt better. He took a porcelain bowl from a shelf, along with a towel and some bar soap and poured water from a kettle into the bowl.

He undressed and began vigorously washing himself, then rummaged through his things to find his shaving mug, brush and razor. A mirror hung on the wall near the door, so he moved the small table there so he could shave, wincing when he nicked his jaw. He washed his face again, then put on the clothes Elizabeth left out for him. He picked up his comb and walked back to the mirror, combing back his disheveled hair as best he could, thinking how he'd better get it cut before he left for Dawson. Then again, why bother? On a trip like that a man might as well not worry about shaving or cutting his hair until he arrived at his destination.

He walked to the back door to check the temperature outside. Cool and rainy. Could he have expected anything else? Seemed more like late evening than morning. He scurried to the privy to take care of personals, then went back inside and took his fur-lined suede jacket from a hook. Under the jacket hung his gun belt and six-gun. Deciding not to wear those just now, he pulled on his jacket, then drank down more coffee to help sober himself more before going through the door that led to the hotel lobby. The manager was at his desk.

"Wheeler, isn't it?" he spoke up, walking up to the man.

"Well, Mr. Brady! You're looking quite a bit better! Glad to see you up and around! Did you enjoy the food Miss Breckenridge brought you yesterday?"

"Yesterday?" Elizabeth must not have said anything to the man about his being drunk. "Yes. It really hit the spot," he answered. "Can you tell me what time it is? And where is Miss Breckenridge now? Her things are gone."

"Yes! I finally had a decent room open up." He winked. "I think she was happy to get a room of her own. She seems like such a nice young lady."

Clint's feelings of guilt kept getting worse. "Yes, she is. Which room is hers?"

"Well, it's upstairs—first door on the right, but she's not there. She went to get something to eat, and then she wanted to try to find someone who might accompany her to Dawson. I told her about a town meeting just up the street where men are gathered to learn more about the trip. But I also tried to tell her there are few men in this town she could trust. She insisted—"

Clint did not wait to hear the rest of the man's sentence. He hurried out the door to find Elizabeth.

Chapter Eighteen

*The simple believeth every word: but the prudent
man looketh well to his going.*
—Proverbs 14:15

"Well, lady, first you have to take either Chilkoot Pass
or White Pass to get to Lake Bennett. If you're real lucky,
you'll still have all your provisions with you. Now, if ya
can't get all yer supplies over there yerself, then you'll pay
about triple what it costs to buy them here, if'n you have
to buy them from those that carry them over for you, so yer
best off gettin' them to Lake Bennett yerself, ya know
what I mean?"

Elizabeth just stared at the bearded, kind-eyed older
man who called himself only by the nickname of Hard
Tack. He was obviously enjoying being able to show her
how much he knew about the trip to the Yukon. He'd rattled
on so fast that she was left totally confused.

"Now, I'd shore like to take ya myself," he continued,

"only I ain't goin' all the way, on account of I take supplies
just to Lake Bennett. I kin git ya that far, if that helps, but
then ya'd have to find somebody else to help you git the
rest of the way, which is by boat up the Yukon River, over
dangerous rapids and all that." He looked her over.
"Ma'am, I'd suggest ya wait till spring myself."

"I'd really rather go now," she answered. "I don't know
what on earth I would do with myself in a place like Skagway
all winter. Besides, I can't afford room and board for that
long. I guess I could get a job, but all I want is to reach my
brother in Dawson and have it over with. There I could rest
at last and truly be home and with someone familiar."

The man scratched his beard. "Well, now, I know that
that group of fellas over there is goin' for sure, leavin' in
a couple of days. One of 'em is a lawyer, so he says. The
others are just friends of his, all businessmen, they claim,
'cept in these parts ya can't always believe what a man tells
ya. I reckon ya can trust them as good as anybody."

Elizabeth glanced at the group of men gathered in a
large tent with about one hundred others who'd come to
hear about what they would need for their trip to the
Klondike. Those here to fill them in were outfitters and
owners of Skagway supply stores, as well as men with
horses, dogs, sleds and boats for sale.

The men Hard Tack referred to were mostly dressed in
suits and overcoats, certainly not men who appeared to
know much about survival in the wilds. Still, as Hard Tack
said, they certainly appeared to be gentlemen who would
at least honor her integrity and would surely protect her if
need be from animals and the elements. She thanked Hard

Tack and walked over to the men, who were intently listening to a man telling them about the proper way to pitch a tent on hard, cold, rocky ground, giving tips on what to do if the snow was deep. It was obvious by comments some of the men made that indeed, they didn't know much about such things. One of them turned to eye her, then removed his hat. "Ma'am?"

Elizabeth took a deep breath for courage, hating to approach strangers with her request. "My name is Elizabeth Breckenridge, and that man over there—" She pointed to Hard Tack. "He's a supplier, and he told me you and your friends might oblige my request."

The man smiled through thin lips and looked her over with rather unreadable brown eyes. He was neither handsome nor hard to look at, with dark hair that seemed too thin for what appeared to be a man only perhaps Clint's age, which she guessed to be late twenties or perhaps thirty. "And what might that request be?"

"Well, I'm headed for Dawson myself, to find my brother, Peter. He's a preacher there." She hoped that fact would cement her own credibility and honor. "I need some kind of escort on the trip, and I was hoping…well, Hard Tack…he said you were a lawyer here with some other businessmen. I hoped that meant you were all gentlemen and that perhaps I could trust you to get me to Dawson. I wouldn't be any burden, I promise. I could cook for all of you, keep your clothes washed and mended, that kind of thing. I can't really afford to pay—"

"Certainly!" the man answered before she could finish. His grin widened. "We'd be honored to take you along with us, Miss Breckenridge!" He touched the arm of one of his friends, a portly, middle-aged fellow wearing a suit. "Jonathan Hedley, meet Miss Elizabeth Breckenridge."

Hedley nodded to her as the first man put out his hand.

"And my name is Ezra Faine, ma'am." He looked at Hedley. "Miss Breckenridge needs an escort to Dawson, wondered if we might be obliged to help her out."

Hedley's eyebrows shot up with pleasure as he grinned, his cheeks actually turning red. "Why, of course we would!" the man answered, too quickly it seemed to Elizabeth. He turned to Ezra and winked.

"We leave in two days, Miss Breckenridge," Ezra told her. "We and our friends would be glad to take you along with us. We'll make sure you get to Dawson all safe and sound. Do you have all the supplies you need?"

Someone in the crowded tent bumped Elizabeth's velvet hat, and she adjusted it as she answered. "Actually no. I mean, I just don't have the money—"

"Not to worry," Ezra told her. "We have brought along plenty of money, and we'll get all the necessary supplies. You just bring along your personal baggage and we'll make room." He leaned closer, grinning eagerly. "You, uh, don't have any other female friends you could bring along, do you?"

Elizabeth frowned. "What?"

The man put an arm around her shoulders and led her aside. "Ma'am, we both know that it's pretty unlikely a woman traveling alone to Dawson is totally proper, if you know what I mean. Now, I'll accept your story about having a brother there who is a preacher. That's what we'll tell the others. But, well, it's possible we could get caught in a blizzard or something like that, which means we'd have to all hole up in a tent together. Now I know that even a woman who's, uh, not so proper, shall we say?—that even she wouldn't want to put up with a whole tent full of men. Me, I'll have my own tent, and I'll see you get to Dawson without charging you one blessed cent, as long as you share my tent with me, if you know what I mean."

Elizabeth's heart fell like a rock. This man thought she was lying about Peter! He thought she was a prostitute trying to hook a free ride to Dawson! Fury and disappointment engulfed her, and she could not hide her tears as she looked at Ezra Faine. "You are a filthy-minded, reprehensible man with not one ounce of manners or honor about you!" she shot back.

The man grasped her arm. "Now, honey, don't get angry. I just wanted to be sure—"

"Let go of the lady," came a deep voice.

Elizabeth recognized it as Clint's. Ezra glanced up at someone tall standing behind her. "What was that?" he asked.

"You heard me. Take your hand off her arm. And if I were you, I'd turn around and rejoin my friends and not say one more word."

Ezra gave Elizabeth a light shove before he let go of her. "Says who?" he asked, trying to look brave and manly.

"Mister, I'm a bounty hunter, so hurting or killing a man means nothing to me. Is that enough of an answer?"

Ezra backed away slightly, looking Clint over and pretending not to be afraid. He moved his gaze to Elizabeth. "He one of your customers or something?"

In the next split second a big fist came from behind Elizabeth and slammed into Ezra Faine's face, sending the man sprawling into a stack of sacks stuffed with beans. One of them broke, spilling the contents onto the wooden floor. Beans bounced about, some of them off Ezra's face. Other men turned to look, and Clint grasped Elizabeth's arm. "Let's go," he told her.

Still fighting tears, Elizabeth left with him.

Chapter Nineteen

*For we must all appear before the judgment seat of
Christ; that everyone may receive the things done
in His body, according to that He hath done,
whether it be good or bad.*
— 1 Corinthians 5:10

Clint walked so fast that he nearly dragged Elizabeth
along the boardwalk back toward the hotel.

"Clint Brady, how dare you!"

"How dare I what? Keep you from making the biggest
mistake of your life?"

"And you haven't made any?"

"I've made *plenty!*" He scooped her up in his arms to
carry her across one of the narrow board crosswalks.

"What are you doing!"

"Keeping you out of the mud."

"Not long ago you wanted to knock me clear out the
back door, if I remember your words correctly!"

"Yeah, well, that's what I want to talk about."

Elizabeth could not help being surprised at how adeptly he picked her up, as though she weighed nothing. He couldn't possibly be anywhere near his normal strength, but he'd clobbered Ezra Faine with startling force.

They reached the boardwalk at the other side of the street, and Elizabeth felt a sudden, surprising surge of happiness and desire rush through her as she looked at Clint Brady by the soft light of the oil lamps hanging along the boardwalk. It so startled her that she fought it vehemently.

"Put me down!" she commanded, tears coming again and making her even more embarrassed and upset with herself.

Clint just stood there with her for a moment, an odd look in his eyes, almost like a sorry little boy—a look that changed to something she could not quite decipher. Sorrow? Adoration? For one brief moment she thought he might actually kiss her!

"Tell me you aren't afraid of me. I'm sorry for what I said, and we need to talk."

"We certainly do! And you owe me a dollar for that wasted food!"

Clint set her on her feet. "It wasn't wasted. I ate all of it." He put a hand to her back. "Come on back to the hotel with me." He started walking again, a little slower this time.

"Why did you hit that poor man?"

"Poor man? Why were you crying?"

Elizabeth wiped at the tears on her cheeks. "I don't know."

"I think it was because the man was insulting you in some way, maybe misunderstood your intentions. Am I right?"

"Yes," she answered, embarrassed.

"You'd go a long way to find a man out of that crowd who'd honestly see you got to Dawson safely. Most would probably have every good intention of helping you out, but men are men, and each one at that tent is out for himself. You get snowed in with any one of them, worse than that, a group of them, and all their good intentions could easily go right out the smokehole and blow away with the mountain winds."

"And I suppose you're different?"

They were nearly at the hotel. "Maybe not, except for one thing."

"Oh? And what is that?"

They walked up the steps to the hotel front door, where he turned to face her before going in. "I care about you."

The comment left Elizabeth speechless for the moment. *I care about you.* What the heck did that mean? As just a friend? As something *more* than a friend? Heavens! What if *that* was what he meant?

The thought made her suddenly self-conscious. What was she supposed to say to him? Should she ask him what he meant? Did she *want* him to care about her as more than a friend? Truth was, deep inside, she did. She'd never really allowed the thought to surface until now. Still, he was nowhere near the kind of man she'd always imagined she'd end up with someday, and he was too old, wasn't he? Heck, she had no idea *how* old he was. Perhaps his size and experience made him seem older than he really was. And for heaven's sake, he killed men for money! He didn't even believe in God any more...or at least so he claimed. She suspected that wasn't true at all. *Dear Lord, what am*

I supposed to say? What should I do? What does this man want? What do You *want?*

Clint led her inside. Elizabeth was glad to see that Mr. Wheeler was not at his desk as they stormed through the lobby and into the back room. Clint closed the door and turned up the lamp. He ordered Elizabeth to sit down in the wooden chair, and Clint sat down on the cot. He took a deep breath, resting his elbows on his knees. Elizabeth waited for him to speak first, still a little wary of him after his drunken threat to her the day before.

"Here's the deal," he told her. "I've rescued you from peril twice, and you just might have saved *my* life. For some reason we keep running into each other and helping each other out. And now I've come to know you too well just to let you go off to Dawson with complete strangers, and too well to…well, like I said, I care about you, which means I could never…you know…take advantage, if the issue were to arise."

Elizabeth felt the odd rush of desire again, a feeling that confused her. With it came an uncomfortable embarrassment at what he meant.

"What I mean is," he continued, "I've come to respect you highly. What happened earlier…I can promise you that won't happen again. I drank that whiskey because whiskey can be a pretty good cure-all for a lot of things. I figured it would make me feel better and heal faster. Fact is, I feel awful. My head feels like it's trying to lift away from my neck, and my chest still hurts, but I think that by day after tomorrow, I could start for Dawson."

"That's too soon."

He put up his hand. "I'm not finished." He coughed before continuing. "I want to apologize for what I said earlier. You can rest assured I've never hit a woman in my life and never would. That was whiskey talking."

"And what if you drink during our journey?"

He held her gaze for a moment, and she thought again how blue his eyes were, how handsome he was.

"Well, I promise not to. You'll just have to believe me. But if I *do* drink—and even if I don't—you have to promise me one thing. One thing, and I'll get you to Dawson safely."

She frowned. "What is that?"

"Don't bring up my dead wife's name again."

So, that was it. Why was it so terrible to talk about Jenny? "And what if *you* bring it up?"

He shrugged. "I won't. But if I *were* to bring it up, it would be because I want to talk about her and…what happened to her…and…our son."

A son! Elizabeth could see just the mere mention of both of them made him agitated. "All right," she told him. "But may I say one thing?"

He eyed her warily. "What?"

Elizabeth swallowed before continuing. "Well, I just want you to know—" *God, help me find the right words* "—that I care about you, too. And the couple of times I did mention your family, I was just hoping to help you cope with loss…because that's just the kind of person I am. My heart is filled with the love of Jesus Christ and with His teachings and commandments, which means He would want me to be His instrument of healing in any way I can. So I just want you to know that if and when you should ever want to talk, I am ready and willing to listen, and I would never, ever judge your anger or the things it has made you do. I look at you and I see someone who I believe was once a wonderful family man who believed in God and in His Son, Jesus Christ."

Clint just stared at her a moment, and she could see a hunger in his eyes, but it quickly vanished. "Now there's another requirement. I don't want to be preached to for the whole journey."

Elizabeth smiled softly. "All right. I'll do my best." She folded her arms. "We never even said flat-out that we would do this, you know—go to Dawson together, I mean. I take it that's the decision you've made, considering the way you walked over to that tent and hauled me out of there and warned me not to trust anyone but you. I'm still not so sure I *can* trust you. But I am going to for the simple reason that I absolutely cannot believe that God didn't bring you into my life for the specific purpose of seeing that I reach Peter safely. If you are the one He's chosen for the job, then I have no choice but to trust you."

Clint actually smiled a little himself then. He took off his coat. "Thanks for fixing things up for me, changing the sheets and all. I'll pay you back for that meal, and I'll pay for your room. You shouldn't have had to take a different one."

"I'll manage."

"Okay, rule number three. Don't argue with me about everything. Whatever I tell you to do, you'll do it, including letting me pay for things. I have plenty of money and nothing to spend it on. I have even more in a bank in San Francisco. And no, it didn't *all* come from killing men for bounty. And yes, I'll explain all of it to you in my own time. And I might add that you have some explaining of your own to do."

Elizabeth raised her eyebrows in curiosity. "Oh? What do you mean?"

"I mean it's kind of strange that a nice young woman like you is headed for Dawson all alone. You said your father had been a preacher in San Francisco, and so had your brother, apparently. You must have belonged to a church. There must have been friends and parishioners who cared about you. Why the sudden rush to head for Dawson so late in the year? It can't be just because your mother died. You act more like someone who is running away from something. What is it you aren't telling me?"

Elizabeth felt the renewed shame and anger she'd felt when the deacons accused her of sinfully throwing herself at Reverend Selby. Would this man understand? Or would he judge her in the way so many men in the church had judged her? "I guess I'll have to answer that the way you said you felt about talking about your wife. I'll tell you when the time is right."

Clint rose. "Fair enough." He walked to the door and opened it. "One more rule," he added.

Elizabeth stood up and faced him. "What is that?"

"While we're traveling together, we lead others to believe we're husband and wife. If and when we come across people who knew us here in Skagway, we tell them we got married."

Elizabeth felt a flutter in her stomach. "Why?"

"Because you'll be safer if others think you're married. I shouldn't have to explain the reason why."

"But…if we sleep in separate tents—"

"We won't. Between lonely men and wild animals, I'm not letting you away from my protection. Besides, two tents mean extra gear to carry. A lot of the time we'll sleep out in the open anyway."

"But…I…"

"You're supposed to trust me. Besides, God sent me to help you, remember? He must mean for you to trust me."

Elizabeth thought about what a big, strong man he was, a man who carried a gun at that. Still, he was right. She'd said herself that God meant for them to travel together. Maybe she'd stuck her foot in her mouth, but what was done was done, and if she wanted to reach Peter safely, she didn't have much choice. Clint Brady was her best bet.

She nodded. "All right. From here on we are husband and wife. And you should start calling me Liz. That's what everyone close to me calls me. It will make us more believable."

"Good enough." He stood aside. "Good night…Liz. Be ready tomorrow morning at eight o'clock to go shopping with me. We need supplies and you need a wedding band. I'll have to go get my horses from where they are boarded and we'll start packing what we'll need."

"Do you know the way?"

"I have good maps, and besides, the trail is pretty well worn by now. We're bound to run into others the whole way."

Elizabeth walked through the door and looked back at him. "Thank you, Clint."

He nodded. "You're welcome. Use the rest of today and tomorrow to rest up. I'll be doing the same."

He closed the door and Elizabeth stared at it for a moment before turning to go to her room. *"Lord, what in the world are You doing?"* she muttered. This was going to be one interesting trip. Not only was Clint Brady a bounty hunter and a Godless man who needed her help in finding his faith...but he'd become more. She'd never thought her trip to Dawson would include a battle with her own heart.

Chapter Twenty

...Oh, my Father, if it be possible, let this cup pass
from me: nevertheless, not as I will, but as Thou wilt.
—St. Matthew 26:39

"I'm glad I already have my own tinware," Clint told Elizabeth, who was watching him yank leather straps and tie ropes and hoist more supplies onto his three sturdy horses. "You can't find a tin plate or cup at any supply store. They're bought out. One man told me that last year you could pick up practically everything you needed for free as you went over the pass, so many supplies were abandoned by men who just gave up."

They stood behind Morgan's Supply Store, loading all the things Clint had purchased for their journey. Elizabeth felt so indebted. He'd not asked her for a dime.

Clint took a moment to glance at the surrounding mountains, and Elizabeth knew he was worried. Every peak showed snow, and the owner of the store where they'd purchased most of their grub, extra blankets, a tent and numerous other necessities, had told them that men who worked for him making deliveries had returned just the day before, giving up an effort to get over the pass to take valuable supplies on to Dawson. A sudden snowstorm had forced them back to Skagway.

"Could very likely be sunny and melting now," the store owner had suggested. "That's how it is here, a storm one minute, springlike·weather the next. And if it does warm up, watch out for a sudden flood. A little mountain water-fall can turn into a raging torrent in five minutes flat."

The news was not inviting.

"Clint, are you sure you're up to this? You're still coughing, and I can tell you've lost weight."

"I'm all right," he insisted as he continued packing flour, pork, beans, coffee, sugar, tea, lard, potatoes, a shovel, two bags of oats for the horses, the tent, blankets and two rifles.

"I should have taught you how to use a gun," he told her as he shoved the rifles into their sheaths. "Could come in handy if a grizzly decides to have us for lunch. Most should be going into hibernation any time, so we might not have a problem. Then, of course, there are cougars to worry about, and wolves. If we're lucky, I'll come across a rabbit or deer so we can save our provisions, and we can always throw out a net every night while we travel the Yukon and eat fish instead of using up the salt pork. I have a good fil-leting knife, and a good hunting knife for cleaning game." He stopped and faced her. "Have you ever cleaned a rabbit or helped gut a deer?"

The thought was not pleasing. "I'm afraid not."

Clint shook his head. "You'll learn soon enough." He returned to his packing.

"I'll do whatever I have to do to help," Elizabeth told him. "I have no qualms about doing anything that's necessary to survive, including—" She eyed his six-gun. *You are traveling with someone who kills men as easily as rabbits,* she reminded herself. Was she crazy? "—including learning to use a rifle," she finished. "For all we know, I might need to know that to help you out of some kind of danger."

He faced her again, this time smiling. "If I am in a fistfight with a bear, I'm not sure I want you pointing a rifle anywhere in my direction," he told her. "If the bear doesn't get me, a bullet probably would."

She was astonished at how a genuine smile transformed him completely, into a handsome, affable-looking man who could be anyone's neighbor. She could not help smiling in return. "Wouldn't a bullet be more humane than letting you be mauled and slowly eaten by a grizzly?"

This time he chuckled. "You have a point."

Elizabeth leaned against a post as he continued packing. He'd given her specific instructions not to try to help. He had a method to his packing, and he didn't want any arguments about it. *I've done nothing but travel and sleep out under the stars for the last four years,* he'd told her.

Hunting men, she'd thought. If she had her way, Clint Brady would be a changed man by the time they reached Dawson. How she would accomplish that, she had no idea. God would have to do it through her.

She looked down at the plain gold band on her left hand.

Secretly, she liked the looks of it, the thought of being a wife someday…someday. She shook away the thought.

Their journey would start tomorrow, early in the morning. She pressed a hand to her stomach, feeling butterflies. Her father must be turning over in his grave knowing she was venturing out alone with a man who in all essence was really still a stranger…a man who sometimes liked his demon whiskey. He'd packed two full bottles of it, *for medicinal purposes,* he'd told her. *Whiskey can clean wounds and help a cough and clear sinuses and kill pain. Any man would be crazy to set out on a trip like this without some good whiskey along.*

She walked around to pat his horses, wanting them to get to know her. One was a black gelding named Devil, who, Clint advised "fit his name." She'd already been instructed to leave Devil to him to handle. Still, the horse whinnied and nodded when she petted his neck and spoke softly to him.

The other two were mares, one a roan named Red Lady, the other a gray speckled horse named Queen. Clint claimed both were easy to handle, especially Queen.

"I have a question, Clint," she spoke up, coming closer to watch him again.

He put an arm over Devil's neck and faced her. "What's that?"

"You've never told me how old you are."

He grinned, and she thought how nice it was to be around him when he was in a good mood. However, she couldn't help wondering if it was only because he was finally on his way to find another wanted man.

"How old do you *think* I am?"

She shrugged, pulling her cape closer. The day was cool and damp. "I can't decide. Early thirties, maybe?"

"Thirty on the head," he answered. "I guess you to be about eighteen."

"I'm twenty," she answered. She saw more questions in his eyes. He probably wondered why she was still single. A man like Clint couldn't possibly understand that the work of the Lord must come before personal wants and needs.

He turned away. "You mean you didn't leave behind some broken hearts when you left San Francisco?"

"Oh, there were a couple of interested young men, but I didn't share the interest." She took a deep breath and looked out at the mountains. "The man I marry will have to be very special, a Christian man who shares my faith and puts God above all else, a steady, settled man who knows his Bible and who will be a good provider and a wonderful father. He'll have to be brave like my father was, brave enough to voice his faith among the unfaithful. And of course he'll be strong and handsome and—"

She suddenly realized how she'd been rambling, like a silly girl fantasizing about a prince. She glanced at Clint and realized that he fit at least part of her description— strong and handsome and brave—but brave in the ways of violence. She felt heat come into her cheeks, and she covered her face. "I'm sorry! That was silly of me."

The words were met by silence. What was he thinking? Did he wonder if she was describing him? Or was he insulted, thinking he didn't fit any of that description? And why on earth did she care *what* he thought!

"Nothing wrong with being particular," he finally answered.

She uncovered her face, and he'd returned to his packing.

"One thing I forgot to tell you," he said, obviously trying to change the subject. "No dresses. We need to go find you some pants that will fit you. Small as you are, that won't be easy. We might have to shop for boy's pants."

"Pants! I can't wear pants! It isn't proper!"

He stopped his packing and faced her, again wearing his "don't argue with me" look. "Where we're headed, lady, you'll be walking knee-deep, maybe sometimes *waist*-deep in snow. I don't think I need to paint any better picture than that. I'll not have you end up with frostbite clear up to—" He looked her over, and Elizabeth felt like a complete idiot for not realizing why she'd have to wear pants. "You get my meaning," he finished. He dug into his pocket and handed her some money. "Here. Go shopping."

"Clint, you've already done too much. I'll never in the world be able to pay you back."

"And I've told you not to worry about it." He took hold of one of her hands and shoved the money into it. "Once I find the man I'm looking for, money will be the least of my worries for quite a while. And like I said before, what the heck else would I be spending it on?" He turned away again to strap on the last bit of supplies. "I have no home," he continued, "no property but my horses and gear, and no one to leave my money to anyway. I might as well spend it any way I want, and right now I feel like spending it on helping you get to Dawson. Now go buy yourself some pants and a warm coat and wool hat, and boots, and anything else that will ensure your warmth. Then go back to the hotel room. I'll put away the horses and store this gear for the night and meet you in the hotel lobby in the morning. We can pack your remaining personal supplies then. And make sure you bring along enough...you know...woman things."

She frowned. "Woman things? You said yourself I can't wear dresses."

He rolled his eyes again. "I'm not talking about dresses. I was married once, you know. I know about those things. Make sure you bring enough supplies along for that time of the month."

Elizabeth was so embarrassed she wanted to die! She couldn't look at him as he mounted one of his horses. "See you in the morning," he told her. He took the reins to the other two horses and rode off.

Elizabeth just stood there, dumbfounded that the man had even thought about "woman things." Embarrassing as it was, it drove home the fact that she'd be traveling with a man far more experienced and worldly than she'd ever known.

"Oh, Lord," she said with a sigh, "how can someone like me get through to a man like that?"

Just as quickly as the thought had come, so did a little voice inside that reminded her of the horrendous task God had given His own Son, Jesus Christ...to die a horrible death on the cross to save sinners like Clint Brady. There could be no greater burden. Jesus had sweat blood in agony over that burden the night before his death. Finding a way to get through to Clint Brady's heart was not so much to ask.

Chapter Twenty-One

There is one lawgiver, who is able to save and to destroy; who art thou that judgest another?
—James 4:12

Elizabeth watched her footing as she led Queen along the foothills of White Pass Trail north of Skagway. The ground was a combination of grass and rock, ranging anywhere from pebbles to much larger boulders. Such cascades of rock meant they were constantly in danger of being crushed to death if they were not on a minute-by-minute lookout for the next tumbling killer.

All of this made it impossible to hurry along the trail. A steady walk was all they could muster. They were forced to travel even slower in places where the trail narrowed to hardly more than a pathway around the side of a precarious ledge. Elizabeth tried not to look down for fear of fainting.

Keeping watch both above for tumbling rocks and on the ground under their feet for smaller rocks that could cause them to lose their footing, kept both Clint and Elizabeth on edge. Elizabeth's feet ached from the long day's walk, and her neck and back ached, mostly, she figured, from fatigue and tension. Clint was worried about how easily his horses could suffer wounds to their hooves or legs.

Elizabeth in turn worried about Clint, who she felt was still not rested and well enough to make this trip. However, there was no arguing with him about it. She could not imagine that finding one man could be worth the misery they were sure to be heading into, and she hoped that secretly he was doing this more for her sake than to find a wanted man. But from what she'd seen so far, money meant more to most men than anything else. Why else would they leave wives and children and comfortable homes and good jobs to literally risk their lives reaching their El Dorado, especially when it was likely most of them would never strike it rich?

Gold. The Bible itself was filled with kings and slaves, untold wealth and horrible poverty. In one parable Jesus had said it would be easier for a camel to go through the eye of a needle than for a rich man to get to heaven, although her father had always taught that what the Lord meant was rich men who refused to share their wealth and who committed sins to obtain and hang on to their wealth. There were generous, compassionate rich men, just far fewer of them than those who would give up just about anything for wealth.

The sad part about Clint was that she suspected the money didn't really matter to him as much as simply finding a wanted man and doing away with him. That was what bothered her most, the obvious deep hurt and hatred in the man that led him to continue the hunt, man after man, as though each new find might somehow be the answer to finding his own peace.

"May I ask just who it is you are looking for?" she spoke up, hoping to relieve the constant tension over the dangers they faced, as well as the unnerving silence. They had walked the last two miles or so without speaking at all.

Clint led the way, although the already well-worn trail, in this second year of the gold rush, was easy to follow on this sunny day. Other pack trains were about a mile ahead of them, which meant that besides watching for rocks, one had to be on the lookout for horse manure.

"His name is Roland Fisher," Clint yelled back. "He's an Eskimo, a half-breed, actually, from up in the Yukon."

"What in the world was he doing down in the States?"

Clint didn't answer right away. They made it to a wide, flat area, where he stopped and looked back at her. "Let's rest the horses for a while." He glanced at the sun, which was getting very close to settling behind a distant peak. "Actually this would be a good place to make camp." He looked around at dark circles on the ground where others had made fires. "Apparently a lot of others thought the same thing. And I think there is a party a ways behind us. They just might end up reaching this place, too. We'd better go ahead and pick the best spot." He walked Devil closer to a sheer wall of rock. "We'll camp here so we'll be out of the way of any others who might decide to head on past us."

This was their very first night on the trail, and one thing Elizabeth was more sure of was that she didn't have to worry about Clint Brady getting any funny ideas in regards to tenting alone together. She had no doubt he was just as tired as she, and that his feet were just as sore as hers were, and that he shared her craving for a good night's sleep.

Clint began untying the ropes that held the canvas tent he'd brought along and continued his explanation of the man he hunted. "Rather than take the chance of never striking it rich in the Klondike when the gold rush began, Fisher decided to go to Skagway and see if he couldn't find a 'get rich quick' job there by taking advantage of all the gold seekers, like any smart man would do."

"What does that have to do with ending up in the States?" she asked.

"Grab the other end of this thing and help me open it up," Clint answered, unfolding the tent. He was breathing heavily and he stopped to cough before he continued. "He was hired to help guard a shipment of gold nuggets on its way to San Francisco. The job paid well, so he took it. The shipment left too late in the year for him to think about coming back before winter, so he stayed on in California, taking a job helping guard a stamping mill at one of the mines northeast of San Francisco."

With the tent all laid out, Clint took down a burlap sack that contained iron tent stakes, then yanked a sledge hammer from its stirrup. He began pounding the stakes into the hard earth, not an easy job, and one Elizabeth knew for certain she never could have done herself.

"Come this past spring," he continued, "Fisher for some reason decided to rob the very bank where he'd been cashing his pay checks. It was situated in a little town north of San Francisco." After finishing one stake, he went on to the next. "He was easy to identify because he'd been there several times. The teller he shot told the authorities who'd shot him..." He looked over at Elizabeth. "Before he died." He returned to hammering. "That teller was a fairly young man with three little kids. He left behind a kind wife and mother who will have a heck of a time raising those kids alone." He stood up and went on to the next stake. "The bank owner, the owner of the stamp mill and some of the teller's friends pooled their money to come up with the reward for Fisher...dead or alive."

Elizabeth relieved Queen of some of her load. "But why would he work guarding gold all that time, apparently being well paid for it, and then just suddenly decide to rob a bank? It doesn't make sense."

Clint rose to walk over to a fourth stake. "A lot of things in life don't make sense. Maybe he just missed home and decided to go back a little richer than he already was. According to what he'd told others he worked with, he had a wife and a couple of kids up in the Yukon. Maybe he figured if he went back there, nobody would follow him that far."

Elizabeth set out a coffeepot. "But you will."

He pounded on the fourth stake. "Why not? I don't have anything better to do, and I feel sorry for the widow who was left behind. I know what it's like to lose one's mate to violence."

A clue. His wife had died violently. The son, too? Elizabeth unpacked bedrolls. "I'm sorry you understand that kind of sorrow. Still, don't you worry about possibly killing an innocent man? I mean, it just doesn't make sense, a man leaving a wife and children to work hard to support them, and then just up and robbing a bank."

"You already said that. And no, I'm not worried about his innocence, because I know he's guilty. The teller identified him, and that's good enough for me. I'll find him and I'll take him back, dead or alive, just like the poster says. That's what I do for a living." Clint rose and walked over to pound in a fifth stake.

"So, because of a poster, you have the right to be judge and jury and hangman?"

He pounded extra hard on the fifth stake. "I told you— no preaching."

Elizabeth walked closer and shoved a support post under the front section of the tent, pushing up on it to raise the front opening. "I'm not preaching this time. Just sort of thinking out loud, I guess."

Clint continued to the sixth stake. "You're the one who says we shouldn't judge, so don't judge *me*, Liz."

"I'm not doing that, either. I'm just trying to figure out why you do what you do." She walked around behind the tent to secure a pole there, hoping she could keep him talking so she could learn more about the complexities of the man. After all...unwanted feelings for him were growing deep inside. How could she possibly allow such feelings for a bounty hunter, of all men? "You just don't seem like the typical kind of man who would choose to be a bounty hunter."

"You've already made that clear, more than once. And quit trying to get information out of me." He pounded in the seventh stake.

Elizabeth began stretching rope from the top of one of the poles to a stake to hold it up. "Foiled again," she answered, hoping to keep the conversation light. One thing she did know was that Clint Brady could become sullen and angry over one wrong word, and they had a long trip ahead of them. She caught a grin at the corner of his mouth and felt relieved that she'd managed to keep to his lighter side.

"I'll finish the tent," he told her. "You take more of the load off Queen and Red Lady and tether them. I'll try to get a fire going. Some hot coffee sounds good right now. So does a good night's sleep."

"Agreed," she answered. She studied the tent a moment. It was meant for two people, but certainly not much else. It was going to feel very awkward sleeping in a cramped tent with a man who was not her husband or even related to her. Then again, she might as well *be* a man, the way she was dressed: woolen pants that were slightly too big for her, a red flannel shirt that was also too big, then covered with a canvas coat, a woolen hat, high leather boots over thick woolen socks, her hair twisted into a bun at the base of her neck so she could pull her hat completely over it... *Lord, I must be just about the most unattractive woman in all of Alaska right now,* she thought.

She walked back to Queen, taking a moment to look out at the stretch of mountains and valleys all around. It would all be so beautiful if it were not so dangerous. Yet she couldn't help feeling safe. She was with Clint Brady.

Bounty hunter or not, he was a strong, able man, and God had led them together. She trusted God above all else…and so she would trust Clint.

Chapter Twenty-Two

These...things doth the Lord hate:... A false witness that speaketh lies, and he that soweth discord among brethren.
                                        —Proverbs 6:16 & 19

"Hello there!"

Elizabeth looked up to see another party of gold seekers approaching. She and Clint sat beside a campfire in front of their tent, and, in spite of the interruption to their quietude, Elizabeth was actually relieved by the visit. For the past hour or so, she'd been fighting the embarrassment of going inside the tent and settling down to sleep beside Clint. She had a feeling he felt just as awkward about it, so they had both lingered by the fire after eating boiled pork and potatoes. The sun was long set, but neither of them had made a move to retire, in spite of being bone-tired.

"I see you have horses," one of the men spoke up. He

walked into the light of the fire, and Clint, wearing his sidearm, rose defensively.

"That's right," he answered.

"Well, if it isn't the son of a bitch who punched me out a couple of nights ago!" the visitor spoke up then.

Alarmed, Elizabeth also rose, realizing there could be trouble. She moved to stand beside Clint. The visitor, Ezra Faine, looked her over, then moved his gaze back to Clint. Behind Ezra stood at least six other men.

"I see the woman found someone to travel with," he nearly sneered at Clint.

"The woman is my wife," Clint answered.

Faine's eyebrows arched in surprise. "*Wife!* You two got married?"

"That's right." Clint put his hands on his hips. "Now, you've commented about my horses and Mrs. Brady, neither of which is your business, so you can keep on going."

Faine stiffened. He glanced back at the others, a couple of whom chuckled. It was obvious Ezra Faine was the leader of the pack of men, all of them carting heavy loads on their backs and traveling completely on foot.

Faine eyed Clint again. "It's dark. Surely you don't expect us to keep going. Any one of us could lose our footing and fall a thousand feet."

"Am I supposed to care?"

"Clint!" Elizabeth spoke up. "There is plenty of room in this clearing. Surely there is nothing wrong with letting them make camp here."

Clint cast her a look of anger and chastisement. "After what this man said to you a couple of days ago?"

"Well, it…it just wouldn't be Christian to make them keep going in the dark."

Faine smiled and tipped his hat to her. "How kind of you, ma'am. And I do apologize for my remarks the other night. I deserved a wallop from your husband."

Elizabeth raised her chin. "You most certainly did."

Faine, his left cheek still visibly bruised and swollen, grinned and faced Clint again. "Friends?"

"No," Clint answered. "But you can make camp here if you want. It's public land. Just stay well away from this tent…and my horses."

Faine chuckled as though it was a great joke. He turned to his cohorts and told them to go ahead and make camp. Their eyes adjusted to the near darkness, and with a three-quarter moon above, the men were able to find an area out of the light of Clint and Elizabeth's campfire.

"Now, about the horses," Faine spoke up to Clint.

"What about them?"

"Well, as you must know, procuring a horse in Skagway is near impossible. Every available horse is grabbed up as fast as it comes off a boat, and for unheard-of prices. In light of that, and the length of this journey, and the weight of our packs, I thought you might be willing to sell at least one horse to us. I am willing to pay four hundred dollars, far more than any of your horses is worth, I might add."

"Maybe in the States," Clint answered. "But on a trail from Skagway to Dawson, you couldn't get me to sell for a *thousand* dollars. Besides that, I've owned these horses for years. They were mine before I even left San Francisco, and they aren't for sale at any price."

Looking angry and chagrined, Faine pursed his lips mockingly. He sighed deeply, looking Clint over. "Well, you can't blame a man for trying."

"There are a lot of things a man can be blamed for," Clint retorted. "Why don't you just go join your friends. And, by the way, I'm a light sleeper."

Faine frowned. "Mr. Brady! Are you saying you don't trust me?"

"That's exactly what I'm saying."

"Clint, the man apologized," Elizabeth spoke up.

"He didn't mean a word of it." Clint nodded toward the others. "Go join the rest of your party," he told Faine.

Faine sighed deeply, glancing at Elizabeth again. "Thank you for at least trying to be hospitable, ma'am. And again, I apologize." He backed away. "And I must say, I can't imagine such a nice young lady marrying such a rude, unfriendly man as Mr. Brady." He took another look at both of them, eyeing Clint's gun for a moment, then left.

Elizabeth turned to Clint. "If they had any bad intentions, you certainly didn't help any with your attitude," she chastised.

Clint grasped her arm a little too tightly and made her sit down on the log they'd been sharing. "Look, I can be as friendly as the next man with people who deserve it. That man doesn't. The rest of them might be all right, but not that one. And it's my bet they all would follow just about anything he told them to do. When it comes to handling men like that, let *me* take care of it. Understood?"

"But a kind word—"

"Understood?"

"Let go of my arm."

Clint sighed deeply, doing as she asked. His tone softened, and he leaned closer. "You have to admit that I know a bit more about these things than you, right?"

Elizabeth frowned. "That doesn't mean you have to be rude to people."

"It does when my gut instinct tells me someone isn't worth trusting," he said, keeping his voice down. "And after dealing with some of the worst of them, my instinct is honed pretty darn well. And I'm telling you that Mr. Manners over there would steal my horses, and you along with them, if he got the chance. Fact is, we're staying an extra day and letting that bunch of fast talkers go on ahead of us. I don't intend to travel with them at my back. Got that? And from now on, when strangers come along, I'll be the judge of who we're friendly with and who we aren't. When men come along to test out your vulnerability, especially when you have something they want, you let them know right up front that you're not to be messed with."

Elizabeth blinked back tears of anger and embarrassment. "It's hard for me to be unfriendly," she answered, her voice quivering. To her surprise, he moved an arm around her shoulders, giving her a reassuring hug.

"Well, it isn't hard for me, so let me do the talking, all right? I'm not asking you to do or say anything you don't feel right about. I'm just asking you to be still and let me handle things. Will you *please* do that?"

Elizabeth nodded. She quickly wiped at a tear. "Do you really think they might cause trouble?"

He gave her one more squeeze before pulling a pre-rolled cigarette from his jacket pocket. "I don't know. I only know I don't trust them, and that these horses are as valuable to us as the air we breathe." He lit the cigarette with a burning stick from the fire. "Sometimes when you set a man straight right off, it saves a lot of trouble later." He took a long, quiet drag on the cigarette. "Now why don't you go inside the tent and try to sleep. I intend to keep an eye on things for a while. And bury yourself good into the sleeping bag. It gets mighty cold in these higher elevations at night, and I intend to open one side of the back of the tent and tether the horses back there…to my ankle. Anybody tries anything, I'll know it right quick."

"It isn't good for you to breathe such cold air."

"I'll wrap a woolen scarf around my face. I'll be fine. I've slept out in colder weather. You're the one who isn't used to it."

Elizabeth finished a cup of coffee and rose. "I'm sorry I interfered."

"Don't worry about it. Just get some sleep. I might need you to wake up early morning and keep watch while *I* get some sleep. We're not leaving until that bunch gets a good head start on us."

Elizabeth felt almost sick from being sore and tired. "If that's what you want." She headed for the tent, going inside and grimacing as she removed her boots. She rubbed her sore feet for a few minutes, then crawled into her blankets, pulling them up over her head as Clint had ordered. She thought how at least the incident had dispelled her nervousness about sharing a tent this first night with Clint. It would likely be a while before he even came inside to sleep. By the time he did, she'd be asleep herself. After tonight, things wouldn't seem so awkward. She just had to get used to it.

"God, watch over him," she prayed. *"Please don't let there be any trouble."*

Chapter Twenty-Three

Deliver me, oh Lord, from the evil man:
preserve me from the violent man...
—Psalms 140:1

Elizabeth awoke to birds singing. She sat up, noticing Clint was not inside the tent. The last she remembered, he was sitting inside smoking, and told her he would take his bedroll outside and sleep there so he could keep an eye on the horses.

She shivered from the cold, thinking how much colder it must have been lying outside in the damp air. She took the combs from her hair and shook it out, then rewound it into a bun and fastened it. Looking down at her pants, she wondered how she must look to others. By the time this trip was over, she'd be an even worse mess from not being able to bathe or wash her hair. She wondered already if she could ever feel or look feminine again.

She pulled on her boots and jacket and crawled out of the tent. Clint sat by a renewed fire, drinking coffee and smoking yet another cigarette. She stood up, rubbing her eyes.

"Finally woke up, did you?" Clint teased.

Elizabeth stretched. "Did you ever sleep?"

"Some."

"You're going to make yourself sick again, Clint."

"I bundled up plenty good. As you can see, our horses are still here."

She glanced at Devil, Queen and Red Lady, then over toward Ezra Faine's camp. The men there were packing up. "I see," she answered. "I really don't think it was necessary for you to lie out in the damp cold all night."

"Well, I *do* think it was. And we'll wait right here until those fellows over there get a good head start on us. You might as well fix us some breakfast. I might even try getting a couple more hours' sleep while you take a turn watching the horses. It will put us somewhat behind, but I'd rather that bunch went on ahead. It will be worth it."

Elizabeth shook her head. "Whatever you say." She headed over to a cluster of rocks behind which she had no choice but to drop her trousers and drawers to relieve herself. If nothing else, this trip would certainly damage her modesty, that was sure. And it would be a while before she felt halfway comfortable in such a position with an unrelated man nearby. She walked back to the campfire and dug a frying pan out of their gear. "Pork and potatoes?"

"Sounds good." Clint was watching the Faine party.

Elizabeth set up a sheet-iron stove and set a black fry

pan over the flames. She dropped in a few pieces of pork, which created enough grease to fry potatoes. She quickly sliced some into the pan, then sat down next to Clint. He poured coffee into a tin cup and handed it to her.

"Thanks for making this," she told him. "Sorry I didn't get up sooner."

He shrugged, keeping the cigarette between his lips. "Didn't matter this morning, since we aren't leaving right away. The horses can probably use the rest, too." He removed the cigarette and drank some coffee, and Elizabeth noticed he wore his six-gun and kept a rifle beside him. "I'll take a bucket to a little waterfall I found in some rocks just around the bend of the trail," he added. "I'll fill it for the horses. I found the waterfall earlier when I walked a little ways ahead." He took one more drag and threw the butt of the cigarette into the fire, then looked at her with a mixture of humor and warning in his eyes. "You won't believe what's just around the bend."

Why did his closeness stir such odd feelings deep inside…a desire to touch him? Elizabeth had to turn her attention to the cooking food. It was difficult to look into those startlingly blue eyes; the man was so handsome in spite of the fact that he already needed a shave. He'd probably have a pretty good beard by the time they reached Dawson.

She stirred the food. "What's around the bend?"

"A view like nothing either of us has ever seen, even though we've seen the Sierras," he answered. "It would be beautiful if not for the fact that we have to go through it. We have three pretty challenging mountains to get across before we reach Lake Bennett, which is where we'll finally be able to finish the trip by way of the Yukon River. But that's a good fifty miles off, and the last climb will be White Pass. From around the bend you can see it, and *white* is a good description. There's a lot of snow up there, Elizabeth. We could lose all three of the horses before we even get there, narrow as the trail is in some places—and it's almost for sure we'll lose them trying to get over the pass."

Elizabeth looked back at Clint's loyal steeds. It was only natural to be attached already, and she realized Clint must be much more attached than she. She knelt by the fire and kept stirring. "I'm sorry. Clint, if you want to go back—"

"No. We'll make it, horses or no horses. But since you have some kind of an in with God, it wouldn't hurt for you to keep praying those three mounts make it, at least to the top of White Pass."

She smiled and looked over at him. "I don't have an *in,* as you put it. But I will do my best." She stirred the potatoes again. "I'd hate for you to lose your horses."

He sighed deeply, watching the Faine party finish their packing. "I can buy more."

So, you won't even let yourself get attached to your faithful animals for fear of losing them, Elizabeth thought. Or at least you pretend not to care.

Clint remained silent as she finished cooking the pork and potatoes. She scooped some onto a tin plate for him and handed it to him with a fork. By then Ezra Faine and those with him were ready to head out, their backs packed heavily. Two men were hitched to a sled like draft animals. They left, passing Clint and Elizabeth on the way. Ezra stopped to address them.

"Shouldn't you two be underway?" he asked with a frown. "There's no time to waste this time of year."

"We'll be along," Clint answered. "I figured I'd let you go first. Wouldn't want to hold you up."

Faine pretended an unconcerned laugh. "You just want us ahead of you, is that it?"

Clint handed his plate to Elizabeth, taking hold of his rifle and placing it over his knees. "Something like that."

"Not exactly the friendly sort, are you?" one of the other men commented.

"Depends on who wants to be friendly," Clint answered. "Word is there are men on these trips who would kill for horses and supplies. I'm just looking out for my own."

"Probably a good idea," another spoke up. It was Jonathan Hedley.

Clint just nodded. "Good luck," he told them.

Faine glanced at Elizabeth, then back to Clint. "Same to you." Again he looked at Elizabeth. "If anything should happen to your...uh...*husband* there...we won't be far ahead, ma'am, if you should need help."

"Thank you," Elizabeth answered. She realized the man didn't believe their story about getting married. If not, did they still think her a wanton woman? "I'm sure we'll be fine."

Faine tipped his hat. "Let's go, men." He plodded on, and the others followed. Elizabeth noticed that Clint watched them until the last man was out of sight around the bend. Then he rose.

"I'm going to make sure they do keep going," he told Elizabeth.

"Clint, just finish your food. It will get cold."

"Put it back in the pan till I get back. It'll keep," he answered.

He picked up his rifle and headed for an outcropping of rocks that hid the trail beyond. Elizabeth looked out at the surrounding mountains, now lighting up from the morning sun. Along the lower elevations across the wide chasm from where they were camped burst a display of splendid color from golden aspens that still hung on to their leaves, mixed with dark-green spruce and crimson undergrowth splashed with the purple and white of flowering autumn weeds. It was all so beautiful against the snowy mountains that rose above the color. She saw something move, then squinted her eyes to focus more sharply on the image.

"A bear," she said softly. It looked small from where she stood, but she surmised it would be much bigger up close. She hoped she'd never find out if that was so.

"What's so interesting?" Clint shouted.

She turned to see him returning. "There's a bear down there," she said, pointing.

Clint walked closer, and it took him a few seconds to see where she was pointing. "Yup, I see it. Looks like a grizzly." He grunted a laugh. "Better there than here."

Elizabeth smiled in agreement. "Look at the colors, Clint. It's so beautiful!"

He looked out at the scene with her, and she thought how in that little moment they shared something. She could feel a little part of what must have been the "old" Clint Brady, a man who could relax and appreciate beauty, but the moment did not last long.

"It's deceiving," he said, suddenly turning away. "Beneath all that beauty is a lot of danger. Come on. I'll finish eating. You can enjoy the view while I get some extra sleep."

Chapter Twenty-Four

*Blessed be the Lord my strength... My goodness
and my fortress; my high tower, and my deliverer;
my shield, and He in whom I trust...*
                                                    —Psalms 144:1 & 2

For the next two days the journey became so treacherous that there was little time for talk. Sleeping in the same tent with Clint no longer worried Elizabeth. Both fell exhausted into their blankets at night, and the exertion had made Clint's cough worse again, so that he was even more drained at night than Elizabeth.

She was glad she'd brought along the smelly liniment. She'd heated it for him, and he'd smeared the mysterious, oily concoction onto his chest himself. He hadn't even wanted to smoke, which was a relief to Elizabeth, who was not so sure smoking wasn't sinful, let alone surely not good for a man. But knowing Clint, he would not care to hear her preach against the habit. *If only that was his only fault.*

On the third day, they reached the first corduroy bridge across the foaming, freezing and very intimidating Skagway River.

"The guide I talked to said we'd have to cross several of these bridges to get to White Pass," Clint yelled to Elizabeth above the roar of the churning water. "After that we'll be in British Columbia."

The memory of her near-drowning came vividly to Elizabeth's mind. She never wanted to experience such a thing again, and the force of the river surely meant it would be impossible to survive the current if one fell in. Apparently Clint saw the fear in her eyes as she stared at the roaring death trap. He walked back to where she stood.

"I'll take the horses across first, then come back for you," he told her. "Don't worry. Thousands of other men and horses have crossed these things."

"Clint, be careful!" she told him. "If you fall into those waters and don't drown, you'll be sick all over again!"

He buttoned his fur-lined coat higher to his neck. The water's spray in this area made it seem colder than it really was. "Don't worry," he told her. He took hold of Devil's harness and started across the wobbly log bridge, constantly talking to the black gelding to keep him calm. Elizabeth's heart nearly stopped beating when the horse whinnied and balked, rearing back slightly and nearly pushing Clint off the bridge.

Clint managed to calm the animal and get him to the other side, a process that took a good ten minutes. He tied Devil to a little pine tree that jutted out of the rocks nearby and balanced his way back across the bridge to repeat the process with Queen and Red Lady. The sweeter-tempered mares caused much less trouble than Devil. Clint tied them and returned for Elizabeth.

"It's not that bad," he told her. "If those horses could make it across, you sure can."

"I should have just come across behind you the second time," she told him. "It's just the memory of falling off the *Damsel*."

"Don't worry about it." Clint moved his right arm around her back, grasping her waist for extra support, then grasped the rope railing with his left hand. Elizabeth clung to the right-side rope and they made their way carefully across the precarious logs. She could not help appreciating the strength of Clint's grasp, and she thought how it seemed like God protecting her through this man.

"Yea, though I walk through the valley of the shadow of death," she shouted.

Clint laughed lightly. He gave her a light squeeze, which surprised her...and was sinfully pleasing. It amazed her that she could think of that in such a time of fear and peril, but it was Clint helping her, reassuring her, risking his life, money and belongings for her. How could she not begin to feel an attachment? Was the same thing happening to him?

She reminded herself he was doing this mainly to reach Dawson so he could hunt for a wanted man. Still, already she was wondering what things would be like once they reached Dawson. Would he simply hunt down Roland Fisher and either kill him or tie him to his horse and leave? Would their own relationship, such as it was, simply end with a thank-you and a goodbye?

The security of his arm around her was unlike anything she'd felt before. It wasn't like a hug from her mother or father, or her brother. It was much more...dangerously more...dangerous because of the things that were happening to her heart, things that absolutely should *not* be happening, let alone so soon into their friendship, if it could even be called that.

They reached the other side safely, to Elizabeth's great relief. It also struck her that she'd been so lost in thought that she hardly remembered most of the frightening short jaunt over the bridge.

"On to the next bridge," he told her, letting go of her. He walked up and untied the horses, bringing them to the edge of the tumbling waters so they could take a drink. As he waited, he looked her over, smiling. "Have I ever told you how utterly ridiculous you look in those clothes?"

She looked down at herself and laughed. "I'm sure I do."

"And now do you understand why I said you had to wear pants and boots? Can you imagine trying to get across that bridge wearing a bunch of slips and petticoats, let alone making your way over this rocky trail?"

"Oh, I do understand," she answered, taking Queen's reins. Clint tied Red Lady to Devil's tail, then grasped Devil's reins and started off again. Elizabeth followed him along a trail that meandered along the opposite side of the river. She always felt easier around Clint when he was in this kind of mood, and she felt better now about the log bridges. The next one would be easier, she knew, because Clint would never let her fall.

For the rest of that third day the trail led them along

endlessly steep gorges, again and again meeting the Skagway River, over more log bridges, the pathway widening, then narrowing again to widths that made Elizabeth's chest tighten. It was difficult to believe they were hardly halfway to the height they must reach at White Pass. They still were not even above the tree line, and she tried not to think about what lay ahead in the awesome, dark granite, angular peaks. When she looked up at the vast bastions of the frigid interior of Alaska and Canada, starkly outlined against a deep-blue sky, she wondered that any man could surmount them, but thousands had, and so would she and Clint.

They moved past rocks that literally seemed to leak trickles of water, as well as splendid waterfalls that roared in Elizabeth's ears. They stopped only briefly at midday for something to eat, then headed into an area where the trail widened considerably, much to Elizabeth's relief. Trees and underbrush gave way to a clearing, where they spotted several men with instruments set up on tripods.

"Surveyors," Clint shouted back to Elizabeth.

They approached the men, one wearing spectacles, all well-dressed and equipped for camping in the area. They hailed Clint and Elizabeth with friendly gestures.

"How has the trip been so far?" the man with glasses asked Clint.

"As good as can be expected," Clint answered. He reached back for Elizabeth. "My name is Clint Brady, and this is my wife, Elizabeth."

The man nodded to her and then turned his gaze to Clint again. "Robert Stokes. We're with the Northern Pacific and are trying to build a railroad to the Yukon so you people don't have to make this trip on foot and horseback."

"A railroad! Into country like this?" Elizabeth asked.

Stokes laughed. "That's what they said back in the sixties when men proposed a transcontinental railroad through the Rockies and the Sierras. But wherever men go, especially when it involves gold, the railroad will follow, ma'am, no matter the obstacles. Never underestimate us."

"Oh, I wouldn't think of it," Elizabeth replied.

"Have many others passed by you today?" Clint asked.

"Two parties—both inexperienced men who have no business trying this trip, but you know gold and men. I suppose that's your purpose also."

"Actually no," Clint answered. "My wife is looking for her brother, who went to Dawson over a year ago to preach, believe it or not. Me, I'm...well, I agreed to take her, simple as that."

Stokes looked him over, studied the pack horses. "Well, you sure don't look like a man inexperienced at this kind of trip."

"I did my share of living under the stars before I got married," Clint answered, with no further explanation. "By the way, was one of the parties who passed by here led by a man named Ezra Faine?"

Stokes nodded. "About four hours ahead of you. He tried to buy a couple of horses from us, but they belong to the railroad. I've got no right to sell them."

Clint nodded, then tipped his floppy-brimmed, leather hat to them. "Thanks. Good luck to you."

"Same to you. There's an even better clearing about an

hour ahead. You should be able to make it that far before full dark."

"Good to know." Clint walked through the camp and continued.

Elizabeth followed, calling out to him once they were several yards from the railroaders. "Are you still worried about Ezra Faine?" she asked. "We haven't seen him and his men for days, and that man said they were a good half day ahead of us."

"Doesn't hurt to check," Clint answered.

Elizabeth could hardly believe he needed to worry about them, but she decided Clint would just get in a sour mood if she pressed the subject. "Do you really think they will be able to build a railroad into these mountains?" she asked, wanting to change the subject.

"Sure they will. Like the man said, where men go, so goes the railroad."

They walked nearly two more miles until they reached the clearing the railroad men told them about. It was indeed a good place to make camp, and burned-out camp fires, flattened grass and small trees chopped down told them that plenty of others had camped here. For now, they were the only ones.

"Look there," Clint told Elizabeth as they unpacked their gear.

When she looked in the direction of his gaze, she spotted two moose. She drew in her breath. "What a grand animal! Look at those antlers!"

"I'm thinking food," Clint answered, slowly pulling his rifle from his gear.

"Clint, they are so beautiful!"

He leaned against his horse and looked down at her. "And there is a reason your God put them on this earth," he answered. He leaned even closer to her. "To feed man." He straightened. "And where we're going, it will be easy to pack meat," he continued, keeping his voice low. "We'll have more trouble with thawing it out than worrying about it spoiling." He retracted his Winchester and raised it, taking aim. "Hang on to the horses," he told her.

Elizabeth grasped the reins of all three animals, then squinted, waiting for the loud noise. Clint stood there sure and easy, and she couldn't help wondering if he'd used that rifle on men. Maybe he only used his six-gun. Either way, it reminded her of what the man did for a living.

He squeezed the trigger, and the horses twitched and whinnied, sidling sideways at the sudden crack of the rifle. One shot. A moose fell. The other one ran off.

Chapter Twenty-Five

Thou shalt not be afraid for the terror by night; nor the arrow that flieth by day...for He will give His angels charge over thee, to keep thee in all thy ways.
—Psalms 91:5 & 11

Clint spent most of the early evening gutting the moose he'd shot. He carved chunks of meat from the carcass while Elizabeth watched, sometimes crinkling her nose. The work was tough, but Clint worked diligently and adeptly, complaining that there was not time to truly preserve every part of the animal, including the hide.

"Indians would cringe if they knew what we're leaving behind," he told her. "They make use of every part of an animal, even most of the innards."

Elizabeth could not imagine using any of the matter Clint threw on the ground.

"We can only carry so much," he continued. "What we do take could save our lives later, even if we have to eat it raw."

"Raw!"

"You do what you have to do to stay alive sometimes, Liz. It's just a shame to leave so much of this poor animal to the wolves, which is why we came so far away from camp to clean it. If wolves decide to make a meal of this thing, I don't want them close to our camp. Even this is a little too close. I'm worried about the horses. What we take we'll have to hang high in a tree till morning. We just have to hope this carcass and innards keep them occupied tonight."

"We haven't even encountered wolves yet. Why are you so sure we will tonight?"

He threw another chunk of meat into a frozen puddle of water at his left side, where other pieces lay chilling. "Ten to one a wolf pack is already skirting around us. They can smell fresh blood for miles, and winter is coming on. They know darn well that it's time to start burying meat for the lean times."

The thought of wolves skulking about, sight unseen, was disconcerting. "What can I do to help, Clint?"

"Go back and build up the fire. I'll skin off as much hide as I can and use it to carry back the raw meat. You can go ahead and heat up some coffee and a fry pan. I'll cut off a few thin slices to cook tonight." He stopped and turned to rinse his hands in one end of the frozen puddle. "Wait a minute," he told her before she left. He shook off the water and wiped his hands on his denim pants, then took his six-gun from its holster, handing it to her butt first. "Take this with you."

She looked wide-eyed at the shooter. "What on earth for?"

He sighed with obvious impatience. "What did I just tell

you about wolves? With fresh blood all over the place, this isn't a good time to be walking about alone without some kind of protection."

She put her hands on her hips. "I've never shot a gun in my life! I've never even *held* one!"

"Will you just do as I ask? And be careful. It's ready to fire. If something comes running at you, all you have to do is cock it and pull the trigger. If you don't hit whatever it is, you'll at least scare it away."

Elizabeth took the gun, holding it by only the handle so that it dangled from her hand.

"For crying out loud, woman, it isn't a snake that will bite you," Clint grumped.

Elizabeth carefully grasped the gun barrel, surprised at how heavy the gun was for its size. She took a better hold of the butt, keeping her finger away from the trigger. "I just...I cock it?"

Clint rose, taking the shooter from her. "This is the hammer," he said, pulling it back with his thumb. "Now it's cocked. If you pull the trigger, and believe me, it doesn't take much pressure, the gun will go off." He grasped the hammer again and carefully let it back to its original position. "When it's not cocked, pulling the trigger isn't easy, so you're pretty darn safe carrying it this way. Just remember that if you need it, you have to pull back that hammer. Okay?"

She studied the gun as he handed it back. "Okay, I guess." She clasped the gun carefully with both hands and carried it back to the campsite, thinking how it would be next to impossible to really shoot it if the need arose. And if it was so difficult to think about killing an animal, how on earth could someone kill a human being?

She set the gun on the stump of a freshly cut tree and tended to the fire, building it up as Clint had instructed. She set the skillet on the coals to heat the pan, realizing only then that the sun had set and it was darker than she had realized. When the fire got bigger, it became difficult to see Clint in the distance.

The horses whinnied then, shuffling around as though nervous about something. Should she yell out to Clint? She left the fire and picked up the six-gun, sitting down on the stump and listening. An odd, low growl came from behind her to the right, and her blood ran cold. Everything tingled from head to foot as fear engulfed her when the growl came again, a kind of low snort actually.

The horses whinnied louder, and Elizabeth felt light-headed as it seemed as though all her blood was pouring into her feet and leaving the rest of her body. She sat frozen, not even able to scream to Clint. Perhaps a scream would make things worse. Maybe moving to turn with the gun would bring on an attack from whatever it was that lurked in the shadows.

But the horses! Clint had made it clear over and over how necessary they were to their surviving this trip. And they were Clint's horses. God knew she had an obligation to watch out for them.

More growls. Now the horses were beginning to rear. They could break loose and run off! That would be a catastrophe! She said a quick prayer for courage, then rose and turned. Red eyes stared back at her, from a height of a good ten feet! What on earth! Coming from the darkness, whatever approached seemed like a giant, demonic beast!

Instead of a scream, all she could muster was a whimper from somewhere deep inside as instinct made her nervously search for the hammer of the six-gun. It was harder to pull back than she'd thought it would be. It took both thumbs to do it. The beast came closer. She fired, but the six-gun was not powerful enough to stop it. She finally screamed Clint's name and managed to fire again, but the beast came even closer. Then, from somewhere behind her she heard two louder shots.

Clint's rifle! The beast was nearly on top of her. It fell, and she screamed as it took her with it, both of them tumbling dangerously close to the fire. Instantly something grabbed her away and tore the six-gun from her hand. She heard four more shots. The growling stopped.

"Clint!" she screamed.

In almost the same instant she was in his arms. "Are you all right?"

"I don't know! I don't know!"

"It was a grizzly! He's dead, I hope. Stay here a minute. I've got to calm the horses so they don't run off. The smell of that bear isn't helping!"

He left her near their tent and ran over to calm the horses, retying them. He returned then to where she sat, pulling her around to the other side of the fire from where the bear lay so he could see her better. He ran his hands over her face, looking deeply concerned.

"Did he take a swipe at you?" he asked. "Hurt you in any way?"

"I don't think so. It all happened so fast," she answered, shaking. "I shot at it, just like you told me to do, but it didn't help!"

"No six-gun will stop a grizzly. And here I was worried about wolves, which we still *do* need to worry about now, what with a dead bear lying here. It's going to be one sleepless night." He heaved a deep sigh. "We'll have to move camp. That bear probably weighs a thousand pounds. There's no way I can drag him away. Do you think you can help carry everything to a different area?"

He held her arms, and she grasped his shoulders. "I'll do whatever I need to do." She couldn't help tears of fright and shock. "Oh, Clint, what if you hadn't managed to bring him down with your rifle?" Without thinking, she flung her arms around his neck. "Thank God!"

His arms came around her in return. "I was more worried I'd hit you with the rifle instead of the bear."

"Not you," she answered without thinking. "You know how to use your guns. You'd never miss."

They stood there a moment…in each other's arms. She thought how he smelled good in spite of not having bathed for days…in spite of just coming from gutting the moose. Around his neck and hair he still smelled good, a manly smell she'd come to recognize as distinctly Clint Brady's.

It took both of them a moment to realize what they were doing…holding each other…enjoying it. The spell was broken by the howl of wolves in the distance.

"Let's get away from here," Clint said, letting go.

Rather stunned by the sweet feeling of being held close in his arms, Elizabeth said nothing as she helped him break camp. She wondered if Clint had felt the same sweet joy as she while he held her. *Dear Lord, am I falling in love? Is this how it feels?*

No! It was wrong to feel this way about a man like Clint. Totally wrong!

Chapter Twenty-Six

Deliver me, O Lord, from the evil man: preserve me
from the violent man; which imagines mischief in his
heart; continually are they gathered together for war.
—Psalms 140:1-2

The days were growing too short. Clint realized that even though it was the end of August and not all that late, it was pitch-dark when they'd resettled their camp. He climbed down from a pine tree where he'd hung the moose hide that held the fresh meat tied inside, only a fraction of what could have been taken from the carcass. The hide hanging in the tree held all the weight they could afford to add to the back of one of the horses.

With a sigh of both weariness and relief, he walked over to sit down on a blanket near the fire. He lit a rolled cigarette, taking a long first drag to further settle his nerves. He noticed Elizabeth's hands shaking as she turned the sliced meat he'd given her, now cooking in the black fry pan.

"What a day," he commented. "Are you sure you're all right?"

"Well, nothing hurts, except the back of my head from hitting the ground. I certainly will have a tale to tell my grandchildren."

Clint grinned. Our grandchildren. The unexpected thought quickly sobered him. What on earth had caused him to think it at all? He felt like cursing her for throwing her arms around his neck. Darned if he hadn't wanted to hang on. He'd enjoyed the feel of her against him, the smell of her hair. The trouble was, that quick embrace was going to make sleeping in the same tent with her more difficult.

"That's for sure," he answered, taking another drag on the cigarette. He'd get over this feeling. It was just from the scare of thinking she'd been hurt. It brought back all the guilt he felt for not being with Jen when she was killed. He might have been able to stop the whole thing. And Ethan. Poor little Ethan. Had he cried out for his daddy when—

They heard growling in the distance, and the horses shifted nervously again and whinnied.

"Wolves," Clint told her, "just like I figured. I just didn't add that grizzly to my figuring."

Elizabeth sat down across from him, looking more tired than normal. Clint suspected the encounter with the grizzly had taken more out of her than she cared to admit. "I'm sorry I sent you back alone. I won't do that again."

She shrugged, pretending it didn't matter. "It's all right. You didn't know. Besides, if I'd been out there with you, that bear might have ripped our camp apart and maybe attacked the horses before we had a chance to stop it."

"Maybe." He felt the odd new tension between them. It was the embrace that did it. She felt funny about it. So did he. He had to avoid talking about it at all costs. This would all blow over.

"I have to say, pulling back the hammer on that gun was harder than I thought it would be. I can't imagine how you do it with one hand."

She, too, was trying to keep things nonchalant. "I should have known it would be hard when you've never even shot a gun before. When we get the chance, I'll have you do a little target practice with the six-gun *and* the rifle. Then we'll hope you never have to use either one again."

She took another deep breath. She was nervous. He could tell. "I agree with you there." She leaned over and turned the meat again. "Now I owe you one again."

"I didn't know we were keeping score."

She laughed lightly. "It just seems like you keep delivering me from death's door. But then, that's why God brought you into my life, to get me safely to Dawson."

There she went again, bringing up God. God had nothing to do with it. He sat there smoking quietly, thinking how, if God was so intent on saving good people, why couldn't He have saved his wife and son?

"Saying God brought us together still makes you uncomfortable, doesn't it?" Elizabeth commented.

He shrugged. "Believe it if you want to."

She didn't answer right away. She dished some of the meat onto a plate and gave him a biscuit along with it. The biscuit was hard, a left-over from the day before; but she'd warmed it by the fire first. "Do you want a knife and fork?"

He finished his cigarette and threw the butt into the fire. "No sense dirtying more utensils than necessary. I'll eat it with my fingers."

She took a couple of pieces for herself, and they both ate quietly. The growling in the distance continued. "That carcass will keep them busy," Clint told Elizabeth between bites. "I don't think we're in any danger, but I'll keep my rifle beside me all night, just in case. It also helps to keep the fire going. They don't like fire. I'll sleep outside tonight to keep watch."

There. Now he had an excuse not to have to sleep next to her tonight in that tent that seemed much too small for a man and a woman together.

"All right." Elizabeth set her plate aside. "God *did* bring us together, Clint. I've gone far beyond doubting that. I just want you to know I truly believe that in my heart, because it means God is watching after you, too. He has some kind of plan for you."

Now came the irritation. Good. That would make it easier to forget about that embrace, the feel of her slender body in his arms. "I thought you promised not to preach."

"I'm not preaching—exactly. I just...well...you think you are a man who makes all his own decisions, and in most ways you are. But there is a Higher Being controlling your life in many ways, Clint. I've grown to care about you, enough to know I can't let you go on thinking there is no God, or that if there is, He's somehow totally uninvolved with your life."

There it was. The very thing he couldn't stand to hear. Yes, now he knew why he didn't want to get too involved with this woman, why he didn't dare care about her. "You don't know anything about real life, or the ways God can totally fail a man!" He let out a rough deep breath.

"Please don't think like that."

"I'll believe what I want! And believe me, the God you're talking about doesn't exist. That God would not have allowed my wife and son to die! And He wouldn't allow men like those who killed them to exist on the face of the earth! He wouldn't allow *evil* to exist!"

To his surprise she didn't back down. "There *is* evil in this world, Clint," she retorted. "It's a fact of life, and knowing it is where *faith* becomes all-important—faith that even when bad things happen, God has a plan for us. He has ways of working around the evil, and no evil on earth can destroy the beauty and peace all of us will know when we reach God's arms in heaven! That's where your wife and child are right now. They are enjoying something far more wonderful than anything they would have known here on earth! You could kill every evil man on this earth, and it wouldn't bring back your wife and son, or bring you the kind of peace only our Lord and Savior can bring you."

"Shut up!" he yelled. "Just shut up! Why are you bringing this up now? I asked you *never* to bring it up!"

She shivered and looked away, saying nothing for the next several tense seconds. "I'm sorry," she finally said, her voice lowered to a nearly unintelligible pitch. "I just thought...tonight's experience just...I don't know. It just made me feel even more strongly that you were meant to come into my life. That in turn...it makes me feel responsible to tell you about God's love to do what I can to bring you back into His arms…the only place where you'll ever find any peace. It's so obvious that you're lonely and hurting. If God brought you to me, then all that is Christian in me tells me I have no choice but to do what I can to bring you back to Christ."

Why was she doing this? He set his tin dish aside. "I am real close to hurrying up this trip till we catch up with Ezra Faine and his bunch. You can finish this trip with *them!*" he snarled. "Now clean up and go get some sleep! *I* won't get much shut-eye tonight, thanks to you bringing up things I have a hard enough time not thinking about—like the fact that my wife and son are *dead!*"

He walked off to check on the horses, pulling another cigarette from a pocket inside his jacket and lighting it. He swore. Why had she said all those things? Why did she keep bringing up God? Why was she breaking her promise to him not to talk about Jen and his precious son?

He could hear her crying. Good. She *should* cry. Maybe she was beginning to see that all her preaching wasn't going to do any good. Maybe she *needed* yelling at. It would wake her up to real life. Besides that, it helped keep him from looking at her as someone he could care about.

Chapter Twenty-Seven

Thou art my hiding place and my shield:
I hope in Thy word.
—Psalms 119:114

Selfish fool! Elizabeth scolded herself as she plodded through fresh, wet snow on their way up the highest mountain they had climbed yet. She hated herself for crying after Clint had yelled at her two nights ago. After all, she'd *deserved* to be yelled at. She wouldn't be surprised right now if God Himself struck her dead.

She'd deliberately said the very words she knew would make Clint Brady explode. And immediately afterward she'd regretted it and cried about it. She had no doubt he'd enjoyed hearing that. God probably had also. After all, she'd said what she had on purpose, just because she was afraid of her own feelings for Clint. All she could think about was how to avoid those feelings, and the best way to do that was to say something that would make him explode at her. When he was like that, it was easy not to like him, and that was what she wanted—not to like him…not to *love* him.

And yet for all she knew God *meant* for her to love him. Who was she to fight her own heart? Who was she to judge, believing that Clint Brady was not right for her, maybe even not good enough for her? How dare she think that *anyone* might not be good enough for her! Everyone was a child of God. Everyone had a right to love and be loved.

Clint had not said one word to her since the night they'd argued, other than to bark orders angrily. Whenever they made camp, he joined her only long enough to help put up and take down the tent and load and unload supplies, or to eat. Other than that, he walked off alone, away from the fire. He'd slept outside, in spite of a snowfall last night.

She almost wished he would scream his head off at her. At least that would open a way to talk again, but she could tell he was determined that all talking was over.

If only they had not embraced after the grizzly had nearly attacked her. That was the most wonderful embrace she'd ever experienced, warm and loving, an embrace that had brought forbidden desires and a rush of pleasant feelings of warmth and safety…and yes, love. And either she was crazy or she was right that she'd sensed the same feelings in Clint. Then she had to go and spoil it all on purpose, all because of her own stupid, girlish fears, not just the fear of falling in love with someone totally wrong for her, but of being with a man at all.

What did she know about men? And for heaven's sake, Clint was ten years older than she! He'd been married, and only the Lord knew how many other women there had been in his life, maybe women like Collette. How could an ignorant young woman who knew little beyond church and family be a wife to a man like that? And why in the world was she even *thinking* that way? Clint Brady drank, often cussed, and he killed men with no remorse. He wore a gun and never hesitated using it...even on men.

She wished she was already with Peter, or that she could talk to her mother. They would know what to tell her. They would pray with her, show her passages in the Bible that might help.

You should be talking to Me.

Where did those words come from? She actually looked around.

God, that's where. He was speaking to her through that still, small voice from deep inside. Yes, she should pray more. She should ask forgiveness for being so selfish and judgmental. Then she should pray to God again to help her please to sort out her feelings, find the right words for Clint Brady. Whether he cared about her or not, she already cared too much about him to let him go on in such bitter loneliness.

The only distraction from her thoughts was the hardship of their journey. The climb had grown steeper and steeper, the pathway more and more narrow, the canyons below deeper and deeper. Her legs felt like bricks, and her breath grew shorter and shorter as they trudged ever higher. If White Pass was higher than this, and covered with deep snows to boot, how in the world would they get over it?

Clint finally stopped at what seemed the highest point,

although stark, gray walls of snow-capped granite rose on both sides of them, much higher than where they stood now, in spite of the climb. When Elizabeth caught up to where Clint stood, she realized why he'd stopped.

"Oh, my," was all she could say. Before them lay another mountain, a much higher mountain. From where they stood they could see several parties climbing it, and several more men coming back their way—giving up and returning. Those climbing it looked like small black dots against a wall of white. In the area just below them they could see abandoned caches, a few dead horses lying stiff and frozen. Between them and the next mountain was more of a depression than a valley, an open area where a few trees grew. A closer look at the entire area brought more debris into focus, more abandoned back packs, tents, more dead horses and a general array of trash.

"What do we do?" Elizabeth asked Clint.

"We make camp down there and let the horses rest for a full day, then we go for it. Part of the problem with losing horses is most men headed for Dawson are in such an all-fired rush that they don't let their animals rest in between. Since we aren't breaking our necks to get there and make the first claims, we can afford to slow down."

"Except for the fact that it's September and by the time we get there it will surely be very wintry. That old guide I talked to back in Skagway told me that last winter a lot of men starved to death in Dawson because they didn't bring along enough supplies. I hope my brother wasn't one of them."

Clint sighed. "Right now my only real concern is getting over White Pass. Then we have to hope that the Yukon isn't frozen shut. We'll reach Dawson a lot faster if we can float a raft on the river than if we have to walk."

"A lot of those men are turning back. It must be pretty bad up there in the pass."

"We'll make it," Clint replied matter-of-factly. He headed down the other side of the mountain they had just climbed, a much more gradual slope that did not lead as far down as on the other side. The lower they got, the more mushy the ground became, until by the bottom the ground was marshy and sported a little grass. Elizabeth suspected there once had been more, but that most of it had been grazed off by other horses that had come through during the summer.

By the time they chose a place to make camp it was nearly dark, yet a few men were still trying to get over the snowy pass. Elizabeth could see their lanterns. She breathed deeply against her frayed nerves. The thought of climbing that pass was indeed intimidating.

They passed abandoned sleds, dead dogs, more bloated horses, their legs sticking up stiffly in death. In the distance two men were arguing about something, and in seconds they were battling each other with fists and feet.

They passed sacks of rotted potatoes, crates of canned goods, tents, saddles, sacks of flour. In some places men were ransacking abandoned supplies, stealing what they could carry. She didn't need Clint to tell her that she'd better keep a close eye on their own supplies, and especially on the horses. By this point of the journey men were getting greedy and desperate. Even she, in all her ignorance of the ugly side of people, could understand that, just from what she saw here.

One returning party passed them, all the men bearded and looking haggard. One of them, whose nose was deeply peeled to an ugly red, nodded to Clint. "Not worth it," he commented. "Just not worth it. I done lost part of my nose to frostbite. And the climb…" He shook his head and continued.

Clint stopped and looked back at Elizabeth. "You want to know the only reason I'm heading on?"

She frowned. "To find the man you're after?"

"Oh, I can find him now or I can find him in the spring. If he's really in Dawson, I have a feeling he's going nowhere the rest of the winter."

The statement confused her. "Then why?"

He looked her over rather scathingly. "Because you keep claiming that your God means for this trip to happen. You keep telling me that He will take care of us and keep us safe." He turned back and kept walking. "We'll see just what kind of a God He really is."

The comment astonished her. So, was he "testing" God? Or was he just making fun of her? Was he out to prove her wrong? That would not surprise her. In fact, he was risking his very *life* to prove her wrong.

Lord, I guess it's up to You to get us through this and prove me right, she prayed quietly. *Just help me know how to handle this man and what to say to him while we do this. Help me act according to Your will…not my own.*

Chapter Twenty-Eight

Behold, thou art fair, my love; behold, thou art
fair; thou hast dove's eyes within thy locks…
thy lips are like a thread of scarlet, and thy
speech is comely…thou art all fair, my love;
there is no spot in thee.
—Song of Solomon 4:1, 3 & 7

Clint tethered the horses, glancing over to watch Elizabeth build a fire with what little wood she could find. They were nearly out of the wood they had bundled to bring with them, which was good in a way; it was just too much weight. Now they were headed over a snowy mountain that would yield no wood at all, and he'd heard that beyond White Pass lay a near wasteland on the trek to Lake Bennett in British Columbia. There they hoped to buy a raft that would float them to Dawson. Meantime, they would probably not be able to build a fire for warmth.

He glanced at the snowy pass. Part of him hated the

thought of dragging his poor horses and a spit of a woman through all that. The sight of so many dead horses did nothing to boost his hopes that Queen, Red Lady and Devil would survive the trip, and the thought of wading through drifts that could be deeper than Elizabeth was tall just made him even more unsure.

What a mess he'd gotten himself into! He turned back to finish tethering the horses, then unloaded more supplies. A fool, that's what he was! This had all started with running down the man who'd grabbed Elizabeth's handbag back in San Francisco. If he'd known what all that would lead to, he would have let the fool of a woman chase the man down by herself. To think that she could actually be right about God bringing them together irritated him no end.

What business did God have in his life anyway? He'd abandoned all faith a long time ago. God shouldn't care *what* happened to him! The Man Upstairs should just let him go to hell in a handbasket and tend to people more deserving. And if He *really* cared about Elizabeth Breckenridge, He would have sent someone else to help her out.

Still, naive or not, she sure as heck had courage. And she was one of the strongest, most uncomplaining women he'd ever met. Through this whole trip, she'd not groaned once about being too tired or too hungry or complained that she had to do too much of the work. She cooked every day, helped put up and take down camp, helped tend to the horses, did everything he told her to do.

He set down some supplies and leaned against an outcropping of rocks, lighting a cigarette. For all that poor woman knew, he'd been sent by the Devil to test her faith, rather than by God. That made more sense. He was just glad they'd had that argument. They were getting a little too friendly as far as he was concerned. The argument had helped end that little problem. And at least she'd had sense enough to shut up about it since then.

He took a long drag on the cigarette, wanting to scream. One minute he was ready to throw Miss Breckenridge over a cliff, the next he was worried she might get hurt or get sick, wondering how he would feel if something really did happen to her. One minute he wondered if she might be right about God bringing them together, the next he thought she was an idiot for thinking that. Most of the time the last thing he wanted was to think about God and faith and all that nonsense, the next minute he really wanted to talk more about it. One minute he wanted to gag her so she'd never again ask about Jen; the next he wanted to tell her everything. One minute he couldn't wait to get to Dawson to be rid of her; the next he was pondering what it might be like to allow himself to fall in love again.

Love! How had that word managed to creep into his thoughts? His head literally ached from thinking too much. Besides, what made him think a woman like Elizabeth would settle with somebody like him anyway? He was ten years older, a bounty hunter, a godless man of no faith at all.

He noticed she'd got the fire going. As usual, night had come early. He threw down his cigarette butt and stepped it out, then pulled his rifles from their boots and picked up the remaining gear he'd unpacked, walking back to the tent. He set the gear aside and sat down on a flat rock near the fire.

"The only good place to tether the horses is too far away to watch them overnight from here," he told Elizabeth. "I'll have to bed down closer to them later. We can't move our tent over there because the ground is too wet and marshy, but at least there is a tree there I could tether them to."

"Fine."

He set his rifle aside, watching her put coffee grounds into a little burlap bag and drop it into the coffeepot. She filled the pot with a canteen of water. Clint thought how at least water would not be a problem on this trip. It was plentiful everywhere. He'd traveled in places where a man would kill for a drink of water.

He noticed circles under Elizabeth's eyes. Surely this trip had been a physical challenge for someone so small and inexperienced, let alone the emotional problems he caused her. "You all right?"

She shrugged. "As well as can be expected, I guess. Just sore feet, but they're better than they were the first few days. How about the horses? Did you check their hooves?"

"I dug out some little stones. The kind of ground we've covered has helped keep them filed down, but they will still need trimming when we get to Dawson, if the poor things make it that far. I brought along burlap to tie on their feet for the trip over White Pass to protect them from the snow and ice."

Elizabeth nodded but said nothing. She quietly proceeded to dig out the trusty black fry pan and filled it with onions and more moose meat. "We're almost out of potatoes," she finally spoke up, "and this is the last of the onions. I have some carrots, and enough flour to keep making biscuits for quite a few days yet. I'll save what's left of the potatoes as long as I can. We'll soon be down to pork and moose, but that, too, will be gone before we reach Dawson. That's about it, although I do still have a few sweet potatoes and some beans. You may have to do more hunting before we make Dawson."

"Lord knows there's plenty of game in this land," he answered. "We've seen bear and moose and deer, rabbits and quail, pheasant, elk. I'm not sure why men should be starving, unless the surge of gold seekers into Dawson has depleted or scared off all the game in that area."

"Maybe most of the prospectors just don't know how to shoot straight."

The remark made him smile. "Maybe."

She finally looked at him. "You could probably make a living just hunting once you get there," she suggested. "For game, I mean."

Their gazes held. "Instead of men?"

She looked back at the pan and turned the onions and moose meat. "You said it. I didn't."

Clint reached over to take a piece of cheesecloth and a cleaning rod from his supplies, then he snapped open one of his rifles and ran some of the cloth through the barrel to clean out the residue. "I should have cleaned this sooner," he commented. "All this dampness isn't good for for steel, especially mixed with gunpowder."

He hated the uncomfortable feeling between them. He wanted it over with.

"Did I tell you I made extra money as a gunsmith at one time?"

"No. You've never told me much of anything. I wasn't supposed to ask, remember?"

She was definitely making this hard for him. He wanted to get a conversation going without making it look obvious.

"Well, I did. That was back when I farmed in northern California. Good extra money." He pulled out the cheesecloth and ran a cleaner piece over the outside of the barrel. "I can take a gun apart right down to the last screw and put it back together again. I can even build a gun from scratch, when I have the right tools. I left all those behind when I—" he hesitated "—left my farm," he finally finished, adding no further details.

He set the rifle aside, then stood up and removed his revolver. "Might as well clean this one, too. I'm going to check on the horses first."

He set the six-gun on a log near Elizabeth and started back to the horses. That was when he heard a rifle being cocked.

"Stand right there, Brady," came a voice out of the darkness.

Chapter Twenty-Nine

These...things doth the Lord hate...a lying tongue,
and hands that shed innocent blood...
— Proverbs 6:16, 17

Elizabeth stayed put where she sat. Her chest tightened with terror. There before the fire stood Ezra Faine, aiming a rifle at Clint! Another man stood beside Ezra with a pistol! She recognized him from Ezra's party, but did not know his name.

"What do you think you're doing?" Clint asked Ezra.

"We lost most of our supplies in the Skagway River when two of our men fell in," Ezra answered. "Now, the way I see it, you have quite a bit of goods left, plus those three horses and a woman to boot. We intend to take them the rest of the way with us."

The second man hurried around and grabbed Clint's open rifle and tossed it into the darkness. Noticing that both men kept their eyes only on Clint, Elizabeth carefully reached over and grasped Clint's six-gun, pulling it under the blanket she'd wrapped around her shoulders because of the chill.

Clint, who did not seem the least bit worried that there was a rifle pointed at him, looked both men over. "Last I knew, stealing another man's property and horses was a hanging offense among miners."

Ezra grinned. "Could be. But we aren't in a mining town right now, and there isn't any law here in this valley. It's every man for himself. Besides, you owe me for that sucker punch back in Skagway, and for moving in on the pretty lady there."

The second man chuckled. "You don't really think we believe she's your wife, do you?"

"Believe what you want," Clint answered. "And if you're going to take what's mine, you'd better kill me, because you don't want me behind you, Faine."

"Clint!" Elizabeth rose and ran over beside him, keeping the blanket around her.

"You'd best stay away, little woman," Ezra warned her. He kept his eyes on Clint. "A couple more of my men are over there untying your horses even as we speak. And the only reason I haven't shot you yet is because I wanted you to know first who is doing this. I don't take kindly to being insulted and embarrassed in front of my friends."

"I call them as I see them," Clint answered.

All the while they talked, Elizabeth moved closer to Clint, until finally she was close enough to move her arm into his as a show of support. "Please don't do this!" she begged Ezra. "What kind of a man are you?"

"He's not what he pretends to be, that's for sure," Clint replied before Ezra could speak. "I had you figured all along, Faine. For all your pretense of being a fancy lawyer, you're no better than an outlaw."

Faine grinned. "Like you said, you call them as you see them."

Her blanket hiding Clint's six-gun, Elizabeth carefully slipped it into Clint's hand.

"You'd better move aside, ma'am," Ezra told her, stepping back slightly. "I wouldn't want this man's blood to splatter on you."

"Do like he says, Liz," Clint told her.

Had she done the right thing? If someone died here tonight, would it be her fault? *God help us,* she prayed inwardly, terrified for Clint.

"Get the woman out of the way," Ezra told the man beside him.

In one split second everything changed. Elizabeth saw fire spit from Clint's handgun...saw Ezra fly backward...saw fire coming from the second man's gun. Clint stumbled slightly. Elizabeth screamed his name, and then came another shot from Clint's gun...the second man went down. Clint shoved his six-gun into Elizabeth's hands. "Stay here!" He picked up Ezra's rifle and ran off into the darkness.

Elizabeth stood there shaking. She was almost sure Clint had been hit. Her breath came in quick gasps and tears filled her eyes as she stared at Ezra and the second man. Both lay near the fire, blood on their chests. They looked dead.

"Dear God," she groaned. "Please forgive me! I couldn't let them shoot Clint without giving him a chance!"

Tears welled in her eyes, and she looked down at the gun in her shaking hands. She could smell the smoke that still wafted from its barrel. She looked out into the darkness. "Clint," she whispered. He'd surely gone after those who were trying to steal his horses. She jumped when she heard another, louder shot. It had to be Clint shooting Ezra's rifle. She could only hope that's what it was, rather than someone shooting at Clint.

What was wrong with these men? She thought about the fist fight she'd seen on the way to camp. Why did men have to be like this? Why had her own innocent father been murdered for the few lousy dollars he'd had in his vest pocket. He'd never harmed a soul in his life. Greed. Lust. Such sinful things led to fights and murder. And how could she blame Clint for defending himself? Surely part of it had been for her sake. These men would have taken her with them if he hadn't stopped them.

Tears stung her eyes as she waited in fear of what might have happened to Clint. Should she run after him, or should she wait here? What if he was dead? Should she use the gun in her hand if men came for her? No! She could never do that! When soldiers came for Jesus in Gethsemane, He did not resist. Still, that was because He knew His calling. He was born to sacrifice Himself for man, and to fulfill the prophecies for the Savior. Surely He understood that sometimes a person must defend himself against evil.

"Clint!" she shouted. "Clint, where are you?"

Finally she heard some kind of commotion in the distance to her left. She and Clint had not even been aware that Ezra and his bunch were camped in the same valley.

They must have been too far away to notice, but if that was the case, how had they known she and Clint were there? Ezra must have had men scouting around for things they could steal when they'd noticed her and Clint.

A tear slipped down her cheek. Where was he? It suddenly struck her that she would feel a loss much deeper than she had thought she would if something had happened to him...much deeper because she was in love with Clint Brady, and there was no denying it any longer. It might be too late to matter.

"Clint!" she screamed again, clinging to the six-gun. How much time had passed? Five minutes? Ten? Two men still lay dead nearby. What was she supposed to do about them? She'd never seen violent death up close like this. But Clint had, and they lay dead from Clint's gun. How could she possibly love a man like that? But she did.

Finally, she heard him yell somewhere off to her left. "It's all right, Liz. I'm coming."

His words were like God Himself reassuring her. He'd become her friend, her protector. Surely if God meant this to be something more, He would help her find a way to bring Clint to peace with himself. This recent incident certainly wouldn't help. He'd just killed two men and probably didn't think a thing of it. But what else could he have done? Such a killing, in self defense, wouldn't be so bad, if not for the fact that Clint Brady sometimes deliberately hunted men down to kill them. That was different. That was what he had to deal with emotionally. That was the Clint she could not love.

Suddenly there he was, walking toward her. She

dropped the gun and her blanket and ran to him. He scooped her up in his arms, and she embraced him around the neck. He held her close.

"Clint, are you all right?"

"I'm fine. That second fella just nicked the outside of my left arm, but it's nothing. It's already stopped bleeding." He breathed a deep sigh as though greatly relieved himself. "I could hardly believe it when you put that gun in my hand. You're something, Liz Breckenridge."

She could not let go of him. "I thought Ezra was going to shoot you right in front of me! And then when I heard those gunshots out in the darkness—"

"I caught two more of his men trying to take the horses. They shot at me. I shot back."

Elizabeth closed her eyes. "Did you—"

"What else was I supposed to do? It was them or us, Liz. Sometimes that's just the way it is. What about you? Are you all right?"

She broke into tears. "Just a nervous wreck," she sniffed. She still clung to him. "I love you, Clint Brady. I'm sorry if that makes you mad, but I love you."

His tight grip loosened just a little. He kissed her hair. "Why would that make me mad?"

"Because *everything* makes you mad," she sobbed.

He lowered her, putting a hand to the side of her face and wiping at her tears with his thumb. "That's my fault... no one else's."

Their gazes held, and in the next moment his lips covered hers. In spite of his beard scratching her chin a little, the kiss was the warmest, softest, sweetest moment she'd ever experienced in her young life. The kiss grew deeper, almost like a branding of her soul, as he pressed her close again.

He left her lips, kissing her hair, keeping her close. "I love you, too." He held her a moment longer while she let the words sink in.

Clint grasped her arms and pushed her away then. "Men are coming over here to help bury these bodies," he said, as though suddenly needing to change the subject. "When I told others camped over there what happened, several men threatened to hang those left if they didn't start heading back to Skagway. I'm sure that's what they'll do come morning. We don't have to worry about this bunch anymore."

Elizabeth hardly heard a word. Clint Brady loved her. Her mind and heart were such a whirl of confusion she could barely breathe.

Chapter Thirty

Thy word is a lamp unto my feet, and a light unto my path.

—Psalms 119:105

Elizabeth could not sleep. The trauma of the shooting, combined with Clint's revelation, kept her mind in a whirl. The camp remained surprisingly quiet the rest of the night, almost too quiet. A little noise would be welcome so her thoughts didn't tumble over in her brain like a raging torrent. Once in a while she heard the howl of a wolf somewhere in the distant mountains, but that was it. This semi valley was almost barren of trees and wildlife, the trees all having been cut down by travelers, the wildlife frightened away.

Clint was involved with taking care of the dead bodies for most of the evening, and she couldn't help wondering how he felt about the fact that he'd been their killer. Did it bother him more than he let on? When he returned to their campfire to eat, he'd picked up his rifle and quietly finished cleaning it and his revolver, saying little. Elizabeth in turn had no idea *what* to say. What he'd told her surely was a big step for him. She suspected she would have to leave the subject up to him as far as talking about it more. She'd offered to look at his arm and wrap it, but he'd insisted he was fine, other than the rip in his coat.

"Maybe you can just fix that," he'd said, before telling her to go inside the tent and try to get some sleep.

Try was the word for it, and hard as she did try, sleep would not come. She lay staring into the darkness, thinking how much more of a strain it would be now to sleep inside the tent together. What did a man expect from a woman to whom he'd professed his love, and who he knew loved him in return? That secret, forbidden desire she'd felt for him had begun to surface, making her wonder at man and woman and lovemaking. The latter would have to wait until marriage, but they were a long way from that. There were far too many matters to be settled first, and until they were, no matter how much she loved him and dreamed of being his wife, there could be no marriage, no consummation of their love.

She sat up when she realized Clint was ducking inside the tent.

"You still awake?" he asked.

"Yes."

"I thought you might be. Come on outside. You need to see this."

Curious, Elizabeth crawled out of her bedroll and pulled on her boots, much more aware now of the fact that she needed a bath and wished she could put on a dress and look nice for Clint. If he could love her in this condition, then it sure must be true love.

She crawled outside to see Clint looking up into the night sky. She followed his gaze and drew in her breath. The dark abyss was a display of moving light, flitting across the sky in mysterious curves and beams and glorious colors. "What is it?" she asked Clint.

"They call it aurora borealis—something to do with the sun and the solar wind. I don't understand it all, but it's beautiful…makes a man feel kind of small, knowing there is something endless out there."

Elizabeth watched, awestruck. "To me it's like…like a sign from heaven…that God is there and all is well. It's like a showing of God's glory, a reflection from heaven's gates."

Clint did not answer.

"In one of my brother's letters, he told me that to him this country was surely the place where heaven begins. Now I know what he meant."

Still no answer. Finally Clint breathed a deep sigh and sat down on his blanket near the fire. "Sit here beside me, Liz," he told her.

Always wary of his mood, Elizabeth obeyed, deciding she must let him do the talking. He lit a cigarette and stared at the flickering flames of the campfire. Elizabeth suspected he was carefully weighing his words. Maybe he didn't love her in the way she thought he'd meant. Or maybe he'd say he'd spurted out the words in a moment of relief that both of them were all right. Maybe—

"About what we said…a while ago…"

Elizabeth didn't know whether to be happy or embarrassed. She'd blurted out those words like a silly schoolgirl.

"I, uh…I meant what I said," he continued.

She sensed this was not the time to throw her arms around him again. "So did I."

He smoked quietly before speaking again. "There is one big problem."

Elizabeth also watched the fire. "You don't need to tell me that."

"Several problems, actually."

"I understand."

He nodded. "Good. One is…there are lot of things you need to know, things I…I'll tell you when I feel ready. Just don't ask me, all right?"

"I won't."

"And then there's…there's the fact that we couldn't be more different. You're a far better person than I am."

"Don't say that. In God's eyes—"

"Don't bring God into this…not right now anyway. I'm just stating a fact, Liz. You're a good, Christian, young, innocent woman. And I'm…far from good or Christian or innocent. And as far as just suddenly giving up what I do—I don't know that I'm ready to do that. I need to do a lot of thinking, Liz…and I need you…" He cleared his throat. "I need you to…just keep praying for me. No preaching. Just praying."

She'd never loved him more. "You know that I will."

He put the cigarette to his lips again, blowing out smoke with another long sigh. "I'm sorry you had to witness tonight's events."

"It couldn't be helped. Besides, I put the gun in your hand, and as far as I'm concerned, God made me do it. He gave me the opportunity to save you from being shot and me from...who knows what. There is nothing wrong with a person defending himself to protect those he...loves."

He took one last drag and threw the cigarette into the fire. "Yeah, well, there's another problem...the fact that I care about you. We have a lot of traveling to do together yet. I just want you to know that you don't need to worry... about sometimes having to share the tent. I mean...it's hard for a man to care about a woman and not want to...show it...if you know what I mean."

Elizabeth felt her cheeks growing hot. "I'm not sure what you want me to say," she answered nervously.

"I'm just saying that until we reach Dawson, and until I come to terms with the turmoil inside my soul, I don't intend to spoil something as...pure and perfect as you are. I respect you too much."

"Clint, I'm not perfect. *No* one is perfect."

"You are in *my* eyes. I just think we need to think about all this, to be careful, to wait till you reach your brother and we both are back to a halfway normal life before we make final decisions. And I come with a lot of leftover hatred and vengeance that I still need to deal with. I just wanted you to know that I'm not sure right now that loving each other is enough to cure the ugly side of me. And until I am able to overcome my past, I see no future. I live day to day, and, believe it or not, I did used to pray. I just...I found no answers. And I still blame God for what I've lost. For now I'm just glad to know that there is actually a little bit of light at the end of the tunnel. I guess watching the sky made me start thinking about all of this."

Elizabeth looked up at the glorious lights again. "There is always light at the end of the tunnel, Clint. The light is the love of Jesus Christ. He understands everything about why we do the things that we do and He wants us to know that He is always waiting with open arms to relieve us of our burdens and our grief. All we have to do is want it and believe in Him."

He rubbed his forehead. "Well, if I never reach that point, it sure won't be for lack of you trying, will it?"

Elizabeth smiled. "It's God who's trying. He's just using me to do it."

Clint cleared his throat and rose. "You'd better try to get whatever sleep you can."

"What about you?"

"I'll, uh...I'll sleep right outside the tent." He finally turned and faced her. "The horses will be all right, now that others know what was going on. Most of the men up here are decent, you know. They aren't all like Ezra Faine."

Elizabeth rose. "How did you know, Clint?"

He smiled almost sadly. "A man leads the kind of life I have the last few years, he learns how to read men's eyes. I had Faine figured all along."

"And what do you see in *my* eyes?"

His previous look of hard anger over Faine quickly softened. "I see light. I see love, not just the love of a woman for a man. It's more than that. I see someone who is full of trust and joy. Those are two things I haven't known for years. My biggest joy in life..."

Visible, sudden tears in his eyes tore at Elizabeth's heart.

"…was my son." He cleared his throat. "Now he's gone. God would have done better to have had someone carve out my heart while I was still alive than to take my son from me." He quickly wiped at his eyes.

"God didn't cause his death, Clint. You haven't told me how it happened, but there is no way God had anything to do with it. All God can do when the evil of the world destroys the lives of innocent people is to take those innocents into His arms and bring them more peace and happiness than they ever could have known on earth. And those who caused the kind of pain you're feeling will suffer horribly, forever, in a burning hell."

He stood up and turned away. "I, uh…I think I'll go check on the horses once more."

His voice was gruff and broken. Elizabeth felt such pain in her heart she thought she might be dying, for it was certain he was walking away so that he could cry alone.

Chapter Thirty-One

He maketh the storm a calm, so that the waves
thereof are still.

—Psalms 107:29

By the second morning of their stay in the valley, Clint was all business again as they packed up to head for White Pass. Elizabeth tried to ignore the fresh graves in the distance when Clint went to get the now-rested horses.

Two other parties of men would join them, among them two men with bruised faces, swollen eyes and split lips. Obviously they were the two who had fought two nights before. Whatever the problem had been, they were jovial enough now.

"They were probably drunk that night," Clint told Elizabeth on the side. "Men get a little crazy when they drink."

"Yes, I know," she answered teasingly.

Clint grinned rather sheepishly, and in spite of his better mood, Elizabeth could not help noticing how tired he looked, with circles under his bloodshot eyes. He hadn't slept much in the last two nights, and she ached for him, wishing he would have let her hold and comfort him. She also noticed he grimaced several times as he loaded their supplies.

"Is your arm hurting you?"

"Some."

"You should have let me tend to it," she scolded.

"The muscle is just sore from being torn by that bullet. I've hurt worse."

Elizabeth stopped in the middle of securing a rope. "Have you been *shot* before?"

"Sure. Comes with the territory."

"Clint!"

"I'm alive, aren't I? No sense getting upset over it now. Let's just concentrate on getting ourselves over that pass. I have a bad feeling that I'd rather be shot again."

Elizabeth finished securing the tent to Queen. "Are the horses going to be able to find anything to eat up there?"

"Probably not, once we get past the tree line. We just have to hope they can make it till we get down the other side."

Elizabeth petted Queen's neck. "Poor things. They've been so faithful."

She looked up at the surrounding mountains as they headed out, several hundred yards behind the first party that left. As they trudged through the marshy land, several men who'd given up passed them going in the opposite direction, most of them wishing them luck…until what was left of the Faine party approached. They, too, had waited an extra day to leave on the long journey back to Skagway.

Elizabeth felt her heart pound when the four remaining men eyed Clint, warily and with hatred.

"You fellas have a nice trip back to Skagway," Clint told them, tipping his hat to them.

He kept walking, and Elizabeth refused to look at any of them as they passed her by, muttering ugly remarks about Clint and Elizabeth. She told herself it didn't matter what such men thought of her and kept walking, glad Clint had not heard the remark. He was too tired and hurt to be getting into a row with four men. After several minutes she looked back to see they were still walking, having already passed the party of men behind her and Clint.

For the entire day they climbed...and climbed, following a narrow mountain trail ever upward in an endless winding until it seemed they would surely reach the top of the world. By late afternoon they were walking in snow, and by evening the pathway opened onto a wide slope above the tree line where the snow was even deeper.

Here again was an area where many had camped. And again they found dead horses and dogs, abandoned sleds and supplies of all kinds. Crates of food were broken open, their remaining contents rotted. Some horse carcasses had been ripped to shreds by wolves.

Clint stopped. There was just enough daylight left to see the great, rising whiteness before them, with a well-worn pathway leading up between mountain peaks. A few men could be seen close to the summit. To see how small they looked only accented how long a climb it was.

"We'll camp here tonight and make the climb tomorrow," Clint told her. "I just hope the horses can paw through the snow enough to find a little grass to nibble on."

Wind howled menacingly in the surrounding mountains, and the party ahead of them was already making camp. Another glance above alarmed her, for the black dots of men Elizabeth had seen just moments ago were gone, shrouded by what looked like a mean snowstorm. A sudden wind billowed snow into their faces.

"Let's get the tent set up quick," Clint told her. "Looks like we're going to get it tonight."

"Clint, those men higher up—"

"We can't do anything about it. Just pray they survive up there." He hurriedly untied the tent. "We'll have to eat raw sweet potatoes or something like that. We'll never get a good fire going in this wind. No sense wasting what little wood we have left."

Elizabeth helped him get the tent set up, not an easy feat with the wind trying its best to blow it back down. The howling grew so intense that they had to yell to each other to be heard. There was no time now to worry about any of the others nearby. Elizabeth could not even see any of them. At times the snow blew so hard she could hardly see Clint.

"Clint, the horses! You didn't even get a chance to tie burlap around their feet!"

"Too late now," he yelled back. "Just get our blankets, and that wolf-skin jacket I bought you." He was already loosening his own blankets and a heavy deerskin coat lined with rabbit that he'd brought for the colder weather. "Get your leggings on," he ordered, his voice carrying on the wind.

Elizabeth obeyed, hurriedly taking down a large leather

bag that held some of her clothes. She managed to pull out deerskin leggings Clint had insisted she bring along. Now she knew why. The deer hair was still on them, and when she pulled them on she could immediately feel how well they blocked the coldness of the wind. She tied them at the waist and pulled on her heavier coat, all the while wondering if the tent might get buried in snow before they even got inside it. She pulled down another sack, the one that held the sweet potatoes, and unhooked a canteen of water from Queen. Then she walked closer to the front of the horse and held Queen's head for a moment.

"I love you, Queeny. You'll be okay, I promise. I've got to go in the tent now. I'm so sorry to leave you out here in this cold wind." Her only consolation was that Queen had grown an extremely thick, long winter coat. She could only pray it would be enough to keep the horse alive.

"Hurry!" Clint ordered.

She pulled on the wolf-skin coat and slung the canteen over her shoulder, then hurried over to the tent. Clinging to the sack of sweet potatoes and the one with more of her clothes inside, she knelt down to crawl inside with Clint. They lay down on a floor of snow, feeling nothing through the heavy animal skins they wore. Elizabeth thanked God that Clint had insisted they buy them.

"Stay close for warmth," Clint told her. "I think we're in for a good one. We might be stranded here for a day or two till the weather clears enough to go on."

"I can't believe how fast it hit," Elizabeth answered, setting the two sacks and her canteen at the side of the tent.

"Turn with your back to me and I'll wrap myself around

you," Clint told her. "We'll put the blankets over us and hope that along with our body warmth we'll get through this."

Elizabeth did as he asked, and she felt safe and protected as he moved one arm around her and bent his knees into the backs of her legs.

"We might as well try to sleep. There's nothing else we can do for now. Let's just hope we wake up again."

The prospect of freezing to death would normally be frightening, but Elizabeth felt no fear in Clint Brady's arms. And if she died right here, she couldn't imagine a better way to meet her Lord than in the arms of the man she loved, lying on top of the world in God's country.

The wind moaned and howled, and the tent flapped wildly. Snow whispered and swished outside, and for the moment it felt as though she and Clint were the only two people who existed in the world.

Chapter Thirty-Two

And the rain descended...and the winds blew, and beat upon That house; and it fell not, for it was founded upon a rock.

—St. Matthew 7:25

A relentless wind howled with such force that Elizabeth thought nothing of allowing Clint to pull her curled body closer against his own for warmth. This was not a time to worry about what others might think about lying together like this, and God certainly must understand why they had no choice. Protocol and propriety had no place when it came to survival, and right now Elizabeth was not so sure God did not intend for them to die right here. After all, it was His choice when to bring His children home.

They lay buried under every blanket they owned, with no choice but to wait for the storm outside to subside. Lying there in Clint's strong arms, his broad chest pressing against her back, her head tucked under his chin, brought to light something Elizabeth had never realized: how easy it would be to let this man love and protect her for the rest of her life, how nice it was to feel so totally safe, and how easy it would be to give herself to this man if he truly wanted her that way, wanted to marry her...if only he would give himself back to the Lord and give up the life he was leading.

She knew he was still not ready for that, and he never would be if he kept refusing to tell her about his past, refusing to open up to her fully, refusing to let God back into his life and heart and soul so that the healing could begin.

Snow whispered around the tent, and both knew it was building dangerously. They were most likely half buried by now.

"I'm so worried about the horses, Clint. The poor things." She pulled a blanket over half her face to warm her nose.

"We could end up buried here so long we'd have to eat them anyway," he answered.

"Clint Brady!"

"Just thinking practically. In circumstances like this you can't let compassion and emotion take precedence over survival, but don't worry just yet. This could end by morning, and instinct will cause them to try to find a place to burrow down out of the wind. Besides, they had some pretty thick winter hair growth already. Let's just hope it's enough to keep them from freezing to death."

An extra strong gust of wind caused the tent to flap wildly.

"What if the tent blows away?"

Clint hugged her tighter. "Then I'll be your tent."

Elizabeth smiled.

"Keep talking, Liz," he told her. "We should try to stay awake as long as possible. And keep wiggling your toes and fingers."

She curled her toes into the soles of her boots, wishing they were heated. "I guess I could tell you the other reason I ran away."

"Ran away? You never put it that way before."

"Well, as I think about it, I realize now that's what I was doing, although I truly did want to find Peter anyway. After our father was murdered, Peter took over his church, then hired another minister and came up here last year. My mother got very ill and died. I cared for her through her illness, and then after she died, it left such a big space inside of me." She sighed.

"You don't have to describe that feeling to me."

More snow swished across the top of the tent. "I'm sure I don't." She squeezed the strong forearms that were wrapped around her middle and proceeded to tell him about living with the Reverend Selby and his wife.

"It was not such a bad life, but I was so lonely after losing both my parents and with Peter gone. I mean, I had friends in the church and all, but it just wasn't the same."

"Then I understand why you'd want to find Peter, but why do you call it running away?"

Elizabeth waited a moment to answer, hating the ugly memories. "I—Reverend Selby…turned out not to be such a proper Christian man…once Mama died."

She felt Clint tense up. "I don't even want to mention what I think you mean by that," he told her.

"You don't need to. I'm sure you're fully understanding what I'm saying." Her eyes teared at the memory of her devastation in realizing that not all professed Christians were what they claimed to be. Compared to the reverend, in many ways Clint was much more Christian. That experience and this trip had opened her eyes to so many things, especially the error of her ways in how she judged people.

"Apparently the reverend thought that because I was young and inexperienced and alone, I—I might respond to his offers to…comfort me. The trouble was, what started with a pat on the shoulder led to quick hugs, never in public, of course, and then he began coming to my room…at night…making very roundabout suggestions."

Clint's grip grew tighter. She had to smile inwardly at his reaction, typical for a man who lived by violence. "Well, then," he told her, "I'm glad I'll probably never meet the man. I'd hate to be accused of beating a church minister to a pulp."

She smiled sadly. "No one would have understood anyway. When I refused to respond to the reverend's advances, he took it as an affront, and it angered him. He decided to get back at me, and he was probably afraid I'd say something first, so he turned around and suggested to the church deacons that in my desperate loneliness I had been making advances toward *him,* tempting him to do sinful things. He told them I would have to move out of the parsonage."

"Don't tell me the people in that church *believed* him!"

"Most of them did. He was a man of God, after all, and I was a lonely young woman who'd just lost her mother— and there I was, living in the same house. Don't forget that the church was run by *men.* Most men seem ready to believe that if something like that is going on, it must be the woman's fault, as though it's all right for a man to be unable to resist temptation. I tried to explain the truth, but I could see they were not going to believe me. When I realized I had to get out of that house, which I had already been planning to do because of the situation, I figured I might as well come here and find Peter, someone who loved me and would help me. I loved helping with church projects and teaching Sunday School. I figure I can do that in Dawson, too."

"What about the women there? You must have had friends. Your father founded the church."

"Yes, he did, but the congregation had grown from dedicated Christians willing to sacrifice to help the church to grow, to complacent, spoiled members who liked having it easy and liked dressing up for church and calling themselves members. I think most of the married women were jealous and wanted me out. Others probably thought they would be looked down upon for defending me. It turned out my best friend, a girl about my age, liked a young man who liked me, so she sided against me, too."

"And these people called themselves Christians?"

"A lot of people *call* themselves Christians, I've learned. Either way, I just knew it was time to leave anyway. Most of the congregation seemed to have forgotten what founding that church was all about—it was to help those who don't yet know Christ as their Savior and Lord."

He kissed her hair. "I knew there had to be more to your story."

"I didn't want to tell you because I was afraid you would

say that was proof that it didn't matter if a man called himself Christian. I was afraid you would say being Christian really meant nothing, but it means a great deal to me, Clint. Christ taught us that we must voice His word, spread it to others and never be ashamed to offer His grace and peace. And Christ alone knows whose heart is sincere and whose is not. Christ knows that *your* heart is sincere, Clint, in spite of what you do. You feel you're helping the innocent by ridding the world of the sinful. You're angry at God, so you're fighting Him instead of working *with* Him, so you—"

"Stop right there."

She closed her eyes, feeling very sleepy. "You're the one who said to keep talking. I can't do that without talking about what's most important to my heart, and that's two things—God...and you."

"You mean I come second?"

She sighed in feigned regret. "Sorry, but you always will." Why didn't she mind the feel of him kissing her hair again? Was that sinful?

"Okay, then, let's get back to what happened. Why didn't you tell me before this?"

"I guess because I figured you'd be like all other men and think it *was* my fault. I didn't know you well enough to know what you'd think, but I've come to look at you as different from others. I see and feel a goodness about you that just...I don't know...I feel comfortable around you now. And because you aren't pious and because you haven't lived a life sheltered within the church, I thought you'd understand better some of the different feelings men and women have. If you'd been one of those deacons, you would have had the courage to speak up in my defense."

"You think so, do you?"

"I know so."

He sat quietly for a moment. "Oh, but there is so much you *don't* know about me."

"That's *your* fault. You've told me about your childhood, where you came from and what you do now. You've just left out the middle part. You can tell me about that whenever you're ready."

There came no response. All she heard was the howling wind.

"You already know my wife's name," he told her after a good ten minutes of quiet. "My son's name was…Ethan. That's my first name. Clint is my middle name. I started using it after what happened so I wouldn't have to hear anyone call out the name Ethan again. I can't stand to hear it, and I almost never say it myself. It makes me think of him." He sighed deeply. "There. That's all you get for now."

She smiled, her eyes drifting shut again. She squeezed his arms with her fingers. "That's enough," she answered.

Chapter Thirty-Three

For every man shall bear his own burden.

—Galatians 6:5

Upon awakening the morning after the snowstorm, they found the opening to the tent covered nearly to the top. Clint shoved snow outward as best he could to keep it from filling the tent when he opened the tent flaps, and once he made a big enough opening, he stood up and shouted to Elizabeth.

"Not as bad as I thought."

Elizabeth was relieved the wind and snow had stopped. She joined Clint to see sunshine and calm. The snow had blown and drifted in such a way that some tents, like theirs, were buried to the point that only the peaks showed, while others were fully in the open. Already several men were out setting up surveying equipment.

"Must be more railroad men," Clint suggested.

They both gazed at the steep climb ahead. A few men

were already moving about farther up on the pass. Elizabeth looked around. "Clint, the horses."

Queen, Devil and Red Lady were nowhere to be seen. "Come on," Clint told her.

Together they trudged through snow that was sometimes waist-deep on Clint, even deeper for Elizabeth, who had to follow Clint to be able to navigate at all. Finally they made their way to an area that had been swept free by the wind, and both had to stop and catch their breath when they spotted a horse on its side in the distance.

Clint muttered a curse and headed in that direction. Elizabeth cared little at the moment that he'd cursed, knowing how bad he'd feel if it was one of his animals, which it was. Elizabeth rushed up to Clint, and there lay Queen, frozen to death.

Clint knelt beside the horse and ran his hand over Queen's neck, saying nothing.

"Poor thing!" Elizabeth lamented, her eyes tearing. She, too, knelt down, leaning over to kiss the horse's forehead. "She'd become such a good friend."

Clint cleared his throat. "She died alone," he said, his voice strained.

Elizabeth knew he was thinking about his wife, or perhaps his son. She put a hand on Clint's shoulder. "I'm sorry, Clint."

He kept his face hidden from her as he quickly wiped at his eyes and drew a deep breath. "We'd better get as much gear off her as we can." He began yanking at saddle bags. "Whatever is under her will have to stay there," he continued. "She's frozen stiff. We'll never manage to move her or turn her over." He coughed deeply, then took a deep breath and wiped at his eyes again. "I sure hate leaving her here for the wolves." He handed Elizabeth the bags and began untying ropes and straps. "I don't think we've lost too much; a sack of flour, maybe, and maybe one of beans."

He worked quickly, and Elizabeth helped, suspecting Clint's deliberate hasty unloading was to avoid talking about the dead horse or how he felt about it...or perhaps to help him stop thinking about his wife and son.

"We'll drag this stuff back to the tent and look for Devil and Red Lady. Let's just hope they're still alive because there is no way we will manage all these supplies by ourselves, certainly not when one of us is a woman. I'm told the Canadian Mounties won't let us into British Columbia without the right amount of supplies. Too many prospectors died of starvation last winter."

It took practically all the strength Elizabeth could muster to help tote more beans, flour and pots and pans back to the tent. Once outside and away from the warmth of hers and Clint's bodies curled together, the calm cold began to penetrate her to the bone. She couldn't help worrying about Clint's condition.

Clint ordered her to stay at the tent then and see what she could drum up to eat without making a fire. Wood was too scarce. She dug out some leftover biscuits as he left again, and even from a distance she could hear his deep cough.

She bowed her head and prayed for Clint's health and that he would find the other two horses. Aching for hot coffee, she bit into a partially frozen biscuit, thinking how fried eggs and bacon would be much more welcome.

After a good half hour Clint returned, leading the other two horses. Hope filled Elizabeth's heart that maybe the rest of the trip wouldn't be so bad after all. She smiled and rose, walking out to greet man and horses, hugging Devil and Red Lady and kissing their noses. "Where were they?"

"Huddled together in a kind of cove created by boulders. Must have sheltered them from the worst of the wind," Clint told her. "Queen always was the dumbest of the three." He ducked inside the tent and came out with the sack of oats they had used for a pillow. "Hang on to Red Lady so she doesn't start something over these oats," he told Elizabeth, opening the oats and holding them under Devil's nose so the horse could eat some of them.

Elizabeth kept a firm hold on Red Lady. The mare was not at all pleased that Devil got to eat first. Once Clint felt the gelding had had enough, he took the bag of oats away and handed it to Elizabeth, telling her to hold it open for Red Lady.

"Devil will be harder to control," he grumbled, gripping the gelding's bridle. As soon as Red Lady started eating, Devil reared, wanting to shove the mare away from the oats.

"Whoa there!" Clint shouted. He yelled more commands, forcing Devil backward and away from Red Lady and Elizabeth.

"Are we leaving today?" Elizabeth asked as she let Red Lady feed.

"Might as well. No time to waste."

Once Red Lady got her fill, Clint packed the oats away and he and Elizabeth took time to eat what was available, both of them longing for hot coffee. They packed their gear then, rearranging supplies meant for three horses onto two.

Clint even put some of the supplies into a neatly-arranged backpack for himself.

"Guess I'll have to take Queen's place," he joked.

"Are you sure you're ready for this?" Elizabeth asked, truly concerned.

"Ready as I'll ever be." Clint hoisted the backpack to a more comfortable position.

"I'm so concerned about that cough."

"It's just one of those things that's going to linger awhile."

Elizabeth donned a second woolen cap, then made ready to tie a scarf around her face against the cold. "I don't like it. You never rested enough back in Skagway."

"Such is life. I just want to keep going now and get this trip over with."

Elizabeth walked up to him, her face now covered. "There are some here who have turned back. There is always next year, Clint." She noticed an odd sadness in his blue eyes.

"No, there isn't. Until I find Roland Fisher, I won't know the answers to a few things. If you've convinced me of one thing, it's that your God pulled us together, and made me fall in love with you. But loving you isn't the whole answer to what still eats at me inside. I don't expect you to understand it. I just know we have to do this."

Elizabeth felt relief that at least he admitted God had something to do with this journey. This was becoming much more than a physical journey to Dawson just to find Peter and a fugitive. It was becoming a journey of the heart, and her own heart was hopelessly immersed in love for Clint Brady.

"I love you, too, Clint."

He pulled the scarf down from her face, leaned down and met her lips in a gentle kiss, then kissed her eyes and pulled her scarf back up. "When we get to Dawson, I'll shave off this beard so I don't scratch your face with it."

She pulled the scarf down again. "I'd appreciate that. I hate for that handsome face to be hidden under all that stubble. But may I have one more kiss anyway?"

Clint grinned. "I'll gladly kiss you as often as you want." He met her lips again, this time in a deeper kiss that suggested he wanted much more. He left her mouth and embraced her. "You have a lot to learn, Miss Breckenridge, and I will gladly teach you once you're my wife."

Elizabeth's heart took a leap at the words. "Your *wife?* Is that a *proposal*, Mr. Brady?" What an odd place and time to have brought up the subject.

He kept hold of her. "I guess it is. It just kind of slipped out. Actually I was going to save this for Dawson." He laughed lightly and hugged her tighter. "This gives you a couple of weeks to think about your answer, if we both live through the rest of this trip."

Not one part of her doubted that Clint Brady would make a good husband, that there was a gentle, kind side to him he'd seldom shown since his wife's death. She rested her head against his chest. "I would like nothing more than to marry you, Clint, but you're right about the rest of it. I can't be your wife until I know your heart is first right with God. That's the only kind of love that truly counts in this life."

"Let's just get ourselves to Dawson for now. That gives me a couple more weeks to think about a lot of things."

Good. At least they could finally *talk* without Clint

blowing up about something. Clint pulled away, and Elizabeth put the scarf back over her face again. "Okay, let's get over the pass," she told him.

She looked up at the daunting incline. It was hard to imagine anyone would make this trip through the pass more than once, but some men made several trips just to get all their belongings over the peak.

"Clint, wait," she spoke up, as he took Devil's bridle.

"What is it?"

She pulled off her scarf again. "Will you...pray with me...that we make it over the pass?"

He stared at her a moment, at first looking irritated, then doubtful. "If you want," he finally answered, "for whatever good a prayer from me would do."

Elizabeth walked up and grasped his hands, bowing her head. *"Heavenly Father, we thank You for getting us this far. Now, Lord, we just ask that You help us get over White Pass without losing one of the horses, or one of our own lives. We know it won't be easy, but Lord, we also believe that You have been in charge of this journey all along, and so we trust You to help us over this most dangerous and demanding part of our trip. And I personally pray that when we reach Dawson I will find Peter well and happy, and that Clint will find the answers only You can give him so that his heart will be healed. In the name of Christ we pray. Amen."*

Clint squeezed her hands but said nothing except, "Let's go."

Chapter Thirty-Four

Peace I leave with you, my peace I give unto you:
not as the world giveth, give I unto you. Let not
your heart be troubled, neither let it be afraid.
                                          —St. John 14:27

Elizabeth soon realized the word *daunting* came nowhere near describing the climb over White Pass. Those who'd gone ahead of them had helped pack down the fresh snow, but that in turn created areas that were too slick. Mixed in with hidden rocks, the sky-high pathway posed not just a taxing test on the human body, but formidable danger.

Added to that was a cold that seemed to penetrate to the very marrow of one's bones. Elizabeth could not help worrying about Clint's health, but she kept reminding herself to trust his health to God. For now all concentration had to be zeroed onto surviving this climb. From a distance it had looked obviously high and long, but once they started, every step only made the peak look farther away. After only perhaps one-eighth of the distance, she shouted for Clint to stop.

"I have to sit down for a while," she told him, nearly in tears.

Clint steadied Devil. "Do you want to turn around?" he shouted to her.

"No!" she exclaimed. "Please just...just stay put for a little while. The muscles in my legs are screaming! If I go any farther they'll give out and I'll fall." Oh, how she hated creating problems because of her own weakness. "I'm sorry," she yelled. "I'm so sorry."

"It's all right," he called back. "I'd come to you but I can't leave Devil! He's too skittish."

Elizabeth nodded, keeping hold of Red Lady's reins as she rubbed at her thighs. How on earth was she going to get all the way to the top? She heard a man scream from higher above them, and yet another voice yelled, "Look out!"

Elizabeth looked up to see a horse sliding down the slope on its back, its legs flailing while it whinnied frantically. One man could not get out of the way in time, and the horse slammed into him, knocking him ahead of it and then falling on top of him, literally shoving him down deeper into the snow. Clint screamed at Elizabeth to get out of the way, and she scrambled back as far as possible without stepping off the trail into a much steeper area. Clint struggled to hang on to Devil while the falling horse slid past him, narrowly missing man and horse. In the next second the horse shot past Elizabeth, one hoof slamming her across the side of the face. She heard Clint yell her name, and for the next few moments everything went black.

When her mind began to clear, the first thing Elizabeth heard was Clint growling at God for letting this happen after she'd prayed for a safe climb.

"Clint, stop it!" she mumbled. "Please...don't blame God!"

"So much for prayer!" he answered. "You've got a swelling bruise on the side of your face with a cut to boot!"

"I'm all right. I just...got knocked a little silly for a minute."

"You could have been killed! Do you know what my life would be like if something happened to you now? Do you have any idea?"

"Clint!" She spoke louder this time, everything becoming more clear. She looked into his blue eyes and, if not for the seriousness of what had just happened and what she knew he'd already suffered in his life, she could have laughed at the look of a lost little boy in his eyes. "Clint, Jesus said that if we had the faith of just one tiny mustard seed we could move mountains. That's just an example of what little faith most of us have."

He closed his eyes and held her close. "We're going back down."

"No, we aren't! I already asked if you wanted to wait and you refused. We've started this climb, and we're going to reach the peak and get partway down the other side by nightfall. If we manage this, Clint, we'll *know* we can make it the rest of the way. Please! I don't even want to have to reclimb what little bit we've already reached."

He sighed in resignation, picking up some snow and applying it to the side of her face. Elizabeth winced with pain.

"I think the cold will help keep it from swelling and bleeding as badly as it would otherwise," Clint told her. He watched her lovingly. "I just hate the thought of anything ruining this beautiful face."

Elizabeth managed a smile. "I think I can go on now. What about the horses?"

"I got someone to come down a ways and hold Devil for me. Red Lady is just standing there like she's out in green fields someplace. I'd have her try to carry you for a ways, but if she should fall, it would probably kill you."

Elizabeth sat up slightly. "The other horse? The one that fell?"

"He's down at the bottom, not moving. The owner scrambled down to see."

"He's dead!" someone shouted from above them. "Broken neck!"

Clint looked up, then back at Elizabeth. "They're talking about the man the horse rolled over."

"Oh, no! What will they do? He can't be buried up here. They could never dig deep enough through the snow."

"That's up to his party," Clint told her. "Fact is, they'll probably just leave him."

"Clint, no!"

"There is nothing else they can do. Others have been left. Don't argue about it or expect me to do something about it. His soul is with God, so what does it matter about the body? With the weight of what has to be carried, it would be impossible for any of those men to drag his body along with them, and don't ask me to do it, Elizabeth. We'll be lucky to get up there with what we have. Surely God understands that much."

Elizabeth closed her eyes. "I won't argue, mainly because I don't want the same thing to happen to you. How could I ever forget something so horrible as having to leave you on this mountain to be eaten by wolves."

She heard a strange gasp, and immediately she sensed a change in Clint, who stood up and turned around.

"Clint, is that what happened?"

He threw back his head. "That's just how it ended," he groaned. "My wife...my little boy...just left out there to the wolves." He shook his head. "And you're right. You never...*ever*...forget."

Elizabeth stood up, her cheek bone throbbing. "Jesus can help you forget, Clint...*and* forgive."

He took several long, deep breaths without speaking or looking at her.

"Hey, mister, I've got to get going!"

Clint looked up at the man holding Devil and Red Lady. "I'm coming!" he shouted back.

"Your woman all right?"

"I think so!"

Clint quickly wiped at his eyes with a gloved hand. "Are you sure you want to keep going?" he asked Elizabeth, still not facing her.

"Yes. I think I can get my legs to work again."

"Just don't pass out on me," he answered. "This time I'll lead *both* horses, at least for the next several hundred yards." He finally faced her with unreadable but bloodshot eyes. "You hang on to Red Lady's tail. That should help a lot with your climb. Let her do some of the work."

"Won't it be too hard on her?"

"Not as hard or as dangerous as *carrying* you would be, even though you don't weigh more than a sack of beans. With you contributing some of the power by walking, it won't be the same as carrying your full weight." He took a closer look at her cheek, frowning with concern. "You took quite a wallop." He pulled her scarf back over her nose. "Keep that nose covered. I'd hate to see you get frostbite on top of everything else."

He climbed back up to the horses and took them from the man who'd held them for him. Elizabeth did as he'd asked and grabbed Red Lady's tail. Again they started climbing. Elizabeth's thigh muscles stung like fire, and her cheek ached fiercely, but she was determined not to say a word. They absolutely had to get this climb over with, and she had to keep going. She kept reminding herself that on the other side of this pass lay the Yukon River and their route to Dawson and Peter, and the final answers to Clint's road back to salvation. Then—with God's blessing—she'd be married to the first man who'd come along in her life to make her want to share her life with him.

At least he's told me part of the horror that haunts him, she thought. So far this was the most he'd ever spoken about what had happened to his wife and son. It was a step in the right direction, but the picture in her mind told her a lot about the reason for Clint's bitterness. It was a wonder the man had any sanity left to him at all.

Chapter Thirty-Five

For the Lord God is a sun and shield: the Lord will give grace and glory: no good thing will He withhold from them that walk uprightly. O Lord of hosts, blessed is the man that trusteth in Thee.

—Psalms 84:11

Throughout their struggle, Clint and Elizabeth passed other dead bodies, both of men and horses. Clint knew the sights were difficult for Elizabeth, but she was learning she couldn't stop and nurse, or preach to, or bury or lend other aid to every soul she met. Just as he still had issues to deal with when it came to his faith in God, Elizabeth needed to understand that God expected only so much of one human being.

Right now he felt he was himself just about past his own limits, both physically and emotionally. They were a good three-quarters of the way up the pass now…so close and yet so far. By God's miracle the horses were still climbing with them. Devil had even calmed down. Both, however, were breathing heavily and sweating profusely. He feared that sweat would freeze on the animals and kill them once they stopped moving.

Higher, ever higher. He couldn't stop thinking about the horror of seeing that horse kick Liz and knock her down. The risk he was taking in falling in love again had instantly hit him. If he lost yet another woman he loved...

She's all right, he reminded himself. He had to stop constantly fearing the worst. That's where faith came in. If only he could have the faith of that tiny mustard seed, maybe he could rest easier, allow himself to be happy. But his anguish over Jen and Ethan continued to haunt him.

He fell to his knees, got up again, thinking how this climb seemed to emulate his own struggle to find peace in his life...constantly falling and getting up again. Every time he found and either killed or took in another wanted killer, he thought he might finally find peace, sure that each man he hunted down would bring an answer to his fierce need for revenge.

He looked back to see Liz climbing on her own now, giving Red Lady a break. What a trouper she was, not just in climbing this mountain, but in sticking to her guns in her efforts to bring him back to God. She was young, but she sure wasn't stupid or weak or silly. In a lot of ways she was surprisingly mature, and dang stubborn. Lord knew, when it came to getting through to his heart, it took a woman like that. She'd knocked a hole in the wall he'd built around himself that no one else, certainly no whore or normal decent woman had been able to penetrate.

"Clint, we're almost there!" Elizabeth shouted, interrupting his thoughts.

Clint looked up. There was the peak, perhaps another half hour's climb! The sight seemed to pump more blood into his legs so he could keep going. His lungs burned like fire, and he could barely feel his feet any longer. The horses snorted and panted, bolting ahead slightly as though they, too, realized they were almost over the mountain.

"Get up there!" Clint shouted. He turned to yell back to Elizabeth. "Grab Red's tail again!"

She pushed ahead and managed to get hold of the horse's tail. She was smiling. Lord, she had to be hurting bad by now, what with that swollen bruise on her cheek and the way her legs must feel. He'd already determined they would camp for a good two days on the other side before heading for Lake Bennett, where they would have a raft built to take them upriver to Dawson.

He could hear some men who'd reached the top shouting and laughing with relief. It was nearing dark. By the time they reached the top it would be completely dark. He'd hoped to get at least partway down the other side before making camp. The higher they went, the colder it got, and another overnight snowstorm could bury them for good up there.

His chest ached fiercely now, and a surge of coughing hit him, but he refused to stop climbing as he coughed. His whole body felt on fire, and he didn't doubt Liz felt the same way. If it weren't for having to guide the horses, he'd carry her on his back. He'd do just about anything for her…anything.

Suddenly even the horses sped up, half dragging both Clint and Liz, who screamed and laughed until they reached the peak. Devil and Red kept going, snow flying. Liz fell, and unable to stop laughing, she let Red drag her for a ways, until finally Clint was able to pull and jerk and shout at the animals enough to stop them.

"You all right?" he yelled to Liz. Her laughter exhilarated him. They had reached a much gentler slope, though still in deep snow, and she lay there on her back still laughing.

"We made it!" she screamed. "We made it! Thank you, Jesus!" She started laughing again, and knowing the horses were surely exhausted enough not to go any farther, Clint let go of them to walk over and fall into the snow beside Liz. He grabbed her and rolled her over, looking down at her.

"We sure did," he answered. He leaned down to kiss her, and they rolled over twice more before he landed on top of her once again.

"We'll make it all the way, Clint," she told him with a smile, her nose red and her cheek bruised.

"I think you're right," he answered. He kissed her again, passion and desire overwhelming him. He left her mouth and nuzzled her neck.

"Clint Brady, people can see us!"

"We're married, remember?"

She pushed at him. "But we're *not* married," she told him with a teasing look. "And I will not let you tempt me this way until you are my husband."

He gave her a look of deep disappointment. "Then be prepared for a hard ride and an arduous trip upriver, because we're going to make Dawson so fast it will make your pretty head spin. Your brother is a preacher, and he's going to marry us."

"Is that so?"

"Yes, ma'am." Clint saw the sudden concern come into her green eyes. "Soon as Roland Fisher, God and I get a few things straightened out, because I've never wanted anything in my life as bad as I want you right now."

He kissed her once more, loving the taste of her, the way she responded to him with pure love and innocence. He realized then just how hard the rest of this trip was going to be on him, but her faith and goodness demanded that he honor her desire to save herself for marriage. Practically groaning with the want of her, he got up and grasped her hand, pulling her to her feet.

"From now on you sleep inside and I sleep outside," he told her with a wink.

"Oh, we're still too high! You'd freeze sleeping outside!" she objected. "And we'll need to put blankets over the horses to keep the sweat from freezing on them. That will leave fewer blankets for us. We'll *have* to sleep together just to stay warm enough."

"I hate to say it, but you're right. Now you're walking dangerous ground, Miss Breckenridge."

She cocked her head. "You'll just have to pray for strength, Mr. Brady." She turned to lead Red Lady to a flatter spot not far from where someone else was camped.

"Gee, thanks. I'll do that," Clint answered. God knows keeping my hands off you will take more strength than it did to climb White Pass, he thought. His goals for reaching

Dawson sure had changed. The innocent Miss Brecken-ridge had no inkling what it was like for a man to withhold from his desire for the woman he loved.

Chapter Thirty-Six

*Hear my prayer, O Lord, give ear to my
supplications: in thy faithfulness answer me, and
in thy righteousness.... For the enemy hath
persecuted my soul; he hath smitten my life down
to the ground; he hath made me to dwell in
darkness, as those that have been long dead.
Therefore is my spirit overwhelmed within me;
my heart within me is desolate.*
—Psalms 143:1, 3 & 4

White Pass, September 4, 1898

Elizabeth spent a good share of the afternoon catching up
on her diary entries. Rather than camp just the other side of
White Pass, she and Clint had slept just a few hours after
reaching the summit, then traveled for half a day down the
other side before making a permanent camp for some much-
needed rest. Several other travelers were camped nearby.

It is still cold enough that we remain fully clothed, wearing our jackets and hats even when we sleep inside the tent. Clint says we should make Lake Bennett after another day of travel, where we will see about having a raft built for us. There is a sawmill there now for just that purpose. My poor Clint is coughing badly again and I worry so that his pneumonia will return, which cannot be good for lungs still recovering from his first bout.

She'd come to think of him as "her" Clint, with feelings of possessiveness becoming strong, as were feelings of desire she'd never known before meeting him. Right now he slept deeply...right beside her, worn out more than most because of his incessant coughing.

She continued.

Clint's strength and determination is to be admired. In spite of the continued pain in his chest he has continued this journey in a fashion most healthy men could not.

My face is healing, with the swelling gone down but an ugly bruise still showing. Some of those we pass look at me strangely and probably think my Clint beats me, something he would never do. Beneath all that roughness lies a good man who I know is searching for God and longing to be a husband and a father again.

She leaned back against a sack of beans and closed her eyes. She was totally, hopelessly in love with Clint Brady.

Before leaving San Francisco, she would not have dreamed this could happen. She so wished someone like her father could have talked to him, helped him through his terrible grief to the light of God. Maybe Peter could do that. She was trying herself, but maybe he just needed to talk to a man. She felt so helpless sometimes.

Wolves howled somewhere in the distance, and Devil whinnied just outside the tent. Clint turned on his back, then sat up. "Everything all right?"

"I think so. I heard wolves howling, but not close."

"I'd better check." Clint picked up his rifle and ducked outside. Elizabeth heard him cough before coming back. "There's a bright moon. It didn't look like anything was lurking around out there." He lay back down beside her and took a deep breath. "You writing in that diary again?"

"Yes."

"What are you writing about me?"

Elizabeth smiled. "I'm sure you can guess."

He stared at the top of the tent. "Yes." He closed his eyes, and the air hung silent for a moment. "She was raped and murdered," Clint said then.

Elizabeth's eyes widened in surprise. The man continually shocked her by blurting out important feelings at totally unexpected times. Her heartbeat quickened at the realization he was finally telling her something about his wife. She waited, afraid that one word might shut him up again.

"She was only twenty-one. I was twenty-six. We'd gone into town for supplies, and I—I decided to go look at some horses for sale at the livery while she shopped and did the banking. Little Ethan was with her. He was—"

Now the words came hard.

"—only two years old…a blue-eyed, blond-haired, chubby-cheeked and happy little boy who knew only joy in life." He cleared his throat. "While they were in the bank it was quietly robbed by four men with guns. No shots were fired, so no one realized what was going on. They rode off with Jen and Ethan, figuring that if they had a woman and child with them anyone who came after them would hesitate to shoot at them. If they had only used them for shields, it wouldn't have been so bad. But once they decided they weren't of use any longer, they…raped Jen…and shot her in the head. Even worse…they shot Ethan, too. I expect he was crying, and they didn't like the noise. Who knows? I only know that if I'd gone to the bank with her…if I'd only gone with her…"

"You probably would have been shot trying to help them, Clint."

"At least then I would have done *some*thing. Just *some*thing. Until you have a child of your own, Liz, you'll never understand how it felt to know my baby was out there somewhere crying over his mommy, wondering where his daddy was…." He rolled to his side, his back to her. "By the time we found them the deed was done…and wolves had torn at their bodies…my precious beautiful wife…and my sweet, innocent little boy."

The last words were spoken with a strained voice, and by the time he was finished his shoulders were shaking in sobs. "That's when I knew—" he groaned "—that there was no God. I'd prayed and prayed and prayed that we'd find them alive."

Elizabeth could not help tears of her own. *Dear God, help me! Help me know what to say!* Should she speak at all? Should she hold him? Here was a big, strong, brave, able, grown man who, since the awful death of his wife and child, had killed other men and likely slept with other women and drank and smoked and gambled and got into fights. Here he lay weeping. To think of what it must have been like finding his wife and child that way. No wonder he doubted God. No wonder he was so full of rage and hatred and revenge. And part of it was aimed at himself, thinking he might have been able to prevent what had happened. Surely his own undeserved guilt made it all worse.

"I miss him so much," he sobbed. "I miss my little boy…his smile…his little arms around my neck. I was his *father*. Fathers *protect* their sons!"

Elizabeth leaned forward, putting her head in her hands, scrambling for the right words. *Lord Jesus I pray that whatever comes out of my mouth will be Your words, not mine.*

Hesitantly she reached over to touch his shoulder, swallowing back a lump in her throat. "I can't begin to tell you how sorry I am, Clint. If I can even come close to helping you feel the happiness you once knew with Jen and Ethan, I'll be glad. But first you have to face the fact that…sometimes things happen that we can't do anything about. A man can't be in two different places at once, and nothing led you to believe that your wife and son would be in any danger that day. So the first thing you absolutely must realize is that none of it is your fault…*none* of it. No one on earth or in heaven above would blame you for not being there."

He took a deep breath and sat up, his back still to her. He reached over for a towel and wiped at his face and nose with it. "This is embarrassing."

"Embarrassing? Clint, you are grieving over the two most important people in your life and the awful way they died! There is nothing embarrassing about weeping over that. Sometimes crying can cleanse the soul."

He took several more deep breaths. "After they were buried—" He made a choking sound. "Putting my son in the ground like that...the hatred burned so deep inside me it's a wonder I didn't literally burst into flames. I wanted to get my hands on those men! I rode with the posse that went after them, and we found them. I...just lost it. The posse surrounded and disarmed them, got ready to take them in, but I started shooting...and kept shooting until all four of them were down before anybody could stop me. I should have been arrested myself, but most of those men with me were friends. They understood. Not one of them ever said a word. People were told they'd been killed in a shootout with the posse."

He ran a hand through his hair and took a rolled cigarette from the pocket of his jacket. He lit it and took a deep drag, ignoring the fact that it made him cough. "After that, killing just those men wasn't enough. I didn't know what to do with all the horrible guilt and sorrow—the terrible emptiness in my life. I packed only what I needed for traveling, went to the sheriff's office and took down posters and left my farm to a neighbor who'd helped me track down those who'd killed my wife and son, and I left. I couldn't stay in that house and see all the things there

Jen loved, and see Ethan's toys, not even one night. I've never gone back. I've done nothing but hunt and kill ever since then. And I left God behind with those graves. He failed me at a time when I needed Him most. Not only that, He failed my wife and my little boy. He let them suffer."

"No, Clint. There has been another power in this world ever since Satan was cast from heaven. Sometimes that power manages to weave itself into the hearts of men, like those who killed Jen and Ethan, and it uses such men to try to defy God and make people stop believing in Him. Then he finds a way into *their* hearts because they have stopped trusting in God.

"I believe that's what has happened with you. Satan is laughing right now at the fact that he's taken a good man and turned him into a killer who hates and distrusts and thirsts for revenge against something intangible, something no amount of killings can satisfy. Satan takes joy in testing a man's faith and cracking it. As long as you continue living the way you do, he will have won, and that's not fair to your wife and child. They don't want you to burn in hell, Clint. They want you to come and join them someday in a gloriously beautiful and peaceful place where you can forever be together. And most of all they wouldn't want you to be suffering like this, blaming yourself, killing men, turning your eyes from God. If you live this way they died for nothing. Faith in Jesus Christ can set you free, Clint. Letting go of the past and giving it over to Him can rid you of the weight of your sins and sorrows. That's why He gave the ultimate sacrifice, His own life, to forgive all sin."

Clint made no reply.

Help me! Elizabeth pleaded again inwardly.

"You just told me what it felt like to lose your son," she continued. "Just think how God felt, allowing His only Son to suffer and die on the cross and doing nothing to stop that. He could have made sure none of it happened, but He knew it *had* to happen, to save mankind and show them the way to everlasting life. Clint, God sacrificed *His* own son to a terrible death for you…for me…even for the men who killed your wife and son. And He let you live for a reason. Only *you* will know deep inside what He wants for you, once you give all your sorrow over to Him and ask His forgiveness for the way you've been living."

He smoked quietly, then finally spoke up. "You've no idea how many times I've put a gun to my own head over the past four years," he told her. "I could never pull the trigger. The one time I finally did—of course I was drunk—the gun didn't go off. I checked it. Every chamber was full. There was absolutely nothing wrong with it, but it didn't fire. That was about a year ago." He finally faced her, his blue eyes bloodshot. "That's when I knew, for just that moment, that God was still with me. I just wasn't ready to acknowledge it or ask Him what He wanted. It's only been since I met you that I've started thinking about that moment."

So open! This was far from the Clint Brady she'd known up until now. That opening to his heart was getting bigger. God was working His miracles.

Elizabeth smiled. "Well, I'm glad I was able to do that much."

He leaned closer and planted a warm, sweet kiss on her lips. "Let's just let it go at that for now," he said then, resting his forehead against hers. "In the last four years you are the only person I've ever told the whole story to…the only one I've let myself break down in front of."

She moved her arms around his neck and rested her head on his shoulder. "It only makes you look stronger in my eyes. It takes a wise, strong man to admit the things you just told me, and not be too proud to cry out for help. Even Jesus Christ wept over the loss of a friend, and again in the Garden of Gethsemane the night before He died, begging God to change what He knew had to happen, and the next day He cried out to His father on the cross, 'My God, My God, why hast Thou forsaken me?' Yet not a stronger man ever lived."

He moved his arms around her and hugged her tightly, again breaking into tears. Elizabeth breathed a sigh of relief that perhaps she'd said the right thing for once. Only time and reaching Dawson would tell. For now she could only hold him…and love him.

Chapter Thirty-Seven

Every man according as he purposeth in his heart,
so let him give; not grudgingly, or of necessity: for
God loveth a cheerful giver.
— 1 Corinthians 9:7

Elizabeth could see the anger in Clint's eyes. The fees being charged for boats built at a sawmill at Lake Bennett were outrageous. Two more days of traveling had brought them here, where for another three days they camped with scores of others, all waiting for their boats. What irked Clint was knowing the owners of the sawmill had them over a barrel. If they wanted to continue their journey, they had to buy a boat here, since traveling the swift-running Yukon River was the only way to continue.

Elizabeth could hardly blame Clint for being upset. The special raft he wanted built was costing him three hundred fifty dollars, a fortune as far as she was concerned, even though it was different from the smaller boats being built for others who had no horses with them.

The only other woman amid the campers was here with her husband. The couple stayed to themselves. Elizabeth felt sorry for them, as they appeared to have few belongings left. Their clothes were tattered, and they slept under a blanket made into a tent by tying rope between two trees and draping the blanket over it.

Longing to visit with another female, Elizabeth had tried talking to the woman once; but the woman just hung her head, asking Elizabeth to leave because she didn't feel well. Elizabeth had prayed for her that night, noticing the woman looked very thin and depressed, and that she and her husband hardly spoke to each other.

This third morning Elizabeth sat by her campfire drinking coffee and watching Clint rearrange some of the supplies in preparation for loading them onto their raft the next morning. Other than "I love you," and the usual necessary conversations of two people traveling together, he'd said nothing more about his past or his grief.

Elizabeth sensed he still felt unnecessarily ashamed for showing weakness. She thought how it was too bad that men thought it humiliating to cry, for crying could be such a release sometimes. It had helped her get over her father's death, and then her mother's. Telling Clint that even Jesus had cried seemed to have helped, but he was back to pretending none of it had happened.

Now she watched him lift ridiculously heavy baggage, probably to show off for her, and she had to smile. Clint Brady was one man who did not have to prove his masculinity. It radiated from every part of him, from his handsome smile to his calloused hands to the way his shirts fit him and the way he walked. Today was amazingly warm compared to the weather they'd experienced getting here, and he'd removed his jacket for the hard work. He'd trimmed his beard this morning and managed to wash, and she could see the handsome man she'd traveled with on the *Damsel* re-emerging.

She in turn had scrubbed her face and neck and changed into the only other woolen shirt and pants she had packed. Next to a real bath, it felt good to at least wear clean clothes. However, these would have to last until they reached Dawson.

She picked up her diary to continue her descriptions of daily events, becoming lost in her writing until she heard Clint talking to someone. She looked up to see the couple she'd prayed for standing there as Clint finished tying some rope. Clint asked them to step closer to the fire. Looking very humbled, his wife appearing to be near tears, the man and woman walked with him to sit down by the fire across from Elizabeth. Clint sat down beside Elizabeth, who smiled at the woman.

"Hello again," she said with a welcoming tone.

The woman just nodded.

"Mornin'," her husband answered. "Name's Hugo Pepper. This is the wife, Earlene."

Elizabeth guessed them to be in their early thirties. "I'm glad you decided to join us," she told Hugo. "I haven't seen another woman since leaving Skagway."

Earlene looked at Hugo as though urging him to go

ahead with something he had to say. Hugo sighed, turning his attention to Clint. "I ain't never done this in my life, mister, but...well, I noticed you forked out a lot of money for your raft." He removed his hat, revealing straight, black, thinning hair. "Well, it's like this. Me and Earlene, we have four kids back home in Seattle. She's missin' the kids so bad she can't hardly stand it. We didn't have much when we left there, except a dream to go to Dawson and maybe find gold and be able to go back and provide a better life for the kids."

He sighed again, hesitating.

"Thing is," he finally continued, "we're already broke. Can't afford a boat to take us any farther, and can't afford the necessary supplies anyway, let alone what it would take to go on into the mountains and survive a winter there lookin' for somethin' we might never find. Earlene, she thinks...well, I think it, too...we think we ought to just go home. There's others goin' back, and if we stick with them we should be able to get back over the pass to Skagway before the pass gets closed up from snow. If we can just get that far, we can probably get by workin' for others in Skagway. That way we could go back home come spring."

The air hung silent for a moment, and Clint gave Elizabeth a puzzled look. Elizabeth turned her attention to the Peppers. "Are you asking us to help in some way?"

Hugo, his pants torn at one leg and his jacket soiled, rested his elbows on his knees and put his head in his hands. Earlene looked at Elizabeth pleadingly.

"Yes," the woman told her. "It's hard for my husband to say it, but we're desperate. We've been watching you and your husband, noticed him sometimes pray with you, so we…I thought you seemed to be Christian people, and that maybe…perhaps you could find it in your hearts to help us out. We just need a little money, something we could use to buy some supplies when we reach Skagway. And we—we need a few supplies for going back. Even just a sack of beans might do it…maybe a little coffee? We did manage to talk someone else into letting us have his tent. It was his partner's, who'd died getting here, so the man didn't want the extra baggage, but he wouldn't give us anything else. It seems once men get this far it's every man for himself. All Christian feelings go out the window." Tears formed in her eyes. "I just want to get back to my children. It took this trip to make us realize that for all our dreams of getting rich up here, the best thing we can give them is love. They need their mommy and daddy more than anything else." She broke into sobbing, and Hugo put his arm around her.

Elizabeth looked pleadingly at Clint, and he rolled his eyes, his old distrustful self kicking in.

"Look, mister, this is the hardest thing I've ever done," Hugo spoke up. "Fact is, what we need more than anything is a horse. My wife, she's got so weak I hate to think about her walkin' all the way back. I'm scared to death she'll take sick and die and never see her babies again."

Clint shook his head and rose. "No. No horse. They are too valuable."

Elizabeth saw the disappointment in Hugo's eyes, mixed with feelings of embarrassment and shame.

"Why don't you go back to your camp so my…husband

and I can talk about this," she told the man. "I'm sure there is some way we can help. And please—" She poured coffee into two tin cups. "Take this with you. You both look like you could use a cup of hot coffee."

Hugo nodded, standing up and taking both cups. "We're obliged, ma'am. Come on, Earlene. Let's leave them be." He glanced at Clint. "You're better than the rest of 'em. I can tell."

He walked off with his wife, and Clint frowned at Elizabeth. "What the heck did he mean by that?"

Elizabeth sat back down on the log they'd shared moments earlier. "Sit down, Clint. I don't want them to hear us."

Grudgingly, Clint straddled the log, facing Elizabeth, who turned to meet his gaze. "You *know* what he meant, Clint Brady," she continued quietly. "You're a better man than most others here, a man who cares more about human beings than gold and possessions."

He closed his eyes in disgust. "How do you know they aren't scamming us? There are plenty of con artists in places like this, you know."

"Don't give me that, Mr. I-Can-Read-a-Man's-Eyes Brady! You know they're telling the truth. And did you see that woman's face? That's no con job. That's a broken woman who misses her babies. And her husband is a proud man who loves his kids enough to crawl on hands and knees for them. That's how asking for help feels to him. You can see that."

He leaned closer, talking quietly to be sure the Peppers couldn't hear. "We need every ounce of supplies we have left. And God knows we need the *horses!* On top of that, they're worth a good three hundred dollars a piece. If I give them a horse, I never see it again *or* the money it's worth! Men don't just *give* horses away, for God's sake! I'm not *that* rich, lady!"

"That poor woman could *die!* God sent them over here, Clint. I know He did. He wants us to help them. And just think, one less horse will make the raft trip a lot easier and safer. I love those horses by now as much as you do. And don't tell me you don't want to give one up just because of its value. You're *attached* to them, as well you should be, but human life is more important. Please help them, Clint. We can live on a little less food and with one less horse. We're so close to Dawson. Once we get there things will be so much easier."

"*Easier?* Have you forgotten the stories we've heard? You'd better be praying your brother wasn't one of them who died! What if *he* needs our help when we get there?"

"God is taking care of Peter. I know it."

"Yeah, well, you think you know an awful lot about God, don't you? God-this and God-that. That God of yours—"

"Clint! You are very close to blaspheming! Please listen to yourself! How do you think we've gotten this far safely? Who do you think saved your life from pneumonia? And who have you already admitted brought us together in the first place? I see you get so close, Clint, and then you drift away again. The old, distrustful, angry, look-out-for-himself Clint returns to take over!" She folded her arms. "I want to help them. You do what you think is best. You're the one with the money…and the supplies…and the horses…and the right to do with all of them as you please."

He let out a long sigh and put his head in his hands. "How does a man win an argument with you?"

"He doesn't."

He sat there several long, quiet seconds. "All right," he finally told her, his head still in his hands. "A pound of coffee, a sack of beans, a sack of flour and..." He threw his head back. "I must be slowly losing my mind." He rose and turned away. "Two blankets and a horse and saddle."

Elizabeth smiled. "Thank you, Clint! God will bless you richly, I know it! He'll make sure the rest of this trip is safe and free of any disasters. Peter will be there when we arrive, and everything will be wonderful! You're a good, good man, Clint Brady."

She quickly lost her smile when his own eyes flashed with belligerence. "We'll find out when we reach Dawson, considering the fact that Roland Fisher is worth *five thousand dollars!* God knows I'll need *that* by the time you're through spending and giving away everything I own!"

Elizabeth's first reaction was to spit back something in her defense, but she held her tongue. She told herself he didn't really mean it. He was just reacting to the moment... angry that he'd let himself give in to his own feelings of pity for Hugo and Earlene. He'd be sorry later that he'd got so mad.

It was the part about Roland Fisher that scared her. She'd almost forgotten about Clint's real reason for going to Dawson. Obviously he had *not* forgotten. The old Clint was still rearing his vengeful, defensive head, and that Clint would take a lot more praying for.

She stood up and faced him. "Thank you anyway. And if things...don't work out between us...I'll find a way to pay you back somehow."

He waved her off. "Forget it. Just go get Red Lady. God knows they'd never be able to handle Devil. I'll gather up the rest of what we're giving them." He scowled. "What *I'm* giving them."

She watched him lovingly, refusing to let this Clint intimidate her. "God loves you, Clint, and so do I."

He shook his head. "Then I guess you're both prone to loving fools."

No, just good men, Elizabeth thought, smiling as he angrily yanked at ropes to untie supplies for the Peppers.

Chapter Thirty-Eight

Be not far from me; for trouble is near;
for there is none to help.

—Psalms 22:11

The first five days of rafting the Yukon were beautiful, filled with sunshine and surprisingly smooth waters. However, Clint's mood was not quite so beautiful and smooth. He wondered if he'd completely lost his mind letting Liz talk him into giving away a perfectly good and valuable horse. Red Lady had meant more to him than he'd realized, and he worried what would happen to the faithful animal. Would the Peppers sell her once they reached Skagway? *If* they reached Skagway? If so, it would probably be to someone who wanted to use her for a pack horse, meaning she'd have to make that trip over White Pass again.

He couldn't believe that he felt a pull at his heartstrings whenever he thought about her. He actually missed her. A *horse!* He missed a *horse!* He wasn't supposed to have feelings like that. The old Clint would never have given her to paupers to begin with. He would have sold her for decent money and then not given her another thought.

It was Liz, that's what it was. She was totally, completely changing him, making him act like a madman. He was to the point of doing just about anything to please her, and that scared him. To go so far as to give away a horse like Red Lady...

Try as he might, he'd been unable to get back into a good mood ever since. He grumped at Liz constantly, but she just breezed around like she didn't even notice! The fool woman had apparently made up her mind that his mood would not affect her. If Fisher was standing in front of him right now, he'd shoot the man down just to show her...and God...that he hadn't changed one bit! He didn't *want* to change. That would mean finally going on with life, which in turn meant he was ready to put what happened to Jen and his precious Ethan behind him.

He couldn't help somehow feeling guilty for that. After the way they died, how could he start living as though it had never happened? What right did he have to be happy again? To love another woman?

He stood at the rear paddle of the raft, steering it while Liz held Devil's bridle and talked to the horse to keep him calm. A fence built around the raft helped Devil feel safer and gave Liz something to hold on to. Devil had been just as skittish as Clint feared he'd be, but the horse seemed to be adapting to floating for most of the day, as long as he could go ashore at night and nibble on winter grass. The problem was there were rapids ahead. This calm mirror of a river could change overnight. The same could happen if a winter storm blew through the canyons they traversed.

He and Liz took turns at steering the raft, and this afternoon was his turn. He liked steering because then he could watch Liz, study the slender form that failed to fill out either her shirt or the men's pants she wore. Today she'd removed her hat and let down her hair, for the sun shone down surprisingly warm. He'd watched her brush out the thick, auburn waves this morning, remembered how perfect she looked when she wore a fitted dress. In spite of the raw weather they'd faced in getting this far, her skin still looked smooth as porcelain, her cheeks rosy from the cold, a bit of color to the rest of her face from daily exposure to the elements.

Her eyes were what ate at his dreams the most—those soft, green eyes that had a way of ordering him around without saying a word. Maybe if he never looked into them again he could ignore any future wishes and maybe even ignore the feelings she stirred deep in his soul. Still, how could he resist gazing into those beautiful green pools? He wanted her. He'd never wanted anything this much since Jen.

Before falling in love again he'd not realized how much he missed having a good woman beside him every night; missed home-cooked meals and sitting by a fire after supper talking about the day. He missed knowing someone cared about him. He thought he was tough enough to never want those things again...but maybe he wasn't.

Now he felt bad for being as grumpy as a bear just out of hibernation ever since giving away Red Lady. He'd barely spoken to Liz, other than to give orders, and although his cough truly was getting worse, he'd used it to feign being too miserable to talk around the campfire at night.

Now he felt obligated to make up for his grouchy countenance and for being downright mean to her since leaving Lake Bennett. Somehow he had to get a normal conversation going.

"Do you have any idea what you've done to me?" he yelled to Elizabeth.

She turned. There was that beautiful smile. There were those full, tempting lips. Her hair shone more red in the sunshine, and it blew in soft whispers around her delicate face. He was glad to see the bruise from her accident on White Pass had faded to a very light green. "Of course I do," she answered with that air of confidence that drove him nuts.

"Giving that horse away was the most foolish thing I've ever done in my life," he told her, "other than falling in love with you."

She tossed her hair in a way that drove him crazy, and he realized she probably had no idea how tempting she really was or what it did to a man to have to travel with her and keep hands off.

"Are you saying you're ready to stop sulking and forgive me for making you give away Red Lady?" she asked with a teasing smile.

He grinned back at her. "I'm only ready to stop sulking. I didn't say I'd forgive you."

She laughed lightly, a sound that reminded him of a delicate bird. She was pure. She was perfect. She was all innocence. She was a devout, practicing, giving, forgiving, loving, trusting, praying Christian. She was everything that he was not. Yes, he *was* nuts. He had no business nor any right loving her, certainly no business and no right expecting her to take him as her husband. He could never live up to her expectations of a truly Christian man. It would be best for her if he left her with her brother once they reached Dawson, then hunted down Roland Fisher and left.

Trouble was, winter would be setting in good by the time they got there. He'd be stuck in Dawson for several months no matter what happened. And how was he going to live in the same tiny little town without seeing her? Worse, how would he *stand* not seeing her or hearing her voice...or holding her...kissing her.

She had some kind of hold on him, all right.

His thoughts were interrupted by a roaring sound ahead. Liz looked back at him. "What's that?"

Clint lost his smile and his happy thoughts. He wanted badly to curse, but he held his tongue. "Hang on to the railing and on to Devil," he shouted. "We must have reached Whitehorse Rapids!"

He'd not expected to come upon this spot until tomorrow. They must have made better time than he'd figured! There wasn't even time to try to get to shore and figure out what to do next. The current had them now, and when he tried to steer to shore the turning rudder only made the raft spin. Now he *did* pray.

The roar became almost painful. The raft rose and fell and whirled and sank. Devil whinnied with terror. The raft tilted·wildly. The supplies broke loose. Liz screamed and fell into the raging, white, churning waters. Devil followed...and so did Clint.

Chapter Thirty-Nine

Yea, though I walk through the valley of the shadow
of death, I will fear no evil; for Thou art with me;
Thy rod and Thy staff they comfort me.
—Psalms 23:4

Elizabeth had no idea where shore was, where Clint was, or the raft...or poor Devil. For this freezing, beating, horrible moment, survival was all she could think of. This was a raging swirl of white water that beat her mercilessly and tossed her like a rag doll, dashing her under to the river's bottom, then tossing her upward again. Whether a person could swim or not made no difference.

Her hip hit a rock, then she kept tumbling and swirling until by some miracle her hands came upon something she could grasp. She hung on as tightly as possible, pulling hard, begging God to help her get to safety. She pulled herself farther, managing to climb halfway out of the water onto what she realized was a fallen tree. Battered and confused, she just held on, clinging to a branch for several minutes, catching her breath and gathering her thoughts.

She looked around, realizing that just ahead the water slowed to a calmer swirl. She saw nothing there. "Clint!" Where was he? "Clint!" she screamed louder.

There came no reply. Only the sound of rushing water hit her ears, until she heard a whinny. Gasping against the cold, she turned to see Devil standing on shore!

"Devil!" she yelled. "Stay there!" Her woolen coat soggy, her boots filled with water, it took every last ounce of strength for her to climb all the way onto the log. She inched her way to shore, where she pulled off the heavy coat, then sat down and removed her boots, dumping water out of them.

Soaked to the skin, she shook from head to foot. She walked in cold socks over to Devil, checking him over. Miraculously, he appeared to be all right. *"Thank you, Jesus,"* she said, tears of emotion overwhelming her. She hugged the horse around the neck. "Devil, you're okay! Now we just have to find Clint!" She kissed the horse's nose, and Devil nodded and shook his mane as though to say he was glad to see her, too.

Elizabeth tied him to a tree, then looked around, screaming Clint's name again. She looked up and down the shoreline, then thought she saw something farther to the south. She ran in stockinged feet toward what she'd spotted.

"The raft!" she exclaimed when she drew closer. "Oh, Sweet Jesus!" It wasn't even broken up! A few things were missing, but she saw that a good deal of the items Clint had tied on were still there. He'd done an excellent job of securing most of the supplies. He was a man who knew about those things…but what about himself? Where was Clint?

Gasping from the intense cold, she took hold of a rope wound around one of the remaining fence posts on the raft and unwrapped it, then hurried across the beach to tie it to a tree so the raft couldn't float away. She ran back to the raft, quickly loosening a tarp and unrolling it. She took from it a dry blanket, thinking what a smart packer Clint was. She wrapped the blanket around herself, including her hair, which hung wet and limp against her head. She felt of it, realizing then that ice had actually formed on some of it!

She scrambled to think what she should do first. Look for Clint? Build a fire? Cover Devil? Yes, cover Devil first. He probably had ice on him, too. A blanket would help the horse's own body heat melt the ice. She pulled another blanket free of the tarp and ran back over to the horse to cover him.

"Clint!" she screamed again. She strained to listen to anything besides the roaring, rushing waters. She thought she heard a voice, and it sounded as though it came from her right, to the north. Teeth chattering and tears still wanting to come due to a terrible longing just to be warm, she left in the direction of what she hoped she'd heard… Clint answering her. She screamed his name again.

"Here!" she thought she heard more clearly now.

"Thank God!" she cried. She ran in the direction of the voice, continuing to call his name and hearing replies. She hurried around a bend in the river, then saw a tall figure of a man staggering toward her. A wound on his forehead was bleeding badly.

Elizabeth ran up to him. "Clint!"

He grasped her close. "Thank God," he said gruffly. "Are you hurt?"

Elizabeth clung to him, hugging him tightly. "I'm all right. My back hurts bad, though, where I was thrown against a rock. And I'm so cold, Clint…so cold!"

"I know."

Elizabeth could feel him shivering, too, and she thought about the pneumonia that had nearly killed him back in Skagway. This could bring it all back, maybe worse this time. "We've got to get back and make a fire, Clint. I found the raft, and most of our supplies were still tied to it!" She looked up at him. "Clint, you're hurt bad."

He touched her face, looking her over. "The important thing is that you're all right. I'm sorry, Liz. I should have been able to help you, but every time I tried to swim to you the waters took you away again." He hugged her close again. "I thought I'd lost you."

"Never. God will never let you lose someone you love again. I just know it, Clint."

He started walking with her then, keeping an arm around her. "Let's get a fire going and get out of these clothes."

"Clint, I found Devil! He's all right!"

"Well, thank God for another miracle," he answered.

Elizabeth made no comment, just glad that he'd attributed their good fortune to God. They reached the raft, where Clint untied another blanket and wrapped it around himself. Elizabeth heard him coughing heavily as they both hurriedly gathered enough fallen wood to make a fire. Both still trembling from cold, they managed to put up the tent with the entrance practically on top of the fire so that they could feel some of the heat inside. Elizabeth threw both bedrolls inside, then started in herself to huddle against the cold.

"Wait!" Clint demanded. "Get your clothes off first...all of them," he ordered.

Elizabeth peered at him from the blanket wrapped around her head. "What?"

"Everything off first. We've got to dry them out."

"Clint, the carpet bags that had my clothes in them are missing. I have nothing to change into!"

"I see my leather supply bags are still there. See if you can find a dry shirt. We'll hang your clothes around the fire and hope it doesn't snow or rain so they can dry out."

"And I'm supposed to share a tent with you, wearing nothing but a *shirt?*"

He put a hand to his head. "Please don't put it that way. Just do as I ask, okay? Besides, you can wrap a blanket around yourself. Would you rather get sick and die?"

"Well, I—I guess not."

"You *guess* not?" He knelt near the fire and put some snow on the wound at his forehead. "Just go get a shirt and do what I ask. And don't worry. I won't look."

Elizabeth knew he was right, but the thought of getting entirely undressed in front of him embarrassed her to death. Could she trust him? Don't be silly, she told herself. He loves you, and he's right. You can't stay in these wet clothes. She ran over to the raft and dug through his things, finding a shirt that seemed to be dry. She hurried back, grabbing her boots from where she'd left them and setting them near the fire. She looked at Clint. "Turn around and warm your back," she told him. "It's too cramped inside the tent to try to do this in there."

He looked her over in a way that made her shiver, but not from the cold. He turned around then.

"*Promise* me you won't look," she asked.

He shook his head as though disgusted with her. "I promise." He started coughing again and wrapped the blanket completely around his head.

"What if more boats come along?"

"Go around behind the tent."

Elizabeth would have preferred to undress close to the fire, but fearful of being seen by strangers, she obeyed. Quickly she stripped off everything, a secret part of her feeling an odd satisfaction at the thought of Clint seeing her this way. After all, if she became his wife... She smiled. Clint Brady would just wrap her in his own warmth and make her feel beautiful and loved.

She pulled on his shirt, the sleeves much too long, and the tail coming to her knees. She was thankful for that much. She rolled up the cuffs and wrapped herself in the blanket again, holding it closed with one hand as she picked up her things with the other and came back around to the fire. "You can look now."

Clint turned again, and the look of pure appreciation and desire in his eyes made Elizabeth's blood flow surprisingly warm. She felt her cheeks burning.

"I'll change into dry clothes and then rig up some kind of scaffolding that we can set over the top of the fire," he told her, "away from the flames but close enough to catch the heat. We'll lay everything on that."

Elizabeth ducked inside the tent, quickly crawling inside her blankets. She waited while Clint changed into dry clothes, then worked outside building some kind of frame to hang their clothes on. It took nearly an hour before he ducked inside the tent and crawled into his own blankets.

"I built up the fire more. I'm just glad we actually found enough wood, considering how used up most things are on this trail." He began coughing again. It took several seconds for him to stop.

"This is the worst thing that could have happened to you," Elizabeth lamented.

"Well, my head hurts more than anything else. I washed off the blood as best I could."

They faced each other. "You have quite an egg on your forehead. It's purple and still bleeding some."

"What about your back?"

"It hurts. I'm sure it's just bruised. We're very lucky, you know."

Clint watched her lovingly. "I know." He leaned closer to kiss her, then turned away, the cough returning. "Let's get some rest."

Elizabeth closed her eyes, listening to the rushing waters nearby. So many miracles, she thought. God most certainly was hard at work keeping them safe.

Chapter Forty

Hear, O Lord, when I cry with my voice: Have mercy also upon me, and answer me.

—Psalms 27:7

A rainstorm kept us from breaking camp for another three days. Luckily our clothes dried almost completely from the heat of the fire that first night, before the downpour began.

Today is our third day back on the river. Clint's cough is much worse, and he's fevered again. He lay sick the entire time we were camped, and has been getting sicker ever since we left. I pray for him constantly, as in spite of his worsening condition, he continues to insist he can handle steerage while I watch Devil.

The rain has turned to snow, and it is getting very cold again. All either of us wants now is to make it to Dawson alive.

Elizabeth closed her diary and put it into one of Clint's bags, as her own carpet bags were still missing. They would probably never be found. She would arrive in Dawson with literally nothing but the clothes on her back. Even her Bible was gone. Thank God she had, for some reason, shoved her diary into one of Clint's bags before the accident on the rapids. It was damp, but intact.

"Let's go!" Clint yelled.

Elizabeth grabbed hold of Devil's reins again and hung on as Clint shoved the raft into the water.

Three more days. Men in a boat that had passed them going in the other direction yesterday had told them they were only about three days from Dawson. Now those three days seemed like an eternity. There was absolutely no time to spare. Clint's face was flushed and his eyes bloodshot from fever, but he insisted on standing at the rudder and doing the steering while Elizabeth stayed beside Devil to keep him steadied.

Elizabeth was worried sick about Clint. He'd never really rested enough after being so sick back in Skagway. Now, having to weather the blowing snow and the searing cold of the water that splashed up and kept his pants damp could surely kill him in his condition. She thought it amazing that he was able to stand all day steering the raft, and she suspected he was only doing it out of a stubborn effort not to show any weakness in front of her. Besides that, they were both desperate just to finish their long, cold, tiresome, dangerous journey.

Twice she'd called out to others in passing boats to ask if one of them might be willing to help steer their raft so that

Clint could rest, but none would help. All were too anxious to reach their pots of gold, and Elizabeth's heart ached to think what little Christianity lay in the hearts of men lusting for wealth. She could see now why Peter felt such men would need the Word of God, if any bothered to listen.

She looked back at Clint. He understood such men. That's why he carried on relentlessly. He knew no one would help. It was up to him now to get her to Dawson and warmth and safety. Actually, that had been his burden through this whole trip. She realized she never would have made it without him, and she loved him all the more for it.

He looked so haggard, so tired and so sick. His face was heavily bearded now, and she'd almost forgotten what he really looked like. Only those blue eyes reminded her. And the determination he put forth now to get them to the end of their journey reminded her of his strength and abilities. He was everything a woman could want in a man, but he still had that last hurdle to cross and his own need to put the past behind him and learn to trust God again.

First they had to reach Dawson in one piece.

Within an hour after leaving camp the wind picked up, howling through the canyon from the south and bringing with it a heavy, wet snow. The direction of the wind helped propel them along the river a little faster, but Elizabeth wasn't sure how much more Clint could handle in his condition. Since they had been back on the river, he'd barely spoken. All he did was try to sleep between fits of coughing.

The only food they had left was beans, a few sweet potatoes and some coffee. They'd used up the last of the oats for Devil, who now had to paw his way through snow to find enough grass to nibble on to keep him alive. The poor horse was looking just as bony and weary as she and Clint.

Last night there had not been enough wood around to make a fire. They'd been forced to huddle together for warmth, and Elizabeth thought how they had already been tested for their ability to stand up to adversity and hard times together. That was one thing they wouldn't need to learn about each other after marriage.

She no longer worried about what others might think of her traveling all this way with a man. This trip had taught her lot about what really mattered in life, and that appearances meant nothing. She often wondered about Collette, how the woman was doing, if anything she'd said to Collette had perhaps helped turn her to God.

In many ways people like Collette and Clint were just as good if not better than Reverend Selby, for all his pretended righteousness. At least Collette and her friends, and men like Clint, were honest about what and who they were. They recognized their own faults and knew they needed to change their lives. And who knew what lay in Collette's past that made her what she was? It was such people who could teach pompous Christians about God's grace and forgiveness.

The river wound through spectacular country, country only God could possibly take credit for. She fully understood Peter's description of the Canadian Rockies, Alaska and the Yukon surely being a gateway to Heaven. Maybe once she and Clint were safe and warm and well, she could fully appreciate the beauty of this land.

Clint refused to stop at midday for anything to eat or

to rest. "The fewer stops we make, the sooner we'll get there," he told her. He stopped only long enough for her to run to the shore and find a place to relieve herself. She in turn just looked away when he warned her he'd be doing the same.

Elizabeth had to smile at how familiar they'd been forced to become without being married. Trust was certainly not something they would ever have to doubt. If Clint were an abusive man, he certainly would have shown it by now, but he'd never been anything but a gentleman, although she had to smile at his sometimes grudging reluctance to behave properly.

He was a good man...too good to be so lost and to be living without love. She knew by now that there could never be another man in her life but Clint Brady. How could she live without him if he chose to go after Roland Fisher and continue the life he was leading? She worried that he still felt he wasn't good enough for her, or perhaps felt God could never forgive him, and so would use that excuse to leave once he found Fisher.

Night came on too fast in this season of short days, but a full moon allowed them to continue after dark, until finally Clint decided to make camp. They tethered Devil, then dug out of the snow an area big enough to pitch their tent. The snow had not let up, and it reminded Elizabeth of the night they'd spent in the snowstorm back at White Pass.

Clint went into another fit of coughing and turned his back to her. Elizabeth turned to put her arms around him from behind. "What can I do, Clint?"

"Nothing." He coughed again. "You wanted me to stop smoking. This sure has done it," he added.

"Clint, maybe we should stay right here for a couple of days. You're killing yourself."

"I'll make it." There came another fit of coughing. "We're too close now. I just hope...your brother *is* there and that he has a decent, warm cabin where we can stay."

Suddenly Devil's frantic, screaming whinnies roused both of them from their quiet conversation. They heard low growling just outside the tent.

"Wolves!" Clint exclaimed. He threw off his blanket and grabbed his rifle, cocking it and ducking outside.

"Clint!"

"Stay there!" he ordered.

At almost the same time Elizabeth heard much louder growling and barking, as well as literal screams of terror from deep in Devil's throat. Wolves must be attacking him!

By the dim light of their lantern Elizabeth found Clint's handgun, and against his orders, she, too, ducked outside just as Clint fired his rifle once, twice, three times. Elizabeth screamed when a wolf attacked Clint from behind. She heard growling behind her then, and she turned and fired, downing another of the vicious attackers.

Clint wrestled with the wolf that had attacked him, and two more of the animals rushed inside the tent, knocking over a lantern, which blazed up and started the tent on fire.

Elizabeth shot at yet another wolf, and the bright blaze of the tent fire frightened the rest away.

By then Clint had a choke hold on the wolf that had tried to maul him. He stood up and literally flung the choked wolf into the darkness, then scrambled to the burning tent to fling out some of their belongings, but the tent itself was too far ablaze to save it or the rest of what was inside.

Clint stumbled backward. "Liz!" he yelled.

"I'm right here!" Elizabeth hurried up to him. "I think I got one or two of them myself!"

Clint wrapped his arms around her. "I got three of them," he panted, "plus the one I choked."

By the light of the burning tent Elizabeth could see his face. Three deep scratches on his right cheek bled profusely. "Clint, you're bleeding badly!"

He pulled away, putting a hand to his face, wiping at blood. "Thank God we left our heavy clothes and coats on. It could have been a lot worse." He looked her over. "What about you?"

"I'm okay. Clint, what if they come back?"

He looked around into the darkness. "I don't think they will, but we'd better spend the rest of the night on the raft." He walked up to a still-frightened Devil, putting an arm around the horse's neck and talking to him softly to calm him. "So much for God helping us finish this trip safely," he spoke up to Elizabeth. "Now we don't even have a tent to sleep under." He broke into another fit of coughing. "We'll have to just sleep under blankets and keep our heads covered." He shook his head and looked over at Elizabeth. "We're in quite a fix."

Oh, what a test of faith. "Maybe God just wants us to realize that all we need is each other, Clint."

Still panting, he shook his head. "Then He sure has a way of teaching a lesson."

Chapter Forty-One

And he led them forth by the right way, that they might go to a city of habitation.
—Psalms 107:7

Elizabeth smeared more ointment onto the deep cuts along Devil's neck per Clint's orders. He'd brought along a supply of the greasy concoction purchased from a livery in Skagway in case his horses developed any kind of infection. Doctoring the horse made Elizabeth wonder about Red Lady and how the mare was doing. A part of her felt bad for talking Clint into giving up the horse, but it had been the Christian thing to do, and was just another reason she couldn't help loving Clint.

After three more days of rafting, the scratches on Clint's face seemed to be healing, with no redness around the long, deep cuts. The biggest problem was his fever and worsened cough. She looked back to see him bent over coughing again.

"Lord Jesus, please heal him! Don't let him die!" she prayed quietly.

The rest of today and one more night—just one more miserable night of sleeping without a tent, and sometime tomorrow they should reach Dawson...and Peter...and safety...and warmth...and help. She could take a real bath, wear a real dress again. Clint could shave and bathe, get his hair cut, feel human again, get some much-needed rest, food and medicine.

Then there would be just that last hurdle, and they could finally be married and share the intimacy they both longed to share. She could imagine nothing more wonderful than lying in Clint Brady's arms, ever safe, ever loved.

She watched ahead, beginning to yearn for just a glimpse of a real town. Maybe they had misjudged. Maybe they would reach Dawson today. More boats pushed past them in the same direction, men paddling wildly, practically racing each other to their destination and to what they were sure were riches just lying in wait for them.

After a few minutes Elizabeth realized the raft was floating toward shore. She looked back and gasped. Clint was on his knees. "Clint?" She patted Devil to keep him calm, then walked carefully over the logs to Clint, who was gasping for breath. *"Oh, dear God! God help him!"*

The pneumonia was back, if it had ever left him! Was he dying before her eyes? Clint couldn't even speak. He collapsed, lying on his side and gasping for breath. The raft floated against a log and lodged there. Elizabeth hurried to their supplies, putting the horse ointment back into them and taking out a blanket and the bottle that held what was left of the smelly, lemony vapor rub. She rushed back to where Clint lay on his side, and for a moment she feared he wasn't breathing at all.

"Clint! Clint, we've got to get some of this liniment on you!" she told him, urging him onto his back. Quickly she opened his wolf-skin coat, the sweater beneath it, then his woolen shirt and woolen long johns, exposing his chest. She poured some of the cold concoction into her palm and began smearing it on his chest, wishing she had a way of warming the liniment first, as she was sure it would be more effective that way.

"Just try to relax, Clint." She began rubbing on the liniment. "I'll do the steering from now on. We'll just have to pray that Devil stays calm the rest of the way. We're so close! So close! And Devil is used to the raft now. He'll be all right. The important thing is keeping you alive!"

She had to keep talking! She finished smearing him with the liniment, then capped the can and rebuttoned his long johns, shirt, sweater, coat. She put the blanket over him and leaned close. "Clint, can you talk at all?"

He just looked at her with fevered eyes, eyes that said he was sorry.

"Clint, I've never known a more able or a braver man. Right now you're down with something even the strongest man can't control. You've *got* to rest the remainder of the way, Clint. It's only one more day! I'll get us there."

Tears stung her eyes. "Don't you die on me, Clint Brady! We're supposed to get married, remember?" She couldn't believe her next words, but she couldn't think of another way to make him want to live. "My first and only man is going to be Clint Brady, understand? It can't be anybody else. It has to be you. You aren't going to deny me that, are you?"

He actually managed a hint of a smile before closing his eyes and rolling back to his side, pulling the blanket over his head.

Wiping at tears, Elizabeth found and dragged over their last five-pound sack of beans, not very large, but big enough for Clint to have something to rest his head on. She knew the logs had to be terribly uncomfortable, but maybe his heavy coat would help cushion him. He was probably too miserable even to notice.

She lifted his head and shoved the bean bag under it, then retrieved a canteen of water, glad that fresh water was one thing of which there was a plenty in this country. She set it near Clint.

"Clint? The canteen is right here. Drink as much as you can. My mother told me once that it's important to drink a lot of water when you're fevered." She lifted the blanket to see his eyes closed. "Clint? Can you hear me?"

He grasped her hand and squeezed it.

Elizabeth's heart pounded so hard with fear for his life that her chest hurt. She turned and grabbed hold of his rifle, which he always kept nearby, and hurried to the front of the raft, using the gun to push at the log that had snagged them, shoving the raft back out into the current enough that it again began flowing toward their destination. She laid the rifle aside and hurried back to the rudder handle and began steering the raft to keep it in deeper waters, surprised at what a hard job it was to keep it steady.

"You have to help me, Lord," she prayed aloud. *"I don't know if I'm strong enough to keep this up."* She was weak from hunger and exposure, but now they were so close. And she had to get Clint to some kind of help. What a horrible ending it would be to their long, hard journey if he died before they reached Dawson!

"Don't let this happen, Lord Jesus," she prayed. *"Don't let me lose him now! I know You want him, but please take him in life, through his faith! Not in death!"*

She wiped at tears that made it hard to see. She had to concentrate. If God saw fit to bring them another night brightly lit from aurora borealis, she would not stop. Maybe she could save another half day of rafting and finally get this trip over with if she traveled through the night.

She wrapped both arms around the rudder handle and held it against her side in order to keep a firm hold.

"Don't let him die! Don't let him die!" she whispered over and over in prayer.

She noticed Clint reach over and take hold of the canteen. He managed to sit up and drink some water, then corked the canteen and collapsed back down to the bean sack, pulling the blanket over his head again. For the next many hours, Clint's taking a drink once in a while was Elizabeth's only way of knowing he was still alive.

She continued her struggle to keep the raft on its course in the surprisingly strong current that wanted to send it right and left and sometimes seemed to want to make it whirl in a circle. Only now did she realize how hard it must have been for Clint to do this in his condition.

She shivered against the stinging cold, dreaming about

the warmth of a fireplace and a real bed, hot food and hot coffee, or better yet, hot chocolate. Her mother used to make the most wonderful hot chocolate.

Through darkness she kept going, and indeed, God led the way with a brightly lit sky that made it possible to see what was ahead of her. Where she found the strength, how she managed to keep going all night long, she could not explain, other than to say that God surely had His hand on the rudder handle or was pushing the raft along with His own hand.

At dawn the raft rounded a bend and she spied smoke rising from a few chimneys.

Dawson!

"Clint! We're here! We're here!" She nearly screamed the words. "It's Dawson! We made it!" Tears of joy streamed down her cheeks. *"Thank you, Jesus! Thank you!"*

She left the rudder handle long enough to kneel beside Clint. "Clint, we're here! You'll be all right!"

His eyes were closed. He gave no reply. Elizabeth realized then that for the last few hours he'd not reached for the canteen, nor had he even coughed. The only sign that he was still alive was the warmth of his fevered face.

Chapter Forty-Two

O, give thanks unto the Lord, for he is good:
for his mercy endureth forever.

—Psalms 107:1

Elizabeth steered the raft toward the only open spot she could find along Dawson's shore, which was packed with boats both large and small. Most of them appeared to be abandoned, most likely by men who no longer cared about the vessels that had brought them here. Many must already be headed into the mountains, in spite of the dire winter that lay waiting for them there.

Still, a good many settlers were right here in Dawson, from what she could see. The little town lay sprawled over several acres and was made up mostly of tents and log buildings. Horses were tied or grazing here and there, poor bony steeds, like Devil, that had managed to actually survive the trip up here.

Plenty of snow covered the ground, but she could see

one street ahead that was churned into pure mud from so much use. She took a moment to look for some kind of steeple, but she saw nothing to indicate a church. Still, what there was of Peter's church was probably no more than a log building like the rest that were here.

"Dear Jesus, please let me find Peter," she prayed quietly.

She realized that until she did, she would have to guard what was left of their supplies and especially guard Devil. She didn't want Clint to lose the last and best of his horses. Most important, she had to find someplace warm and dry for Clint and start nursing him back to health, if it wasn't already too late to save him.

She searched her brain, trying to determine how she would get Clint, Devil and their supplies into town so she could find Peter. If she could get Clint onto Devil, maybe she could somehow drag their supplies, but she needed something to put them on. Then again, Clint would never be able to climb up onto Devil. She'd pack the supplies on the horse and figure out a different way to get Clint to help.

She felt ready to collapse herself, and her arms and shoulders screamed with pain from handling the raft's rudder for nearly three days by herself. Instinct told her to first look for Clint's handgun, hoping God would understand she actually might need to shoot anyone who tried to take anything from her or keep her from getting help for Clint.

"I'm so sorry for such un-Christian notions, Lord, but what else can I do?" She looked around frantically, spotting what looked like an abandoned dog sled. *"Thank you, Jesus!"*

She ran to retrieve the sled, dragging it back to where she'd tied the raft. The sled surely belonged to someone, but if the owner tried to make her give it back, he'd face a six-gun until she got Clint to help! *Then* he could have his sled back.

She saddled Devil, grimacing with the pain in her shoulders and arms. She then untied their supplies and loaded them onto the horse, reserving softer things like blankets and sleeping bags for the sled. Those things could be used to make a bed for Clint.

Relieved that so far no one came running to claim the sled, she tied all supplies as best she could, having learned from watching Clint. God only knew how long she would have to drag things around town before she found Peter, so everything had to be secure. She wanted to cry from the pain in her shoulders as she worked frantically, and reason told her she'd never be able to lift or help Clint from the raft to the sled. Maybe she could get him to stand up and walk by himself.

Too much time was passing. More men arrived. Some glanced her way, then went on about their business. No one offered to help. It reminded her of the parable in the Bible wherein a wounded man lay robbed and beaten at the side of the road, ignored by priests and others of his own race, until a Samaritan, a natural enemy, came by and helped him.

Finally everything was tied onto the sled. So far no one had come to claim it. She hurried back to Clint, kneeling beside him. "Clint! Clint, we're here! Please, please try to get up! I found a sled and I packed our supplies on it and tied it to Devil. I can go find us someplace warm and dry now. You've got to get off this raft!"

He groaned.

"Clint! Please help me help you. I can't get you up by myself."

His eyes opened to slits of red. She shivered at the sight of him, fevered, bearded, scabbed cuts on his cheek. Was he dying after all?

"*Please,* Clint! I can't lose you now! We'll find Peter and get you well first."

He just stared at her for a moment, then slowly turned and got to his knees. He tried to stand, using her for support, but he collapsed again. "Can't...breathe," he answered, before a fit of ugly coughing terrified her.

Elizabeth looked around to see another boat arrive with four men in it. "Help!" she yelled to them. "Please help me get this man onto our sled! He's sick!"

They looked her way, a couple of them shaking their heads.

"Hey, it's a woman!" another yelled.

"Well, I'll be. She purty?"

"Can't tell. She's wearin' pants!"

They all laughed.

Feeling desperate, Elizabeth pulled Clint's six-gun from her belt and aimed it in their direction, firing it once.

All four men sobered and jumped away as the bullet pinged into their boat.

"Hey, lady, what do you think you're doin'!" one shouted.

"I need help!" she screamed. "I've asked dozens of men for help the last two days, and you're all so bent on finding gold you can't take three minutes to help a man who might be dying! Please get over here and help me, you ungrateful, un-Christian creatures, or I swear I'll shoot all of you!"

She used both hands to point the six-gun, surprised at

her own words, knowing she would never back them but hoping these men believed she would.

The men looked at each other and mumbled something back and forth. "Come on," one of them finally said.

"What do you want, lady?" another said as they drew closer.

Elizabeth stepped off the raft and backed away. "All I need is for you to pick up my husband and put him on this sled and secure him so he can't fall off. That's all! You can be on your way after that."

The man shrugged. "Well, considerin' you've got a gun pointed at us, I guess we'll oblige you," the man answered.

They all grinned and chuckled as they stepped onto the raft and managed to pick up Clint. It took all four of them to do it because of his size. They watched Elizabeth warily but with obvious humor as they laid Clint onto the sled and secured him, then stepped back. All the while Elizabeth continued to hold the gun on them.

"That good enough?" one of them asked.

Elizabeth took a quick look. "That looks fine." She slowly lowered the gun. "Now, you can go on about your business. Jesus Christ will bless you for helping me, even though it was at gunpoint. And if I were you, gentlemen, I would think about what is more important in life—gold, or doing the Christian thing for another human being."

A couple of them frowned and shook their heads, while the other two appeared rather sheepish and guilty.

"Yes, ma'am," one of them told her.

The four of them turned away and returned to their business, and Elizabeth put the six-gun back into her belt, breathing a sigh of relief. *"Thank you for not making me shoot them,"* she prayed softly. She hurried over to Clint and leaned close. "You'll be all right, Clint. Just a little farther to help now."

To her surprise he opened his eyes and looked at her with a soft grin. "You...did good...six-gun Lizzy."

She smiled through tears. It was the most he'd said in nearly two days, and it meant he was more lucid and hadn't lost his sense of humor. It was a good sign! "I love you," she told him, leaning down to kiss his cheek.

She walked up to Devil and patted the horse's neck. "Okay, boy, see if you can pull your master into town. And don't get feisty on me."

Devil shook his mane and whinnied, then took off at a slow walk. Elizabeth was not about to try to make the horse go any faster, sensing this was the best the poor, starved animal could do, and wary of doing anything that might make him rear.

"I'll get you to a stable and get you some real good hay and oats and a much-deserved rest, Devil. I promise. We just have to find help for Clint first."

She headed into town, such as it was, Devil's hooves and her own boots splashing through muck and mud, dragging the sled through puddles and slime, across more snow, a patch of ice, more mud, passing saloon after saloon, from whence came the sounds of laughter of both men and women and jolly piano-playing.

They passed several supply stores, a livery, restaurants, nearly all establishments nothing more than tents. Then came a hotel of sorts, made of logs, numerous log houses and more tents used for private living, it appeared, two land offices and three different log buildings that bore signs on the front reading Claims. From not far away came the sounds of a sawmill, and up in the mountains came the occasional rumble of an explosion, dynamite, most likely, as men blew away pieces of mountain to find veins of gold.

She passed yet another saloon, astonished that men could drink so much that in such a little town there would be a need for so many such establishments. Yes, Peter's work was definitely needed in a place like this.

A painted woman came out of the closest saloon, not bothering to cover her bared shoulders and the whites of her breasts against the cold. Elizabeth glanced at her and then kept going.

"Hey!" the woman called out. "Stop!"

Curious, Elizabeth halted Devil and looked at her again.

"Elizabeth?" the woman asked, coming closer.

Elizabeth felt a wave of incredible relief. "Collette!"

Chapter Forty-Three

Praise ye the Lord. I will praise the Lord with my whole heart, in the assembly of the upright, and in the congregation. The works of the Lord are great, sought out of all them that have pleasure therein.
                                        —Psalms 111:1 & 2

Elizabeth literally ran to Collette and hugged her.

"Collette! When did you get here? Oh, I'm so happy to see someone I know!" Was she actually hugging a prostitute as though she was her best friend? What was happening to her? She pulled away, and a couple of men who'd been standing outside the saloon walked closer.

"Hey, Collette, who's this little beauty?"

"Get out of here!" Collette ordered. "Go inside and have a drink on me. This is a proper, Christian lady, and don't you dare forget it!"

The men looked Elizabeth over and left, and Collette smiled. "I don't believe it! You actually made it!"

Elizabeth wiped at tears of relief. "We did! I can't believe we never ran into you."

"Well, I've been here five days."

"You must have left before us then. I can't believe you were probably right ahead of us the whole time, especially since you got off the *Damsel* in Seattle. We got held up because of a shipwreck, and then in Skagway because Clint came down with pneumonia and almost died, and then we had so many misfortunes along the way that slowed us even more, and now Clint is terribly sick again! I've got to get him some help. Is there a doctor in this place? Do you know anything about a church? My brother, Peter, came here to start a church and minister to the miners. Do you know about him? Do you know where he is?"

"Whoa, little lady!" Collette put an arm around her and they walked over to the sled. She took a close look at Clint. "You're right, he's bad sick."

Clint opened his eyes and grinned. "Collette," he muttered.

"It's me, handsome." She turned to Elizabeth, and Elizabeth realized the woman must have seen the sudden, uncontrollable jealousy in her eyes. She laughed lightly. "Don't worry, honey, he's never been a customer of mine."

Elizabeth reddened. "I'm sorry. It's just that…we're going to be married, Collette. It's such a long story, and right now I'm scared he'll die."

Collette put an arm around her again. "Honey, men like Clint Brady don't die. And yes, your brother is here in Dawson. Leave it to somebody like me to find out about everybody in town the first couple days I've been here." She pointed to two cabins on a hill several hundred feet ahead. "Right up there. The bigger building is his church, the smaller one his residence. He's married, you know."

Elizabeth's eyes widened in surprise. "What!"

Collette nodded. "I remembered what you told us about having a brother here, so I looked him up myself soon as I got here, told him I'd seen you and that you definitely were on your way. Found out he has a wife. She's Chinese, and she's carrying."

"*Chinese!* Aren't they pagans?"

Collette shook her head. "This one is a Christian. Did you think just because someone is Chinese they can't become Christians and can't marry somebody like your brother?"

Elizabeth looked toward the cabins again. "I just never thought…"

"Never thought you'd marry a bounty hunter, either, did you? Or that a prostitute would go to church and think about changing her life?"

Elizabeth looked back at her. "I've learned a lot, Collette, about people."

Collette smiled. "I bet you have. Why don't you just go on up there and find your brother and get Clint some help? I have to tell you, honey, that I've actually been praying for you. Can you believe it? I'll never forget what you did for me and my friends."

"How are they, Collette?"

"All right, as far as I know. I got Francine and Tricia settled and decided to find me some men to travel with and went ahead and came up here. Left the very next day after I got off the *Damsel*."

Elizabeth grasped her hands. "I'm so glad you did, Collette. It's so good to find someone I know."

Collette's eyes teared as she waved Elizabeth off. "Right now you'd better get Clint to some warmth." She pulled off Elizabeth's woolen skull cap and let her red hair fall in tangled swirls. "Just wait till he sees you all cleaned up and wearing a dress again. He'll stumble to the altar fast as he can get there." She laughed and shoved the hat into Elizabeth's hands, heading back into the saloon.

Elizabeth thought how strange it was to be so happy to see such a woman. *"Thank you for getting her here safely, Lord."* She pulled the cap back over her head and went back to Devil. "Come on, boy." She headed up the street and on up the hill toward the two cabins Collette had pointed out to her, her heart pounding with great joy and relief. She couldn't help urging Devil into a faster trot and then she began yelling Peter's name as she drew closer to the cabins.

"Peter!" she cried again. "Peter, are you there?"

She pulled up to a hitching post, and the cabin door opened. A man stepped out, accompanied by an obviously pregnant but very young and lovely Chinese woman.

There he was, red hair and all! "Peter!" Elizabeth left the horse as Peter called her name in return. In the next moment she was in her brother's arms at last!

"Peter! Peter! Peter!" She wept.

"Thank God!" Peter cried in return. "You made it! You really made it!"

"Yes, and I have so much to tell you!" She pulled away, wiping at tears. "Oh, Peter, I have someone with me who needs help. He might be dying of pneumonia! We've got to get him inside near a fire and start warming him up. I still have some ointment a horse doctor gave me back in Skagway that might help. We have to heat it up and smear it on his chest." She pulled at him, half dragging her brother over to where Clint lay. "His name is Clint Brady, and he's a bounty hunter, only I think I've talked him out of that because we're in love. As soon as he's well you have to marry us. He brought me all the way here, and he saved my life so many times, and I even saved his a couple of times. Peter, it was such a long, long journey, so many dangers, but we made it through together, and—"

"Wait! Wait!" Peter turned her, grasping her arms. "A *bounty* hunter?"

"Yes, but—"

"You *love* him?"

"Yes, and he loves me and we're going to be married!"

It was obvious Peter was having a hard time digesting everything she was telling him. "I know I'm spilling all this out too fast, Peter. Once we get Clint cleaned up and put to bed and get some hot tea or something like that into him…" She glanced over at Peter's wife. "Oh, tea! Oh, my goodness, Chinese people know all about tea, don't they? Does your wife have tea here? Maybe she knows of some kind of herbal tea that might help Clint." She ran up the steps and hugged the woman. "I'm so happy Peter is married. And you're having a *baby!* How wonderful!"

The woman laughed lightly and bowed slightly when Elizabeth let go of her. "Am honored to meet sister of my husband," she told Elizabeth.

"And I'm so happy to meet you, too!"

"*Elizabeth!*" Peter nearly shouted her name. "How did you know about Summer?"

"Summer?"

He nodded toward his wife. "Her Chinese name is Lanyi Peng. In English it's Summer."

"Oh!" Elizabeth ran back down to Peter. "Collette told me. I saw her in town and she told me how to find you."

"Collette?" He shook his head. "Oh, yes. She told me about meeting you back in Seattle or somewhere, and what you did for one of her friends." He stepped back and looked Elizabeth over. "And look how you're dressed—like a boy!" He ran a hand through his red hair. "Liz, I can hardly believe this is the innocent—and rather ignorant, if I might say—little sister I left behind! Making friends with prostitutes and bounty hunters! Accepting my Chinese wife as though it's perfectly natural for me to marry a Chinese woman. Talking about being in love and—" He looked closer. "Is that a *six-gun* in your belt?"

"Oh!" Elizabeth pulled it out. "Yes. It's Clint's. He's very good with it. He's shot a lot of men with it. Peter, when I met him he didn't even believe in God anymore, but he's changed so much. I think I've helped him find his way back to God. I have so much to tell you about all of this."

"*That's* no surprise." He put his hands on his hips. "You, little lady, are sounding more and more like our father. Could it be you understand why I came up here? Do you actually see people the way I do? The way father saw them?"

"The way *God* sees them, Peter. Yes."

"What on earth made you leave in the first place?"

She calmed down, closing her eyes and sighing. "You won't believe it when I tell you, but all I know now is that I was *supposed* to come here, for a whole lot more reasons than I first thought. Let's just get Clint inside for now. Can you find somebody to take care of his horse? His name is Devil, and he's in bad need of getting his hooves filed and having new shoes put on and getting a decent meal of oats and hay and a warm place to stay and—"

Peter put a hand over her mouth. "First things first. I'll help Clint inside, and then I'll bring in the rest of your supplies. *Then* I'll take care of your horse."

Elizabeth felt as if she was dreaming. They were really, really here! Summer, a tiny woman with kind, dark eyes led her inside, telling Elizabeth she would do all she could for Clint. The two of them prepared several blankets in front of a stone fireplace and Summer built up the fire while Peter helped Clint into the cabin and to the bed the women had made up for him. They took off Clint's coat and pulled off his boots, and Summer began heating the liniment Elizabeth gave her, as well as heating water for tea.

"I take care of putting liniment on him," Summer told Elizabeth. "You need sleep. In there." She pointed toward a curtained doorway.

"Oh, but that must be yours and Peter's room."

"Is fine. Peter would want you sleep comfortable. We will be busy cleaning up your friend. I shave him, put liniment on him, keep him warm."

"But I should—"

"You have been through much. I'll bring you hot water. You wash and go to sleep."

"I have to admit, sleeping in a real bed sounds wonderful." Elizabeth removed her jacket, for the first time realizing how filthy and smelly it had become. "Oh, Summer, I don't even have any other clothes to wear! We lost them in the river."

"I have American woman dresses. We look same size... except for this!" She laughed and touched her swollen belly.

Elizabeth smiled. "I'm so happy for Peter."

"And *I* am happy that you accept our marriage. You are a good sister, just like Peter says you are. We have both prayed hard that you get here safely." She led Elizabeth into their bedroom, taking a quilted robe down from a hook on the wall. "You wash. Wear this for now. We find you a dress when you wake up."

Elizabeth looked around the tidy room, decorated with a few Chinese vases and pictures. She realized she still had so much to learn about other people. Sitting down on the bed, she pulled off her hardened, cracked, worn boots and damp socks that were full of holes.

Summer returned with a kettle of hot water and poured some into a wash bowl on a stand near the bed, where a bar of soap and a towel lay. "You wash. I bring you hot tea and some biscuits. Then you sleep."

Much as Elizabeth wanted to stay with Clint, she knew he was in good hands, and that she wouldn't be any good to him if she got sick, too. Sleep. Yes, that's what she needed.

This all seemed so unreal. She'd known this day had to finally come, and yet they had been traveling and living out of doors for so long that she felt strangely out of place. Her whole world had been turned upside down the past month, and she would never be the same.

She washed and put on the blessedly warm robe. Summer brought her the tea and biscuits, and she barely finished her second biscuit before she felt her body shutting down. She could relax now. She could really, really relax. She walked to the curtained doorway to look out and see both Peter and Summer undressing Clint. They would take good care of him. Surely now he would be all right.

Tired. She was so, so tired, not just physically, but tired of the constant worries and dangers, the relentless, bitter cold. She climbed into a feather mattress and pulled several quilts over herself.

A real bed! *"Oh, thank you, thank you, Jesus,"* she muttered before everything went dark and she drifted into the most blessed sleep she'd known since leaving San Francisco.

Chapter Forty-Four

*...I found him whom my soul loveth: I held him,
and would not let him go.*
                                    —Song of Solomon 3:4

Dawson, September 19, 1898

Elizabeth awoke to voices. She turned on her back, staring at the log ceiling and trying to remember where she was, and as she stretched, enjoying the glorious softness of the feather mattress, she remembered the previous day's events.

Getting out of bed and retying the robe that Summer had thoughtfully left for her, she walked over to peek through the curtain and saw Clint, sitting up in a rocker!

"Clint!" She walked through the curtain. He was washed and shaved...and looked far more handsome than she'd remembered. "Clint, you look wonderful! How do you feel?"

He looked her over appreciatively, and she pulled her hair

behind her shoulders, suddenly self-conscious, wishing now
that she'd brushed it before exiting the bedroom.

"Your brother tells me I'll live," he answered with a grin,
followed by a siege of coughing.

"He has a long way to go to get his strength back," Peter
told her. He and Summer sat at a homemade kitchen table.

"Well, I guess you and Clint have made your own in-
troductions," she told Peter.

"Oh, yes." Peter grinned teasingly. "I even know you've
slept in the same tent with this man for the past month."

Elizabeth reddened. "It wasn't—"

"Don't worry," Clint told her. "He understands. He
made the trip up here himself, you know. He knows what
it's like."

Peter sobered. "And I'm eternally grateful to Clint for
helping you get here safely. We've been talking about a lot
of things."

Elizabeth looked back at Clint. "Oh? Like what?"

Clint rested his head against the back of the rocker, closing
his eyes. "Like Jen and Ethan...and you and...everything."

Elizabeth looked at Peter again. "When did you do all
this talking?"

"All morning."

"All morning?"

Peter looked up at a clock on the fireplace mantel. "Well,
you've been sleeping just about eighteen hours now."

"What!"

"The sun is about to set, dear sister. You got here about
five o'clock last night and it is now one o'clock in the afternoon of the next day."

Elizabeth covered her mouth. "Oh, my! I'm so sorry! I should have been helping—"

"No. You should have been *sleeping,*" Peter interrupted. "It's the best thing for you. Besides, it gave me and Clint time to talk about all the things you would have told me anyway. If you're going to marry this man, I want to know everything about him. And I also want to be sure he's right with God. We've been talking and praying. He knows he's lucky to be alive, and that there has to be a reason for that, which is his love for you. But there is one more matter to be cleared up first."

Feeling confused, Elizabeth sat down at the table, looking over at Clint.

"Roland Fisher is here in Dawson, Liz," he told her. "Peter knows who he is, but he didn't know he was a wanted man." He coughed again and pulled a quilt closer around his shoulders.

Elizabeth glanced at Clint's gun belt and six-gun, which hung on a hook on the wall near the fireplace. One of his repeating rifles was propped against the same wall underneath the six-gun. She looked back at Clint. "And?"

"And I'm going to go find him."

Her stomach tightened. "And?"

He shrugged. "I don't know. God has something in mind, I'm sure. The only way I'll find that out is to find the man and talk to him."

"What if he realizes who you are? Misunderstands? What if he shoots at you?"

Clint glanced at Peter, then back to Elizabeth. "Then I won't have any choice but to shoot back. I'm hoping that won't happen, but at least I won't be going there to shoot him first for bounty. I don't want to do that anymore, Liz. At least I don't think I do. I have to see the man first. I have to find out if I can look another murderer in the eyes and not want to kill him. It's just something I have to do before we can get married. I've told you that all along. That hasn't changed."

Elizabeth looked down, toying with a tie on the front of her quilted robe. "I see."

"It's time to put all this in God's hands, Elizabeth," Peter told her. "You've got to trust Him, and you've got to trust Clint that this is something very personal to him. This is a battle he has to fight alone. You can't help him."

Elizabeth felt like crying. Why had she thought that once they arrived here Clint would just drop his past and they would marry and live happily ever after, even if Roland Fisher was in the same town? "I know," she answered. She looked at Clint as a tear slipped down her cheek. "You won't go right away, will you? I mean, you're far from well, Clint. You need to be well and strong before you face that man."

He nodded. "I know. In the meantime I don't want anyone saying anything to Fisher about me being here and why. Don't go trying to warn the man, thinking he'll go away and that will solve everything. It won't, Liz. I'll just go after him. Besides that, we have no idea how dangerous he is. Peter says he has a wife and kids and seems to be a perfectly normal family man, but that doesn't mean he's not dangerous. So don't go do something stupid. Will you promise me that?"

Elizabeth slowly nodded. "I promise."

"Good." Clint gave her a smile. "Now, come over here and sit on my lap. I don't think Peter will care."

Peter chuckled. "Just watch yourself. She's still my sister and not your wife yet."

Elizabeth was never more sure that she wanted to be Clint's wife. She walked over to him and gladly sat down and curled up in his lap, resting her head on his shoulder. "I love you," she told him. "And I'm scared for you."

He moved his arms around her and kissed her forehead. "Don't be. You know darn well I can take care of myself, and besides, you're the one who's always said to trust God, aren't you?"

He was talking about God as though he truly believed again! How she loved her brother. She'd known all along Peter would know the right things to say to Clint, and Clint was apparently seeking God's love and forgiveness. Surely nothing could change this, not even Roland Fisher.

She snuggled closer, relishing the safety of his arms, breathing deeply of his scent, feeling no fear of allowing Clint Brady to make her his own.

Chapter Forty-Five

I opened to my beloved; but my beloved had
withdrawn himself, and was gone:... I sought him,
but I could not find him; I called him, but he gave
me no answer.
—Song of Solomon 5:6

The next three weeks were the most joyous, pleasant days Elizabeth had ever known, even though, compared to San Francisco, life here was about as rugged as a person could experience. It was enough to be warm and to have hot food, even though often it was no more than broth and biscuits because of a need to be as sparing as possible. No one could tell what kind of winter lay ahead, how deep the snows would become, how difficult it might turn out to be to find game, which had been extremely thinned out because of so many prospectors shooting everything in sight for food.

Summer's clothes were simple but clean and nicely starched and pressed. It felt so good to wear slips and

dresses again that Elizabeth felt beautiful in anything she
wore. Peter had promised that by next year more supplies
would arrive and Elizabeth would be able to find cloth to
make more clothes for herself. Clint slept in an unfinished
loft, and he'd bought a cot for Elizabeth to sleep on in the
main room. Clint's healing time was spent in long talks
with Peter, sometimes about what might happen to
Dawson, since yet another strike had been discovered
farther west and men who'd had no luck here were already
planning to leave Dawson in the spring.

To Elizabeth's delight, Clint attended church services
with her. Even Collette came a few times, something that
warmed Elizabeth's heart. It seemed things had come full
circle. She was leading a more normal life again. And she
felt so much more complete now that she'd learned about
a different way of looking at people like Collette and the
Chinese and the Eskimos and even the prospectors who
seemed to care about nothing but finding gold. All were
God's children, and all needed to hear His word.

It was midmorning, and she sat at the kitchen table
writing in her diary while Summer stirred a rabbit stew in
a pot hanging in the fireplace.

With each passing day Clint grows stronger. He's
gaining back some of the weight he lost on the journey, and it warms my heart to see how much Peter
likes him. Summer's baby is due any time, and so we
all stay close, playing checkers, telling stories about
our adventures. Clint and Peter sometimes have to dig
pathways through the snow to get to the horse shed.

These are the happiest times I've had since before father was killed, and I can't wait to become Clint's wife, but one thing still has to be settled, something Clint has not discussed and I dare not mention. Roland Fisher. Even though Clint has been attending church and talking and praying with Peter, he still has not mentioned giving up on finding Mr. Fisher so we can be married.

"I think the baby is coming!"

Elizabeth quickly put down her pen at the words, closing the diary and rushing to put her arm around Summer, who looked ready to fall. The woman bent over in pain, and Peter came to take Elizabeth's place, helping Summer to the bedroom as he ordered Elizabeth to get some towels and extra blankets ready. "And make sure the hot water kettle is full!"

Elizabeth obeyed, grabbing more towels from a cupboard in the main room and rushing into the bedroom to retrieve more blankets from a chest while Peter helped Summer undress. She hurried over to the bed and aided Peter in getting a flannel nightgown on Summer, who then curled up on her side in pain.

"What should I do now?" Elizabeth asked Peter.

"I don't know. Wait, I guess…and pray." He looked at Elizabeth, terror in his eyes. "I don't know a thing about delivering babies, and there's no doctor in this town."

"I don't know anything, either!" Elizabeth answered. She reached across the bed and Peter took her hands. They prayed for a safe delivery and for Summer's health.

It was the beginning of five more hours of screams and waiting and praying and wiping perspiration from Summer's brow. Elizabeth wanted to cry over Summer's agony, but felt helpless to do anything about it. *The pain is just a natural part of childbirth,* she remembered her mother telling her once, but Summer's groans and screams were unnerving.

Through it all Clint stayed in the main room. Elizabeth wondered what was going through his mind as he'd been awfully quiet throughout the ordeal, just sitting in a rocker staring at the fire in the hearth.

Finally Summer insisted the baby was coming, and, scared to death she'd do something wrong that could hurt the mother or baby, Elizabeth ran out into the main room.

"I don't know a thing about delivering babies! Not a thing!" she told Clint, as she wrapped a towel around the handle of the hot water kettle that hung on an iron hook over the fire. "Do you?" She faced him, noticing an odd look of sorrow in his eyes. "Clint?"

He met her gaze. "I helped deliver Ethan."

"Then you can help with this!"

He closed his eyes and rested his head against the back of the rocker. "She's not my wife. It wouldn't be right."

"There is no doctor in this town, Clint, and Peter and I don't know a thing about this! And you and I owe a lot to Peter and Summer. Don't tell me it's because she's not your wife. Surely having a baby is very different from...I mean..." She felt herself blushing. "Having a baby is surely a beautiful thing. Besides, I don't think that's your problem. It's the *memory* of Ethan that's bothering you, isn't it?"

His eyes shot open, and for an instant she caught a

glimpse of the Clint Brady she'd met on the docks, angry, full of vengeance. He looked away then, saying nothing.

"Clint, we might need you. You decide whether or not to help Summer. I can't make you do it." She hurried into the bedroom, where Summer sat partially sitting, grasping her belly and groaning.

"It is coming fast…and now!" she lamented. "I can tell!"

Peter looked at Elizabeth with a pleading look. "I don't know what to do!"

"Neither do I, but Clint said he helped deliver his son."

Peter glanced at the doorway, then back to Elizabeth. "This could be very hard on him, Elizabeth. It's the loss of his son that has been the hardest for him to deal with. Anything that reminds him of it—"

"I know. It's his decision. I've told him so. Let's just do what we can to keep Summer comfortable for now."

The next several minutes were agony, physically for Summer and emotionally for Peter and Elizabeth, who put aside her modesty for the more important job of trying to help deliver her precious niece or nephew while hoping both mother and child would be all right.

God, why do You keep giving me such challenges? she secretly asked. *Help me know what to do. Please make Clint get in here and help us!*

"Clint, the baby is coming!" she yelled then when she was sure she could see a head emerging.

Summer screamed with the pain, and her whole body was drenched with sweat.

Another push. The head came out, but the baby's face was purple.

"Clint!" Elizabeth yelled. "Something's wrong!"

"Clint, please!" Peter yelled. "Something is wrapped around its neck!"

In the next second Clint was in the room. He walked around the other side of the bed and leaned closer. "Looks like the feeding cord! I saw a foal delivered this way once. It choked to death. Get a knife!"

Peter ran out of the room, returning in seconds with a carving knife. Clint grabbed it and ordered Elizabeth to hold the lantern closer. He moved two fingers between the cord and the baby's neck, then carefully slid the knife under the cord.

Elizabeth held her breath as Clint deftly cut the cord and pulled it away from the baby. "Once the baby is out we have to cut the cord near the baby's belly and tie it off with something. Get some sewing thread," he ordered Elizabeth.

To Elizabeth and Peter's relief, the blue began to drain from the baby's head, replaced by a pink hue.

"Thank you, Clint," Peter said, tears in his eyes.

Elizabeth grabbed some thread from a sewing box, and in moments the baby was fully delivered. Clint cut the cord, and Elizabeth quickly tied thread around what was left of the cord still attached to the baby's belly.

"You just leave it attached and after a couple of weeks it falls off by itself," Clint explained.

If not for the seriousness of the situation, Elizabeth would have laughed over the clumsy efforts of the three of them. If she was lucky, she'd be delivering her own baby in another year or so…Clint's baby. She could think of nothing more wonderful in spite of the pain she'd seen Summer suffer.

The woman lay quieter now. "What is it?" she asked.

Elizabeth quickly and instinctively dug membrane away from the baby's nose and mouth and laid the child on a towel at the end of the bed. She looked up at Clint. "It's a boy!" she said.

"Make it cry," Clint said.

"What?"

"He's not breathing." He picked the baby up by its feet and began lightly smacking his back. The baby spat and coughed and broke into a loud, healthy wail.

Peter and Elizabeth both laughed and hugged each other.

"It's a boy!" Peter told Summer. "Sweet Jesus, it's a boy!" He kissed Summer. "Thank you, darling! You're the most beautiful woman in the whole world!"

Clint laid the crying child on Summer's chest and put the towel over him. He looked at Peter. "Massage her stomach and get the afterbirth. You'll be able to tell when she's rid of it. The doctor who tended to Jen after Ethan was born told me a woman could die of infection if you don't get out all the afterbirth." He turned to wash his hands with some of the hot water, then congratulated Peter. "I think it's time I left the room. And by the way, your son won't stop that howling until he's had his first real food."

"Thank you, Clint! Thank you!"

"Looks like a fine, healthy baby," Clint replied. He glanced at Elizabeth, and she saw the pain in his eyes. And there was something else there—the memory of what he'd lost because of men like Roland Fisher. "It's time," he told her.

"Time for what?"

"You know what." He headed for the door.

"Clint?"

"I know where the man lives," he said as he left the room. "I'm going to get this over with."

Panic filled Elizabeth as she looked at her brother for help.

"Wash your hands and go with him," Peter told her. "I can't leave now!"

Elizabeth quickly washed her hands and dashed out of the room.

"Be careful!" Peter called out to her.

Clint already had his gun strapped on and was reaching for his wolf-skin coat.

"I'm going with you!" Elizabeth told him.

"No, you're not! It's too dangerous!"

"You can't stop me!" she nearly screamed at him. She grabbed a long, woolen cape that belonged to Summer as Clint stormed out the door. Elizabeth hurried after him.

Chapter Forty-Six

But I say unto you, love your enemies, bless those
that Curse you...pray for them which despitefully
use you, and persecute you...
— St. Matthew 5:44

"Clint, give the man a chance to defend himself!" Elizabeth yelled as she ran to keep up with him. "Let him tell his side of the story!"

"He murdered an innocent man who had a wife and three children!"

"You don't know that for certain. Clint Brady, if you go over there and just shoot him I won't marry you! I *mean* it! All men deserve a trial by jury and you know it. Roland Fisher has a wife and children, too. Don't forget that!" She slipped and fell into the snow. "Oh, I could shoot you *myself!*" she blurted out as she straightened and brushed off her skirt.

Clint finally slowed down and turned, letting her catch up.

"Ethan Clint Brady, do you love me?"

He just stared at her with those steely blue eyes.

"Well? *Do* you?"

"You don't need to ask that."

"Then don't *do* this!"

"Why can't you understand that I *have* to do this? If *you* love *me,* you won't try to stop me!"

Elizabeth wiped at angry tears. "Fine! Just give him a chance."

"I never said I wouldn't."

"Those guns say different!"

He rolled his eyes and grabbed her arm. "Come on. Just stay out of the way when we get there, understand? For all we know the man will try to shoot me before I open my mouth!"

"I wouldn't *blame* him, from the look in your eyes, and coming at him with a rifle and a six-gun!"

"Yeah, well, it all comes with the territory." He half dragged her along, his long strides too much for her.

"Do you have to be in such an all-fired hurry? We've been here almost three weeks, and Peter said the man is still here, so a few extra minutes won't make any difference."

He stopped again. "Lady, are you going to turn into a nag when we get married?"

"*If* we get married—yes—if that's what it takes to keep you on the straight and narrow." Now she saw those blue eyes softening slightly. He actually grinned, but there was still a hardness about him that she hadn't seen for a long time.

"Well, then, I guess I'd better take that into consideration before legally putting a ring on your finger." He literally jerked her closer. "If I didn't want you so bad, Miss Breckenridge, I'd smack you and tell you to go back home and get out of my life."

She held his gaze boldly. "Go ahead and try."

They stood there staring at each other until both broke into smiles. In the next instant he was kissing her, a long, hard kiss, as though to brand her. He pulled away and grabbed her hand, pulling her along with him again.

Elizabeth was momentarily speechless. All she could do was pray that whatever happened next would bring Clint the answer he was looking for.

They walked a good half mile, Clint splashing through puddles and mud, on over snow already flattened by people, sleds, horses and such.

"How much farther?" Elizabeth asked.

"Just up ahead. Peter said it's a cabin with a horse shed right beside it that has a big set of antlers on the front of it. That must be it on the hill there to the right."

"Well, at least we're out of town so no innocent people can get hurt if there is trouble."

He looked at her with a frown. "Oh, so now you admit there could be trouble not of my doing?"

"I didn't say it wouldn't be of your doing. If you didn't go after him at all we wouldn't have to worry about it, would we?"

Clint frowned before walking a little farther with her, until they were within a few yards of Roland Fisher's cabin. He pulled Elizabeth over to a broken-down wagon. "Stay here, understand? Don't you dare come out until I tell you to."

With a sigh of disgust, Elizabeth ducked behind the wagon. "If you say so."

Clint started out again.

"Clint, be careful!"

"Always am," he answered as he kept walking.

Elizabeth peered over the top of the wagon. *"God, don't let anything bad happen,"* she whispered, blinking back tears so she could see better.

Clint approached the cabin, rifle in hand. Just then a man wearing a fur-lined jacket appeared from the horse shed. Clint stopped.

"Roland Fisher?" Clint shouted.

The man ducked back inside the horse shed, and Clint went to the ground. A shot rang out, and Clint cried out, shaking his head. He'd been hit! He leveled his rifle then and fired back. Almost instantly they heard a child's scream, followed by crying.

"Clint! Are you all right?" Elizabeth screamed.

"Creased my head!" he yelled back. "Stay down!"

He took aim again.

"Wait!" Fisher shouted, running out of the shed with his hands raised. "Don't shoot! My little boy is hurt!" He sounded ready to cry. "Please! Let me tend to him! He's only two years old!"

"Stay right there!" Clint ordered, getting to his feet and keeping his rifle leveled. "You Roland Fisher?"

"Yes, but I didn't do what they say I did! I swear I didn't!"

Elizabeth ran from behind the wagon, as a woman and two other children came out of Fisher's cabin. The short, round woman also looked Indian, and terror shone in her dark eyes.

"Roland!" the woman screamed. "What's happening?"

Clint walked up closer to Fisher and made him open his coat. Clint felt for other weapons. He stepped back again. "Why in hell did you shoot at me?"

Hearing her little son's scream, Fisher's wife ran to the horse shed to tend to her son. "I heard a rumor you were here but sick. I've heard of you! You've killed many men! I was afraid you would not wait to let me tell you what really happened!"

"So, you *know* about the robbery and killing!"

"Yes! But it wasn't me! Please, let me tend to my little boy, and then I will explain!"

Fisher, a round-faced man with dark skin and a mustache, looked pleadingly at Elizabeth, who stepped up to Clint to see blood pouring from a crease across the right side of his head.

"Clint, let's see what's wrong with the man's son."

"He shot him, that's what's wrong with him!" Roland lamented. "I heard you were a killer of men, but not of little boys!" The man turned away and ran to the horse shed.

Clint looked at Elizabeth, and she saw the horror in his eyes. "*Is* that what you've become, Clint? You've gone after men because of your own little boy's death. Has that brought you so low as to kill a little boy yourself?"

His jaw flexed in what Elizabeth suspected was a surge of emotional turmoil. He handed her his rifle and wiped blood away from his right eye. "Hang on to that." He walked to the shed then, and Elizabeth followed to see Fisher's wife bending over an adorable, dark-skinned, round-faced little boy who was crying in her arms. The woman sat rocking her son and carrying on in her native tongue.

Fisher knelt in front of her.

"We have to get him into the cabin," he told his wife.

Mrs. Fisher looked up at Clint with terror in her eyes, tears streaming down her pudgy cheeks. "Please! You have done enough. My husband is not guilty! Just let us take Toby inside and get him some help!"

"I might be able to help him myself," Clint answered, his voice strained. Blood still streamed down the side of his face from his own wound.

So much blood, Elizabeth thought. *So much violence. Please, Lord, let this end for once and for all!*

Fisher's other two children, a little girl who looked perhaps four years old, and another boy of about six or seven ran into the shed to see what was happening. Both of them cried at the sight of their wounded little brother.

"Let's get your little boy inside," Clint told Fisher.

Fisher, also crying now, took the boy from his wife and lifted him. "I am sorry, Amanda," the man told his wife. "I should not have shot first."

Mrs. Fisher looked at Clint. "Blame the *bounty* hunter!" she seethed through her own tears. She grabbed her other two children and shoved them ahead of her, hurrying after her husband.

Elizabeth felt sick inside for the way she knew Clint had

to feel right now. Her feelings were verified when he turned and jerked the rifle out of her hands. To her amazement he retracted it several times to spit out the remaining bullets, then took the rifle by the barrel end and swung it hard, smashing it against the corner post of the horse shed. The rifle broke in half.

Chapter Forty-Seven

A new commandment I give unto you, that ye love one another; as I have loved you, that ye also love one another.

—St. John 13:34

Elizabeth said nothing as she followed Clint into Fisher's house. She knew she didn't *need* to say anything. What had just happened said it all. Inside the cabin, the still-screaming little boy lay on the kitchen table, stripped to his waist. His parents were bent over him, trying to stop heavy bleeding at the boy's left side near his waist line.

"Let me have a look," Clint asked Fisher.

"Don't touch him!" Mrs. Fisher screamed at Clint. "*Child* killer!"

Clint shoved Fisher aside and bent over the child, and Mrs. Fisher tried to grab the baby away.

"Let me look at him!" Clint growled at her. "I know how to treat bullet wounds."

Mrs. Fisher put a hand to her mouth and backed away, pulling her other children with her.

Clint ordered Fisher to get some whiskey. "It's just a flesh wound," he told the man. "The way he's screaming, he's sure not hurt bad. He's just scared."

"What would you know about little children?" Mrs. Fisher spat at him.

Clint seemed to wilt. He grabbed the little boy and pulled him into his arms. "More than you think," he told the baby's mother. He picked up what looked like a clean towel nearby and pressed it to the little boy's side, then carried him to a rocker and sat down with him.

With his left arm around the child's waist, he held the towel against the boy's wound with his left hand. He moved his right arm around the baby's back and held him close so that the child cried against his neck. Clint began rocking and talking soothingly to him.

"It's okay," he told the baby. "Everything will be okay. Nobody is going to hurt you. Never again. Never again." He kissed the boy's straight hair, stunning everyone else in the room.

Frowning, Fisher looked at Elizabeth.

"He lost a little boy of his own to murderers," she told the man, struggling against tears that were a mixture of remorse and relief. "He was the same age as your son." She looked at the baby's mother. "Mrs. Fisher, Clint would never deliberately harm a child. I know that he's truly sorry."

The woman walked closer to her husband and took his arm. "Who are you?" she asked Elizabeth.

"My name is Elizabeth Breckenridge. I traveled here with Clint to find my brother, Peter. He's the preacher at—"

"We know who Peter is," Fisher broke in, studying Elizabeth with a frown. "You do not look like the type of woman who would travel with a bounty hunter."

Elizabeth took a handkerchief from a pocket of her skirt and wiped her eyes. "Mr. Brady was every bit a gentleman all the way here. In fact, we're going to be married. What happened here…it's a long story, Mr. Fisher, but it…had to happen." She looked at Fisher pleadingly. "You should know that before we came in here Clint smashed his rifle in half. I think he's done with the life he's been leading the past four years. I hope that when your little boy is better you'll let us visit…let us explain."

Little Toby actually stopped crying and fell asleep against Clint's chest. Clint wiped at his own silent tears. "Tell me your side of what happened, Fisher," he spoke up, his voice sounding like that of a tired, beaten man.

Still frowning with a mixture of curiosity and disbelief, Fisher walked over and took a chair near Clint. Elizabeth dared to move an arm around his wife, who broke down and actually hugged her. "I thought he'd killed my baby," she wept.

Elizabeth looked past her at Clint and saw deep remorse in those blue eyes that minutes earlier had been so full of the old, angry Clint. She led Mrs. Fisher to another chair, then went to stand behind Clint while Roland Fisher gave his side of the story.

"I was at that bank," he admitted. "I'd gone there often. I went down to San Francisco because I'd heard a man could make good money there. That was two years ago, before the gold rush here. But I am not a man to go looking for gold anyway. A man's family can starve and die while he's digging for his pot of gold, you know?"

Clint leaned his head back and closed his eyes. "Yeah."

"So me, I stayed north of San Francisco. I had a good job there at a stamp mill, made good money. I figured to work there another year, saving up my money so I could come back here and afford supplies for my family. We have never had much. I saved my money at that bank, went there often to make deposits, so they knew me well. The day of the robbery, I was there. I was taking out my own money, you see? My own money. I was going to come home because I missed my wife so. She had not even given birth to Toby yet when I first left. I was worried."

"So you went to the bank. If you got your money out and left before the robbery, how did you even know there had *been* a robbery?"

"But I *did* know. When I got there, I walked in on the bank teller stuffing money into a bag. He looked like he was in a big hurry—looked startled when he saw me. *He* was robbing the bank, you see? I surprised him, and he pointed a pistol at me. I jumped on him to try to stop him from what he was doing, and we struggled. The gun went off and he was shot! I was really scared then. I am Eskimo. He was a bank teller. Probably lots of people in town knew him. He was not the type ever to tell the truth. I knew I would get blamed for trying to rob the bank, and because I am a penniless Eskimo, a stranger not from San Francisco, people would believe him.

"So I—I gathered just the amount of money to match my savings, and I ran! I did not know what else to do! That teller…I did not even know until now that he died. Either way, even if he'd lived, he would not want anyone to know what he tried to do. He must have told whoever found him that I was robbing the bank and that *I* shot him, that the gun was mine. I hoped that once I got back up here to Dawson, no one would bother coming after me.

"I did not rob that bank, Mr. Brady. You check with them. I took only nine hundred dollars. I had a voucher saying that was my savings. I will get it! I can show you. You check with them. They will tell you only nine hundred dollars was taken."

"My husband has never carried a gun," Mrs. Fisher told Clint. "All he has is his hunting rifle, and he didn't even take that with him to San Francisco. And does he look like the kind of man who would carry a fancy little pistol? He told me that's what kind of gun it was. You check with them. They'll tell you it was a small pistol that banker was shot with."

Clint reached up with his right hand to grasp Elizabeth's hand. "I already know that much, and how much was taken. The teller died after telling the doctor you were the one who shot him and robbed the bank. He knew your name because you had been in there so often." He slowly stood up. "Where can I lay this baby?"

"Here!" Mrs. Fisher led him to a large, wooden cradle. "Lay him here. Has the bleeding stopped?"

"I think so." Clint bent down and laid little Toby into the cradle. "He'll be all right. Just keep that wound clean.

Pour a little whiskey on it. He won't like it, but you don't want it to get infected."

He straightened and rubbed his eyes. "I can't tell you how sorry I am," he told Fisher. "I never would have shot back if I'd known there was a child in that shed."

Fisher stood up. "I was foolish to fire at you in the first place, especially with Toby in there. I believe you when you say you are sorry. The problem is, do *you* believe *me?*"

Clint studied him a moment, then walked closer and put out his hand. "I believe you."

Roland shook his hand firmly.

"There is still five thousand dollars on your head," Clint reminded him. "I'll write the sheriff in San Francisco and explain what happened—get that bounty off your head. They know me well—know I wouldn't lie about it. If I don't get it straightened out, someone else might come up here looking for you, so I'd lay low for a while. If you suspect anything about someone, send for me. I'll take care of it."

"I am grateful."

Clint glanced at Elizabeth, then back to Fisher. "No, Mr. Fisher. *I* am grateful. Coming here to find you changed my life in more ways than you could know. Someday I'll explain all of it. Right now I'll just leave you and your family alone, but I'll want to come back and check on your little boy in the next few days."

Fisher nodded. "You will be welcome."

Clint looked over at Toby, then leaned down to untie the strap that kept his holster close to his leg, after which he unbuckled his gun belt. He pulled it off and walked over to hand it to Elizabeth. The blood on the side of his face was beginning to dry to an ugly crust.

"From here on the only thing I'll be doing with guns is repairing them for other people," he told Elizabeth, "or maybe some hunting."

She took the gun belt, saying nothing.

"Let's go home," Clint told her. "You have a wedding dress to make, and I have a cabin to build so we can have a place of our own."

Elizabeth threw her arms around his waist, the gun belt dangling from one hand. "I love you, Clint Brady!"

He sighed, pressing a hand to her back. "Call me Ethan. It's okay now. Clint Brady the bounty hunter no longer exists."

Epilogue

*Therefore if any man be in Christ, he is a new
creature; old things are passed away;
behold, all things are become new.*
—2 Corinthians 5:17

Dawson, October 30, 1898

Such a long journey. In so many more ways than
one. My Ethan is everything I knew he would be in
a husband, kind, gentle, protective, devoted. Peter
baptized him before we married, and he has fully
given himself to the Lord, who I know in my heart
has forgiven Ethan for whatever lies in his past. Now
there is only a future full of joy and love waiting for
him, and I pray that already his life grows inside of
me. I want to give him another child just as soon as
possible.

She put down her pen and looked out a window of their new cabin to watch her Ethan chop wood. The thought of what it was like to lie with him still sent chills of womanly satisfaction through her. They had no idea if they would stay in Dawson forever, since because of the gold strike farther west, rumor was that Dawson could become a ghost town by next summer.

When Elizabeth had asked Ethan what he would do then, his response was, "We'll go where the Lord leads us."

Such beautiful words coming from a man who just under three months ago was ready to hunt down yet another man for money.

She continued writing.

God works in such strange but beautiful ways, His miracles to perform. Who would have thought, when I left San Francisco, that I would be married and settled just three months later? And to a man like Ethan Brady?

Life was good...so good that sometimes she felt as though she was just dreaming. She was not afraid of the long winter to come, after what they had survived getting here. Ethan was a good hunter. They would be all right.

Ethan and Roland Fisher have actually struck a friendship. And little Toby is fine now. He loves Ethan, and he runs to him every time we visit. I now know why God led me to this place. It was so that I might have the chance to change Ethan Brady's life and bring him back to God. However, I was only the voice. Everything else is thanks to God, not me. I was His instrument, and so was Peter—and even Roland Fisher.

She heard Ethan stomping his feet at the door then. He came inside the one-room cabin that Peter, Roland and others from the church had helped build in just three days. They even had a wood-plank floor. They slept on a feather mattress on a rope spring attached to a homemade bed of pine, and Elizabeth used a large stone fireplace with an oven built into the side for her cooking and baking. It also heated the small cabin just fine.

Elizabeth set her pen aside. "Are you hungry? I think the rabbit stew is done," she told Ethan.

"Sounds good to me. Chopping wood is mean on a man's appetite. I could eat that whole pot of stew. Got coffee?"

"You know I always do." Elizabeth got up and removed a blue porcelain coffeepot from over the fire, grasping it with a towel. She came to the table and poured some into a tin cup Ethan had left there that morning. "There you are." She looked up to see him staring at her. "What is it?"

"I just can't quite get over the fact that you're my wife."

Elizabeth grinned. "You might not be so happy about that a few years from now when I'm older and fatter and I'm nagging you endlessly."

Ethan laughed, rising. He picked her up in his arms and whirled her around. "You will always be beautiful to me,

Mrs. Brady." He looked around. "What was it you said Peter called the Yukon? Something about heaven?"

"Where heaven begins," she answered.

He kissed her nose. "For me heaven begins right here, with you in my arms."

Elizabeth smiled, hugging him around the neck. "Heaven is also knowing God's grace right here on earth, and understanding the full meaning of love." She kissed him softly. "And I do so love you, Ethan."

"And I love you. Did I ever properly thank you for saving my life?"

"*God* saved you, Ethan, not me."

He studied her lovingly. "Well, I sure like the messenger He sent. I'll never question the Good Lord again."

Elizabeth relished the feel of his strong arms holding her. Her joy at knowing Ethan was truly right with God again made her heart burst with love for him. God truly did answer prayer, for even now life fluttered in her womb, Ethan's life. She had no doubt the child would turn out to be another son for Ethan Clint Brady.

She decided she'd kept her secret long enough. It was time to tell him about the baby.

* * * * *